BETRAYED

HAZEL HILL

POLICE & FIRE
BOOK TWO

LIZ BRADFORD

Stand on the Rock
Publishing LLC

Stand on the Rock Publishing LLC

liz@lizbradfordwrites.com

lizbradfordwrites.com

Print ISBN: 978-1-960692-04-7

Cover Design by Emilie Haney at EAH Creative https://www.eahcreative.com/

Comprehensive Edit by Teresa Crupmton at AuthorSpark, Inc. authorspark.org

Copy Edit by Sharyn Kopf https://sharynkopf.wordpress.com/

Scripture quotations are taken from The Holy Bible, English Standard Version. ESV®
Text Edition: 2016.
Copyright © 2001 by Crossway Bibles, a publishing ministry of Good News Publishers.

*This novel is a work of fiction. Names, characters, businesses, places, events, locales, and
incidents are either the products of the author's imagination or used in a fictitious manner.
Any resemblance to actual persons, living or dead, or actual events is purely coincidental.*

Andrew 2001-2007
Carey Ann 1997-2002
Jeb 2008-2023

... forgiving each other; as the Lord has forgiven you, so you also must forgive. And above all these put on love, which binds everything together in perfect harmony.
Colossians 3:13–14

Chapter One

Seventeen Years Ago—September

Sixteen-year-old Logan Jackson ran down the dark hallway of the abandoned asylum, eyes set not on the flag he was supposed to be capturing, but on one of his best friends—AJ. Her long blond hair swooshed as she darted into one of the side rooms.

He followed. But she slipped out another door, a giggle giving her away. Zipping through the doorway, he expected to see her, but instead he ran into their classmate Miles.

"Dude. What are you doing?"

Logan needed to think fast. He wasn't about to admit to the guy AJ had gone to homecoming with last week that he was chasing her, even if Logan and AJ had been friends since they were eight. "I'm sneaking through to get the flag. Will is across the hall." His other best friend was on the opposing team.

"Have you seen AJ?" Miles asked.

"Why are you asking?"

"She denied me a kiss after the dance. Thinking tonight might be better."

Logan tried not to swallow so loud Miles heard him. "I think she's saving her first kiss for her wedding day." A total lie. "So you'd better set your sights on the flag we're supposed to be capturing. Or better yet, go keep an eye out for the cops."

Logan didn't dislike Miles. He was a great guy and a good friend, but seeing him dancing with AJ last Saturday had sparked something inside of Logan he couldn't identify. No, he could. It was jealousy, but he didn't want to admit it.

But maybe he was ready to admit he liked her a lot more than a best friend should.

Miles slapped him on the back and pointed in the direction Logan had come from. "I'm headed this way. I'm on defense. Go get the flag. I refuse to let Cooper gloat in my face again."

Logan snickered. Will Cooper did like to gloat.

Miles left.

Glancing around the dark shadowy room littered with remnants of this being a mental hospital, Logan wondered where AJ had disappeared to.

A soft chuckle came from behind some old equipment. He lifted his flashlight and clicked it on. "AJ?"

"Get over here, you fool."

He climbed through the junk. "How did you get back here without him seeing you?"

"He's a dolt." She grabbed Logan's hand and tugged him down beside her where she crouched behind an exam table of some sort.

She wrapped her hand around his bare elbow. This must have been an electrical shock therapy room for the way the volts blasted through his arm.

"We probably should go find the flag."

She pulled him close. "Why'd you get all tense when Miles said he wanted to kiss me?" She leaned so close he couldn't breathe.

He couldn't find his voice.

She licked her lips.

He looked away. "Gosh, AJ."

She giggled. "I'm sorry I went to the dance with Miles."

He relaxed a little into her nearness. "You don't need to apologize for that. Like you said, I'm the fool."

"Not hardly." She leaned her head on his shoulder.

He dropped to the floor and drew her to him with his free arm. But what was he doing? This was his best friend. Did she understand what was actually going on inside of him?

A blood-curdling scream shook the ancient windowpanes.

Logan grasped AJ's hand. They climbed out from behind the junk and darted into the hall, where they dropped each other's hands.

Staying close, they ran to the end of the hall; the doors to the giant lobby were propped open.

In the lobby, they found Kristen lying on the ground beside the wide staircase that led to the next level.

"What happened?" one kid asked.

Another kid ran to Kristen. "Are you okay?"

Kristen jumped up and let out an equally terrifying laugh. "Ha. Gotcha! And your flag! We win."

Someone stomped up behind AJ and Logan and shoved them apart. Daryl. He barreled toward Kristen. "That's just wrong." He snatched her arm and shoved her against the dilapidated plaster wall.

Logan started toward him. He wasn't going to let some jerk hurt a girl on his watch. But AJ gripped his arm.

"Leave him. He's not going to actually hurt her. And she deserves a good smack for scaring everyone like that."

Will came up on AJ's other side and hollered at Daryl. "Leave her alone. We won fair and square."

Daryl let go of Kristen and turned to Will. "Was it your idea?"

"Nope. I simply found it and tossed it to her. What she did when she reached base was up to her. Let's play again. The night is young."

Will, always the negotiator and fun-seeker.

Daryl leveled a glare at Will. "Same teams?"

"I don't see why we'd mess up what works." Will's grin was stupid big.

Logan groaned at his friend's gloating. "Whatever. Let's play."

Everyone scattered. As Will walked away, he slapped Logan on the back. "You two are just going to have to try harder this time."

AJ squeaked a giggle.

Will turned back around and raised his eyebrow. "You weren't even trying." He shook his head. "I won't tell Daryl; don't worry." Will left.

Logan started to leave the lobby too, but AJ grasped his arm and went up on her toes. In his ear, she whispered, "Find me in the attic."

She bolted up the wide staircase to the next level.

His heart thudded against his ribs in reaction to the way her hips swayed with each step she took. His body urged him to chase after her, and all his self-control was required to keep himself from following her. Hopefully, he'd have enough left when he found her.

He dashed down the hall where the teams were fanning out, hiding their flags. He went straight for the stairwell at the end of the building. Up the rickety stairs and into the long hallway that stretched the length of the building.

Without a doubt, AJ had made it up here before he did. He only had to find her.

The attic was dark. The moon hardly cast any light through the holes in the roof. He didn't want to turn on his flashlight. Sneaking up on her would be so much more fun.

If he could, he'd come up behind her, snaking his arms around her waist. But he had to find her first without her seeing him.

With careful steps, avoiding the creaking boards as much as possible, he crept along one side of the hallway. Of course he didn't trust that she wouldn't jump out and scare the pizza out of him.

At each room, he slowly peeked around the corner. Nothing but dilapidated furniture, cobwebs, and rotting boards.

Halfway down, and he still hadn't found her. He'd need to change tactics.

He stood still. Where was she? Listening intently, he waited.

A faint sound echoed farther down the hallway.

He crept toward it.

A bat swooped through the air by his head.

He gasped—nearly screamed. After grunting at the little creature, he was tempted to swing his flashlight like a baseball bat and knock the flying rodent into tomorrow, but he was the one disturbing its home. He advanced toward the sound he'd heard.

"Logan?"

AJ. Why was she calling for him? Was she throwing her voice again to try and trick him as to where she was? Will had taught her how to do that when they were about ten, which had led to some annoying rounds of Marco Polo.

"Logan?" A hint of panic etched her voice.

"AJ? Where are you?" He followed her voice as she called again. He clicked on his flashlight and searched the remaining rooms.

"AJ!" He couldn't find her.

"Logan." Her voice was nearer.

"I'm coming."

She whimpered. Closer. He had to find her. Was she hurt?

He turned into the room and swept it with his flashlight.

There. The floor had collapsed beneath AJ, and she had fallen through up to her armpits.

"Logan?" Her voice wavered.

"I'm right here. I gotcha." He tested the boards between them, not willing to risk making it worse. They seemed secure. He dropped to his knees behind her and touched her shoulders. "Hey."

"Logan!" She sniffed back her tears.

"What's hurt?"

She shook her head. "Just scrapes. I might have twisted my ankle. But nothing more. It gave out from under me when I came into the room. I'm stuck."

"Do the boards in front of you seem secure? It's probably better if I go over there to pull you up."

"They look fine. I can't move my arms enough to test them."

He stepped over her and knelt, grateful he was wearing jeans. He leaned down to her face. "I'm going to slip my hands under your armpits. Wrap your arms around my neck, and I'll lift you out."

She nodded.

As soon as her grip around him was tight, he lifted her by first pushing on the floor behind her, then by rising until he was nearly standing upright.

Logan held AJ tightly to his chest, all of her curves melding to him. If she had fallen all the way through to the floor below she could have died.

"Thank you." Her voice cracked with residual fear mixed with relief.

"Of course. I can't do life without you."

She leaned back and cupped his face in her hands. "You mean that?"

"Yes."

"But just like, as friends?"

He drew her back to him. "More."

Her eyes gleamed in the light of the flashlight reflecting off the wall. "I was hoping so."

He brought his hand to the back of her head and directed her face closer to his. "Please confirm that what I said to Miles was the lie I believed it to be. You aren't saving your first kiss, are you?"

"I was saving it for you."

He couldn't get his heart to settle enough to make his voice work, but finally muttered, "Same."

Leaning in, he met his lips to hers. He didn't know what to do. Neither did she. They'd figure this out together. He moved his lips, and she responded in kind.

He released her lips and opened his eyes. Her bright blues shone back at him.

His best friend. His first kiss. His only love.

He was just a kid. It was foolish to think too far down the road. They had so much life ahead of them, but he didn't want to do it with anyone else. He wanted to grow old with her. He wanted to promise her forever.

Present Day—Mid-August

Saturday afternoon, Officer Logan Jackson jumped from his squad car and ran toward the corner gas station at the edge of downtown Hazel Hill where two other squad cars were already parked. A man lumbered from the building. Daryl.

Logan stopped short of the slightly taller man. Every muscle in Logan's body constricted, but he refused to let Daryl see it. How had he forgotten this was the station his former friend owned?

Daryl snarled at him. "You."

"What's the call? Where are the other officers?"

Daryl shook his head as if to break his train of thought. "They went that way. The thief ran out the door about the time the officers arrived."

"Thanks."

Daryl nodded.

Logan ran down the street, cut into an alley between the houses, and spotted Zara with her gun drawn. She pointed around the corner and motioned for him to go around from the other side.

He passed her and rounded the other corner. They nodded to one another and darted around the garage.

Logan's heart thundered. The call had indicated the robber was armed. Logan was a cop; the reality was that at any time he could face down death at the end of a barrel. Some days he thought that would be easier than facing the rest of his life.

But at the same time he wasn't sure he was ready. Life wasn't what he'd dreamed it would be, not even close. And he wasn't right with the Lord, even if he faked it pretty well for those around him.

He swallowed hard and turned the next corner.

Zara came around the opposite side. They both lowered their weapons to not point them at one another.

Will came out from around a fence, pushing a heavily tattooed man in cuffs. "I got him."

"Well done." Logan nodded to his friend.

The radio crackled and reported a motor vehicle accident only a few blocks from where their squad cars were parked.

"That's really close. I'll go, if you two have this under control."

Zara nodded. "We got it. Go."

After reporting in, he cut through some driveways and tried to avoid Daryl. But the man caught him.

"Well? Where are you going?"

"To an accident. Cooper got the suspect. It's taken care of." Logan got in, avoiding any further conversation with the man he detested.

He flipped his lights and siren on and raced to the accident.

He was first on the scene. A one-way street intersected with a two-way in a residential area where old houses and ancient trees towered. A green coupe appeared to have t-boned a brown sedan and pushed it into a black minivan. After radioing in, Logan bolted to the closest vehicle. The air bags had deployed.

The window was down. Logan pushed the airbag out of the way. "Are you okay? Are you hurt?"

A young man's battered face appeared. He groaned. "Yeah, I'm fine. What happened?"

Logan reached in and turned off the engine. "That's a question I want to ask you in a minute. Hang tight for a minute. Let me check on the others."

"Sure." The guy groaned again.

The middle car did not look good, but the driver was probably okay since the direct hit was to the back door. He hoped there wasn't a child sitting behind the driver.

Logan snapped his mind away from the dark thoughts that threatened. *Focus.*

He knocked on the window covered by an air bag.

The airbag deflated, and a man's profile appeared. Miles?

Too many familiar faces today.

Miles rolled down the window about four inches before it refused to go any further.

"Hey, Miles. Go ahead and turn off your engine."

"Logan?"

"Yeah, dude. The engine."

"Oh, yeah." Miles blinked but turned the key.

"How are you feeling?"

"Doozer of a headache."

"I bet. I'm gonna check on the other vehicle, okay? Don't try to move. The fire department will be here soon." Logan tried not to growl at the thought. There were plenty of teams of firefighters in the city. Maybe *she* wouldn't be working right now. But a quick glance around reminded him the accident was in *her* house's district.

He went around Miles's sedan and found the minivan empty. Thankfully, it appeared to have been parked.

A fire truck's siren echoed off the houses before it came into view. A block down, it turned the wrong way onto the one-way street and stopped near the end of the minivan. An ambulance pulled up too.

Sure enough, AJ and her crew jumped out of the fire truck.

Seriously! He managed to keep any curse words that wanted to come out inside. This town wasn't so small they'd both respond to the same call, right? Apparently, it was.

He sucked it up and went to Captain Ty Washington and reported what he knew. "Miles Blumetti is probably good and stuck."

Logan accidentally made eye contact with AJ.

Their eyes stayed locked for a moment before she shifted and broke the connection.

Logan clenched his fists. He needed to focus on helping.

AJ took a deep breath as she strode toward the vehicles. Why was Logan here? And why did he have to look at her with such disgust? She didn't want to admit how much she missed him. He surely wouldn't understand.

It didn't matter; she needed to work.

Brennan and Emily, the EMTs on their team, were already helping the young man out of his green coupe. So she went to the sedan.

"Miles!"

"Well, if it isn't AJ! You going to save me from this mess?"

"That's my goal. How are you doing? Other than stuck?"

"Can't complain about life. Other than being stuck in this car."

She chuckled with him. "We'll get you out of there. Now that they have the young man out of the other car, we can get it out of the way and then see what we need to do to get you extracted. How are your legs?"

"Sore. I can feel everything and move my toes easily. I'm pinned but fine."

"Good."

Brennan would have to check him over, but it seemed Miles was not suffering from anything major. Perhaps a concussion but nothing worse.

The other car was towed away and Don, one of the firefighters, and the new guy, Seth, worked the Jaws of Life to get Miles extracted. There was nothing else she could do, so she went and waited near the truck with Ty and Emily.

Logan was there too. She ignored him and stood next to Emily. There'd be plenty more to do soon enough.

Between cuts of the roaring Jaws of Life, a young child's giggle floated on the wind from the house next door.

She tried to see where the child was and spotted a little boy of about four on the deck of the house. He was adorable.

The Jaws ramped up again.

AJ took a few steps to keep an eye on the little boy, who seemed to be out back by himself. Where did he go?

On instinct, or maybe it was a Holy Spirit prompting, she wandered over. She seemed to remember that house having a pool, though she couldn't see over the fence.

The Jaws took a break and a distinct splash met her ears.

She busted into a sprint and hurdled the fence. Where was the boy?

A little body floated face down in the middle of the pool. She reacted without a thought beyond saving the child from drowning. She ran and jumped in.

She came up beside the boy, but the pool was deeper than she was tall. She grabbed the boy and swam to the edge. But her boots and turnout pants weighed her down.

Why didn't she take them off before she jumped in? She should have. She knew better.

AJ fought with all her might to keep the little boy above the water and get to the side. With one hand she tried to release her suspenders from her shoulders, but the boy began to sink without her holding him up with both hands, so she abandoned that attempt. She kicked. They had to get to the side or at least stay up. Her feet hit the bottom of the pool. She pushed off and burst to the surface. The edge was closer, but not close enough. They sank again.

A hand reached in and gripped her arm. The person at the end of that hand hauled her up and to the side of the pool. She found footing on a small ledge on the edge of the pool and lifted the boy onto the concrete.

Logan helped. Logan was the one who had grabbed her? He had saved her. That fact shocked her as much as the cool pool water had shocked her lungs.

But had they saved the child?

She lifted herself from the pool and the two of them assessed the boy.

He wasn't breathing. She started chest compressions.

Emily appeared beside them. "AJ, I got it."

She couldn't stop. She had to take care of the boy.

Logan grasped her arm and drew her aside. She fell into his arms, and he held her.

They stood like that for what seemed like an eternity before the boy began to cough.

"Breathe, AJ." Logan rubbed her back.

She finally looked at him, meeting his eyes.

They stepped back from one another, and AJ ran to the boy.

A woman came out of the back door. "What on earth? West!"

AJ stepped in and held the woman while Emily helped the little boy cough up as much as he could.

"He's all right," AJ reassured the mom. The processing of what might have been sank in, and the woman wept.

Logan said, "I recommend taking him to the ER to be sure his lungs are clear."

Secondary drowning was just as scary and dangerous as first. The mother nodded, but AJ wasn't sure she'd heard his advice.

As soon as Emily gave AJ a nod, she released the mother to go to her son. She scooped him up and held him close. AJ glanced at Logan, but he was already gone. She didn't blame him. Never had.

Chapter Two

Fifteen Years Ago—October

Seventeen-year-old AJ tossed the air horn to Will as they ran up the steps of the old insane asylum. Logan might need to be admitted after what they had planned. But what she really hoped to come from this little joke was mending a bit of the rift that had formed between them over the last couple of months. He always loved dishing out practical jokes. Now it was his turn to be at the butt of one. She wanted this to end in them laughing, wrapped in each other's arms.

After he'd kissed her two years earlier in this very place, they'd gotten serious-ish. But six months ago, when her mom had moved out, AJ had gotten self-consumed. She hadn't meant to push Logan away, but life got busy. He was playing baseball and was always at practice or games. She was busy navigating whose house she was supposed to go to when.

In the lobby of the asylum, Will removed his backpack and took out a white sheet, a pulley system, and some rope. They hung it up so it would fly down the stairs as Logan came through the front door.

AJ checked her watch. They were running low on time. "Hurry, Will."

"I am." He tied off the rope, and they darted down the hall and set up another similar contraption.

She took a speaker and old Walkman out of her backpack and set it up behind a door.

Will walked past her and peeked out the window. "He's here."

They finished their setup and hid. Armed with the air horn, AJ ran to the end stairwell and up to the top of the stairs.

It didn't matter how many times they got yelled at for sneaking around this place, they continued to do so. Other than that time she fell through the floor, no one had gotten hurt.

Will had gone to the basement. Whichever way Logan went to find the promised prize, he'd run into one of them eventually.

AJ leaned over the half-wall and watched for Logan. She heard him screech, most likely at the flying "ghost" in the front. He hollered Will's name and hers.

She waited. It was simply a matter of time before he walked down that hallway and into this stairwell. They'd laid out the clue to bring him this way.

Biting her lip, she prayed. *God, help Logan and me figure things out. I hate the weirdness that's been between us. We had talked about going to the same college next year. Does he even still want that?*

Last week she'd seen a flier for a different college sticking out of his notebook in English class. She'd wanted to ask him about it at lunch, but as he'd come to the table with his food, with a smile meant just for her, some of his baseball friends had pulled him aside. And the conversation didn't happen.

She fiddled with the air horn, holding it at the ready for when Logan walked through the door below.

Something touched her side and snaked around her waist.

She screamed.

Her hand clenched the air horn, and it blared.

The canister plummeted over the railing.

Arms tightened around her waist and the familiar scent of the boy she loved met her nose as he nestled his chin between her head and shoulder.

"Gotcha."

She grunted. "You didn't follow the puzzle."

"You know I hate riddles." He tightened his arms. "I've missed you."

She hugged his arms and sniffed back the emotions that threatened. "Same." Spinning in his arms, she raked her fingers into his hair. "Why do we keep letting life get between us?"

"I don't know. But I'm still yours. Always."

"I love you, Logan Jackson. Are we still going to the same college?"

"Of course." He stepped back from her. "Why would you ask that? Did you apply to Gardner Webb?"

"Yeah, did you?"

"Duh. Will did too."

"Good."

He fiddled with the hair falling in her face. "Then what's the problem?"

"You had a Duke flier in your notebook last week."

"The recruiter was at school. I told him I'm going to a Christian college."

She nodded. "Okay."

"With my girl." He winked.

She relaxed and stepped toward him, closing the gap he had created. "If I'm still your girl, make sure we spend some time together."

"I'm sorry."

"Me too." She went up onto her toes, a more necessary task than it had been even a year ago, and met her lips to his.

When they drew out of the kiss, he touched his forehead to hers. "Let's go convince Will this place *is* haunted."

She giggled. "I like the way you think." She took his hand and led him down the stairs.

Present Day

Logan tried to shake off his irritation at Will as he walked out of the locker room and onto the deck around the country club pool. He hadn't wanted to come to this ridiculous event, but two minutes after he'd poured himself a glass of whiskey, Will had shown up on his doorstep and wouldn't take *no* for an answer. Logan needed that whiskey after seeing AJ save that boy this afternoon. But he didn't want Will to see it, so he hid the glass in the cabinet and popped a breath mint before answering the door. Now on the pool deck, Logan glanced around at who all had come.

AJ sat on a lounge chair talking with Emily and Jenna, sisters whose parents owned this pool and hosted the first-responders party every August.

AJ's muscular-yet-feminine body looked amazing in a swimsuit, as always.

He really needed that whiskey.

Logan put his bag on a chair as far from AJ as he could manage.

"Hey, Logan!" Ty called from the pool. "We need some more cops to wallop in a game of water volleyball. Get in here."

At least a game would distract him. Hopefully. He needed to keep his thoughts in the here and now. "Sure." He kicked off his flip flops, removed his t-shirt, and jumped into the water.

The game got off to a good start, and the country music blaring in the background did the trick.

Brennan spiked the ball, and Will missed it, sending Will underwater. When he came up, Brennan was laughing. "Too many donuts, Cooper!"

Will wasn't the beanpole he had been in high school, but the man did not overconsume donuts. Even Logan had to laugh at the jab.

Will splashed him. "Whose side are you on?"

The game continued, as did the razzing. As much as cops and firefighters always had one another's backs, they thoroughly enjoyed acting like squabbling siblings.

After the cops pummeled the firefighters in the first game, someone shouted for a rematch.

Logan's competitive side took over. "You're on."

One of the firefighters hopped out of the pool. "I'm out. AJ, take my place."

"You got it." She jumped in on the side of the net opposite Logan.

He avoided eye contact and spotted Jenna sitting nearby. "Jenna, you want to play? I can give up my spot."

"Nope. I'm good." Jenna waved the idea away. She was, after all, sitting there in cutoff jean shorts and a baggy t-shirt.

Logan was stuck. *Focus on the game. It's fine.*

So he tried. Yoda would be disappointed.

Pretend like she's not there. AJ made his blood run hotter than hellfire.

Megan served for the cops. The ball went straight to AJ. She passed it to Ty who hit it over the net to Zara. The volley continued until Logan was able to jump and spike it down right on AJ's head.

"Ha!"

"Jerk."

"Oh, come on AJ. It's a beach ball. You're fine. Should have *used* your head."

She snarled at him.

"Didn't take a long enough nap at work today?"

Will shoved Logan to his new spot as their team rotated for serving. At least AJ wasn't right in front of him now.

The game continued and the insults flew. Wise cracks abounded—cops were better than firefighters and vice versa.

Eventually, Logan and AJ ended up back in their starting spots across from one another.

She came to the net. "You're going down, Jackson."

He met her there. "To Chinatown? I could go for some Chinese food."

"You know what cops and firefighters have in common?" she asked. "They all grow up wanting to be firefighters."

He rolled his eyes.

Will and Zara laughed.

AJ knew Logan never dreamed of being a firefighter, but he wouldn't give her the satisfaction of laughing at her ridiculous joke.

"You know why God made cops?" he asked.

She glared at him.

"To give firefighters heroes. Today proved that."

She shoved him. "That little boy would have died if I hadn't seen him outside."

"And you both would have died if I hadn't pulled you out."

"I'd have been fine."

"You keep telling yourself that."

She grabbed the net. "I have to. It's not like you ever told me."

"I'm sure Daryl told you all you wanted to hear."

"Let go of the past." She released the net.

"Hard to when it flaunts itself in front of me day after day."

"I flaunt nothing."

Every muscle in Logan's body tensed to the point of snapping. "You're here, aren't you? Every time I turn around."

"Why do you have to be such a selfish jerk?"

"I'm the selfish one? Seems like you're the one who—"

"Knock it off," Will yelled. "Play the game or get out of the pool."

Logan smacked the water, splashing AJ. "Fine by me. I'm out."

He was done. He didn't care that it was nearly eight miles to walk home or that it was over ninety degrees even at six o'clock. He needed to get away from AJ.

Chapter Three

AJ hated herself. With her back to the pool, she wrapped the towel around her body. Why did she and Logan always have to go at it? She shouldn't have responded to him the way she did. She wanted to treat him better. The bridge could never be mended if she always stooped to the same level of nastiness as he did.

She dried her face and hoped her eyes looked like she'd gotten too much pool water in them. However, everyone had seen that foolish interaction. Could she get away with storming out of the pool party the way Logan had?

Probably not.

Zara picked up her towel from the chair beside AJ. "Are you okay?"

"Yeah, I'm fine." Her roommate was going to notice the tension in her statement.

"I take it the words I couldn't hear weren't real nice?"

AJ snorted. "We've said worse. Don't worry about it. Let's go enjoy the fun. I want some of that pulled pork Brennan has been raving about smoking forever." Maybe food would settle the turmoil in her stomach.

Will joined them, his face taut with tension. "Should I go after him?"

She shrugged. "Up to you. But did he tell you what happened after the car accident this morning?"

Will shook his head.

She gave him the shortest version possible, sticking to the facts.

Will drew in a sharp breath. "Maybe I should—"

"He likes to wallow by himself. The walk may do him some good. Maybe check on him on your way home?"

"I'll do that." Will put his arm across her shoulders and hugged her tight.

She leaned her head on him and fought another round of tears. But a hiccup of a sob slipped out.

"I'm sorry, AJ."

"I know." She was so grateful Zara had helped repair her friendship with Will.

Zara stood there staring, confusion wrinkling her brow.

AJ still hadn't told her the whole truth, or much of it at all. She reached out and squeezed Zara's forearm. "I promise I will tell you. I just ..."

"It's okay. Now's not the time. Let's get some food."

And they did that. AJ bottled it all up and set it down at the feet of Jesus. He'd help her deal with it later.

The rest of the evening was more relaxed. AJ felt the weight in her heart but was able to enjoy time with her friends and co-workers.

She spent a good amount of time sitting on the side of the pool simply chatting with Megan, who had been through some tough times but was seeking God. AJ wanted to be there to help point her in the right direction. Not that she'd done a good job of that when Logan had been here.

Brennan called Megan over to play another game, so AJ got up and walked across the deck.

Will hopped out of the pool and approached her. "I think I'm going to head out and check on Logan. Just so you know how to pray for him, he had alcohol on his breath when I picked him up."

"Still? Or is this new?"

"Newish."

"Thank you for telling me."

Will set his hand on her shoulder. "Seemed like you should know."

She nodded.

Zara joined them and wrapped her arms around Will's waist. "If this guy is leaving, I'm ready to go too."

AJ agreed. "Let's get out of here then. I'm tired."

Will left and the women took a moment to tell people goodbye before they exited through the locker room.

The roommates silently got in AJ's car and drove home. She knew Zara was dying to ask questions but also seemed to recognize that if AJ started in, she wouldn't be able to drive. She didn't have it in herself to talk right now anyway. Once they got home, AJ planned to go straight to bed and cry herself to sleep curled up in Jesus's arms.

She missed the simpler times with Logan. As much guilt as their high school/college relationship held due to their propensity to break rules, they'd had fun.

Thirteen and a Half Years Ago—March

Hand in hand, eighteen-year-old Logan walked AJ up the front steps to her dad's house. Her dad had set a stupid-early curfew for her lately, especially for a Friday night. They would graduate in two months; they were practically adults. Logan didn't understand. But they'd figured out ways around the stupidity.

He drew AJ into his arms and kissed her cheek, then whispered in her ear, "Got to make it look like I'm actually telling you good night."

She giggled.

The front door opened, and the screen door slammed back against the siding. "You're late."

AJ stepped away.

Logan looked at his watch. By two minutes. Even so, he kept his mouth shut. The last thing he needed was AJ's dad thinking any less of him. If the man knew what Logan and AJ had been doing at the movie theater …

"Inside, AJ. Logan, get lost."

"Yes, sir. Good night, AJ."

"Bye." She waved at him as her dad grasped her arm and tugged her into the house.

Logan turned and walked away slowly.

Her dad's voice carried, despite the closed door. "You need to have a little more self-respect, girl. And if that boy respects you, he'll respect the rules and the boundaries you should have set up. You aren't married and aren't gonna be anytime soon. Stop trying to wake up something that should stay dormant until your wedding day."

Logan didn't hear AJ's response or anything else from the house. He *did* respect AJ. Where did her dad get off suggesting he didn't? Maybe they shouldn't be fooling around as much as they did. For two years they'd kept it above board, but in the last six months, it had gotten harder to keep his hands to himself. AJ didn't help. But he knew it was his duty to treat her right.

Logan drove his car down the block like he did on a regular basis and parked it. Tonight he only had to wait half an hour before AJ opened the passenger door and slid in.

"Wasn't that a little fast?"

"Eh. I slammed my door and locked it. He tried talking through it for a few minutes before I turned my music on. He'll leave me until morning." She snickered before leaning over and kissing Logan with entirely too much intensity. "Where to tonight?"

He put the car in gear and drove to a secluded parking lot. He knew he shouldn't. What if they couldn't stop themselves from going too far? He should drop her back at home and not play with fire. He should stop them. But he didn't want to.

The next morning, eighteen-year-old AJ stared at herself in the bedroom mirror. Whether she felt like a million bucks or the scum of the earth was a toss-up. How was it possible to feel such a dichotomy of emotions at the same time?

God, I know Logan and I shouldn't have ...

The prayer stopped there. She couldn't find the words. The guilt was too much. And what made the guilt even worse was the elation she felt as she remembered when skirting the line became crossing the line.

But she loved Logan so much. They planned to get married one day, eventually. If her dad would let them.

Maybe he'd be outside working when she left her room, and she wouldn't have to talk to him. But she was hungry so she couldn't hide in there all day. Did her dad know she had snuck out last night? Would he simply look at her and know she and Logan had gone all the way?

She tossed the towel at her reflection. Taking a shower hadn't helped remove the guilt. After getting dressed, she took the risk and wandered to the kitchen to get some breakfast even though it was noon.

Her dad was sweeping the living room. "It's about time you got up."

She froze for a moment. *Act natural.* "Morning, Dad. What chores do you need me to do today?" Deflect, that was the best solution, right?

"Just the normal ones. Are you going out this evening?"

"Yeah, Will is having a movie night at his house." She opened the fridge and stared. She needed to eat something, but the door stood as a shield, blocking her dad's scrutiny.

"Fine. Back by ten."

"Of course."

"AJ." Her dad waited until she looked at him. He looked sad. "I love you."

"I know, Daddy." She closed the fridge and went to him. "I love you too."

He encompassed her with his arms. "I want what's best for you."

"Of course. Me too. Do you hate Logan?" *You will if you find out what we did last night.*

"No. He's been your friend forever. He's a good guy. But he's a young man, and I know what that's like. You need to protect each other."

"Yes, Daddy." Too late. She should have stopped them. But she hadn't wanted to.

Chapter Four

Present Day

The day after the pool party, AJ went grocery shopping to grab a few things before her shift at the fire station early the next morning. With a basket on her arm, she wandered down the frozen-treats aisle. Oh how she wanted to eat away her sorrows. After the pool party, she had cried herself to sleep as she'd anticipated.

Zara had knocked on the door and asked if she was okay. She'd said she would be. It wasn't a lie; Jesus held her and would sustain her like He always had. No matter how far she had wandered from time to time, He always accepted her back with open arms.

She picked some frozen fruit bars. Healthy and delicious, better than the cheap vanilla ice cream she loved so much.

After adding some yogurt to her basket, AJ headed to the cereal aisle for some granola. She turned down the aisle and halted. Logan stood in front of the granola.

She needed to suck it up and apologize for being a jerk at the party. With a deep breath, she walked toward him. "Hey."

He glanced at her and stiffened. Snatching a package from the shelf, he appeared to read the back.

"About the other night ..."

"Whatever." He put the package in his basket and walked away.

She deflated. She sniffed back emotions that threatened, tossed her granola in the basket, then went the opposite direction.

Before she could leave the aisle, a tall man came around the corner heading toward her. Daryl.

"AJ! Hey, girl!"

Her insides quivered. She needed to run in the opposite direction but couldn't. Be kind. And get away. "Hi." She tried to walk around him, but he blocked her.

"I've missed you. We should hang out again."

"No, Daryl. I'll see you around." She tried again to go around him.

"I think I can change your mind. Just give me a chance." He moved into her space.

She took a step away.

He reached out to stroke her hair or face, but she side-stepped and darted around him. She was done with trying to be polite. She needed to leave the store. But she wanted her veggies.

Just shy of running, she hurried to the produce and snagged what she needed, being less picky than normal. Heading to the checkout, she groaned. Logan was in one of the open lines and Daryl was in another.

Daryl waved to her to join him.

Logan. As much as he hated her, he was a cop and would keep her safe even if he didn't want to.

She jumped in line behind him.

He glared at her. "Why are you over here? Go by him."

She shook her head.

Logan drew closer to her, putting his face less than two feet from hers. "If his bed is better than mine, wouldn't his checkout line be too?"

She clenched her teeth together, willing the tears to stay put. As much as she feared Logan's emotionally damaging words, she was more scared of Daryl trying something physical.

Logan finished checking out, and one glance at Daryl told AJ he'd be done about the same time she was.

"Logan, would you wait and walk out with me?"

"Why on earth would I do that?"

She looked toward Daryl and prayed Logan would see the terror in her eyes.

He must have because he made a big deal of sighing and said, "Fine."

He waited while she checked out her items, and they exited the store. Logan seemed to keep a close eye on Daryl.

She spotted Logan's motorcycle parked an aisle over from her car. "Grocery getting on a motorcycle. That's got to be a challenge."

"Eh. I always do it."

"Just can't get too much at a time."

"Yep."

"About the pool party—"

"Don't."

"Don't what? Talk to you? Apologize for being mean?"

"Whatever. Just put your groceries in your car and get lost."

She placed the bags in the trunk and turned to him. "Logan, when will you talk to me again?"

Without turning his stone-set face toward her, he said, "Never."

The world crashed down on her, crushing her beneath its weight.

He stared across the parking lot, still not looking at her, missing how much that little word hurt her more than anything.

"Daryl's gone. You're fine." Logan didn't even glance back at her before he walked away.

She had to fight to stay upright. Leaning heavily on the side of her car, she made it to her seat before the grief overwhelmed her.

Chapter Five

Logan's hands shook as he held the handlebars of his Honda Shadow. He'd heard her harsh intake of breath at his *never* comment. But he was so angry. Why did he always bite at her with his words?

In all honesty, if he never talked to her again it would be too soon. No. That wasn't true. He missed her, never had stopped loving her even after all these years. She was his first love, and he'd never love another.

With the flick of his right wrist, he opened up the throttle and pushed his luck with the speed limit on the country road that led around town toward his house. He'd write himself a ticket later if he had to.

Slowing as he entered town, Logan maneuvered the streets at a more reasonable speed. A block from his house, he spotted Miles getting out of his rental car. Logan pulled to a stop at the curb. "Hey, Miles."

He walked over to Logan. "How goes it?"

"I was going to ask you the same. You were the one in a car accident. Nothing broken I take it."

"A concussion and some bruises. Nothing that won't heal easy enough."

"Excellent. It could have been a lot worse."

"For sure. Haven't heard the kid's excuse for running the stop sign, but I hope he has good insurance. Thankfully, I wasn't carrying a load of supplies in the car."

"Pharmaceutical sales, right?"

"Yep. Keeps me busy and traveling." Miles ran a hand through his hair and winced. Must have hit his injury.

"A bright point was seeing AJ's face when I came to after the accident."

Logan kept his groan internal and smiled. "No doubt."

"I still don't understand how I missed the opportunity for something more with her after homecoming sophomore year."

Logan wanted to laugh but kept it to himself.

"Maybe I should see what she's up to."

"I wouldn't do that."

"Still hold a candle for her, huh?"

"Trust me. Find someone else."

Miles raised an eyebrow as if he hoped for a further explanation.

"I've got to get my groceries home. I'll see you around." Logan revved his motorcycle to avoid hearing anything Miles said, waved, and drove away.

He turned the corner and spotted a teenage boy taking off from his carport. What on earth?

Logan accelerated and followed the kid, but he cut through a yard and into the woods.

There was no way Logan would catch him there. He stopped and contemplated what to do. He could drive around and see if he spotted the kid coming out on the other side, but there was a creek back there, and the boy would be able to follow it and come out anywhere. Better to go home and see if he stole anything or caused any damage. Too bad Logan hadn't gotten a better look at the teen.

Back at home, he didn't find anything out of place.

Once the groceries were put away, Logan poured himself a glass of whiskey and sat at his kitchen table. He slammed the whiskey back and poured a second glass. He normally kept it to one glass, but it didn't numb him enough anymore.

At work the next day AJ had done nothing but stew in her frustration with Logan for three solid hours. She'd cleaned the kitchen at the fire station from top to bottom. She'd remained cordial to everyone who talked to her, firmly cementing a wall to hold herself up and keep her emotions inside. She was going to need a nap soon though. She hadn't been able to sleep at all after the definitiveness of Logan's *never* last night at the store.

She put the cleaning supplies under the sink, and her phone dinged.

A text message from an unfamiliar phone number.

She opened the message.

> Been thinking about you. We should meet up.

What? Who was this from? It didn't matter, she wasn't going to meet up with anyone. She deleted the text.

Probably should have blocked the number too, but she didn't think of that until the message was gone.

She shoved her phone back into her pocket and went to find Ty, since it was their turn to clean the fire truck.

Out in the truck bay, Ty filled the buckets while AJ grabbed the sponges and tossed one to Ty. She took a bucket of sudsy water, set it beside the truck, and started scrubbing.

Ty stood there watching her.

"What?"

"You doing okay?"

The wall holding her up crumbled, and she slumped against the truck. "No."

"I didn't think so. Not after that save the other day."

"It's not even that. It's Logan. Not only did we have that nasty exchange at the pool, but yesterday we ran into each other at the grocery store."

"Talk to me, AJ."

She couldn't help but notice Ty called almost everyone else by their last names, but not her ...

"What's to say, Ty? He hates me, and I hate that. I want to fix things, but he won't even let me apologize."

Ty dipped his sponge into his bucket. "Seems like it's going to take an act of God on his heart to make a change."

She snorted and climbed to the top of the truck. "Why can't he be a decent human being? It doesn't matter if I'm nice or not. Anymore, he's just a jerk." She grunted and set to scrubbing the top of the engine.

The harder she scrubbed the more her frustrations took on a physical manifestation. She hated herself for how she'd wronged Logan. She hated herself for not confronting the ways he'd wronged her. She hated herself for not loving him like Jesus would.

That's what she needed to do. Love him. But how could she when he did nothing but push her away?

Tears blurred her eyes, but she scrubbed her way toward the back of the truck.

Her heal hit part of the truck, and she lost her balance. She yelled but couldn't catch herself. She slammed her back on the truck and went off the side.

When she hit the ground, the world went black.

Chapter Six

Twelve and a Half Years Ago—March

Logan trekked across his college campus looking for AJ. He should be studying for the quiz he had in an hour, but he needed to talk to her about the email the dean sent out to the entire school. They were looking for the culprit who caused extensive damage to the school fountain three days ago. He and AJ didn't do it, but they knew who had. The school policy about keeping rule-breakers' secrets was severe. If they didn't tell and it came out they knew, they could be kicked out. The email gave them until Friday afternoon to come forward with information. Three days.

He needed to find her.

Pushing open the glass door, he entered the student center. Maybe she'd stopped by for a snack after class. He hoped she had cooled off enough since their latest fight to talk to him. They were fighting so much anymore. He chalked it up to the stress of the semester, but he had a sneaky suspicion it was deeper than that and rooted in the fact they were living less than holy lives.

Of course, bringing up the idea of ratting on Eric would probably spark another fight since the reason they knew what Eric did was because he'd caught them getting frisky in the dugout. But Eric was going to want them to keep his secret as much as Logan wanted Eric to keep theirs. What was he supposed to do?

He popped his head around the corner and looked in the student lounge for AJ, but she wasn't there. The first place he'd tried was her dorm room. He burst through a pair of double doors and strode toward her favorite tree. It was a nice day; maybe she was studying outside.

As he fought to keep his stride cool and steady, he debated what to do. Turn Eric in so they didn't get expelled, but risk Eric ratting on them and get expelled anyway. He kicked a rock across the ground.

They'd chosen to come to this small private Christian college because they both wanted to grow in their faith while learning from a biblical worldview. What they hadn't accounted for was being expected to live by certain standards, standards they'd been failing to live up to for about a year now. Their entire freshman year had been spent creatively breaking the rules. They'd tried to stop having sex, but it seemed impossible.

He should just marry her, but he couldn't figure out how to make that work yet. They needed to make more money than their little campus jobs provided before they could afford one of the apartments. He'd crunched the numbers. The dorms were cheaper. And as soon as they got married, they'd have to get their own insurance because they probably couldn't stay under their parents' any longer. Why did growing up have to be so complicated?

Then there was the matter of AJ's dad. The man hated Logan, at least he was pretty sure. And Logan couldn't blame him. If he ever had a daughter ...

Logan slowed and let out a deep breath. What if AJ got pregnant? He shook his head. They were being stupid on so many levels.

Where was she? They had to talk about all this. Not just the Eric situation, but also what to do about getting married. They needed to have that conversation. Maybe it was time.

Only one more place he could think of to look for her. The library. Perhaps she was studying there or had picked up an extra shift. He climbed the steps and entered the large building.

One of the other students working at the circulation counter caught his eye and pointed upstairs. Logan nodded his thanks and bounded up the stairs. He found her hunched over her books at a table at the end of the library. She didn't look up, so he slipped between the bookshelves and skirted around her and came up behind.

He slid his hands over her eyes. She giggled and gripped his hands, tugging them down around her until he was hugging her. He kissed her cheek.

"Hey, beautiful."

She giggled again, but her entire body was rigid, gripped with tension despite the soft chuckle and affection.

He took the chair next to her. "Are you okay?"

She plucked a piece of paper from under her books. "Look what I found." She'd completely ignored his question. The paper was an advertisement for a sale on motorcycles. "Isn't this the one you wanted?"

"It is. But it's too much money." He was saving first for a ring, second for a motorcycle.

"You're getting there."

He shrugged. He'd wanted that motorcycle since he was a kid, but at this point, he wasn't sure it would ever happen.

Logan took her hand. "Did you see the email from the dean? They want anyone who knows something about the Kool-Aid in the fountain to come forward."

"I'm not turning Eric in. If we turn him in, he'll—"

"We could always give an anonymous tip." Logan may have been humiliated when Eric jumped into the dugout while running from security and caught Logan with his pants down, literally, but Logan had seen Eric gripping the grocery bag full of empty Kool-Aid packets. They had a responsibility to pass on the information.

AJ's hand rested in his, but her touch lacked its normal intimacy.

The weight of their actions suffocated him despite trying to ignore it for the last year. But they would get married; it was just a matter of time.

"We can't. Eric will know it was us. We can't." She jerked her hand away.

"AJ, they find out we knew but didn't report him, we'll get in just as much trouble as Eric."

"We'll get in more trouble if they find out what we've been doing. We've broken more rules than ... ya know." She kept her voice low, but it was tight.

"What are we supposed to do?" He drew closer to her with his arm across the back of her chair and rested his other hand on her thigh.

She closed her eyes, jaw tighter than the knots in his stomach. Moisture snuck between her eyelids.

"What are you thinking?"

She shook her head. That loosed the tears, and they poured onto her cheeks.

"I can't do this." She pushed his hand off her thigh and slammed her books shut. "Tell if you have to, but leave me out of it." She shoved her books into her backpack and stood.

"AJ, we can figure this out."

She looked him square in the eyes. "No, we can't. It's over, Logan. I love you, but I just ... I can't keep arguing and sneaking around." Her entire body shook, but she was going to stand by her words.

He couldn't say anything. He needed to fight for her, but he didn't know how.

Flinging her bag over her shoulder, she turned her back to him. "AJ ..."

She walked away.

"AJ, I love you."

She paused her retreat. "I know. Goodbye, Logan."

His heart walked away, leaving him bleeding, completely gutted, at the study table. She was his one and only. He could never love another. Would never.

Chapter Seven

Present Day

Logan held his hand on his Taser and stared down the teenagers they'd caught making a mess of a crime scene. Today, he was very glad he wasn't a detective. All he had to do was respond to the call. Detective Wyatt Remington, just back to regular duty after getting shot, and Detective Doug Ramirez would get the joy of sorting out what had happened.

A ring tone that sounded like his rang in the distance. He patted his pocket. Maybe it was his phone.

Zara had also responded to the call and was standing closer to his squad. "Jackson, that's your cell." She pointed into his car.

"Answer it?"

"Sure."

Wyatt turned to Logan. "We'll take these guys in. They can sit in the car and wait." He directed one of the teens to stand and head for the detectives' unmarked car.

"Logan!" Zara's voice held urgency.

He spun toward her. "What's wrong?"

Her face was ashen, mouth agape. "It's the hospital. Your *wife* has been in an accident."

The words slammed into him, and the world stopped.

His wife. What had happened?

He looked at Doug. "Take my squad?"

"Go."

He tossed Doug his keys. "Zara, drive me."

"Are you going to tell me—"

"No." He was shaking and couldn't breathe. The last thing he could do was explain to Zara the past twelve-plus years.

He slipped into her passenger seat, and she got in, handed him his phone, and drove.

He dropped his head to his hands and tried to pray. How bad was it if they called him? He really had been a jerk to her. His wife. He hadn't called her that in years, but it was the truth.

With lights and sirens, they reached the hospital in five minutes. Leaving Zara in the dust, he bolted through the emergency room doors. But she was right behind him.

The nurse at the desk nodded to Logan and pressed the button to open the door. "She's in the third room along the back."

"Thanks." Logan darted down the hallway and turned.

Ty stood in his path.

"Is she okay?"

"She'll be fine." He didn't let Logan pass.

"Let me see my wife."

"I don't know that I should." Ty crossed his arms.

"She's my wife."

"Is she?"

"Yes. And who made sure they called her emergency contact?"

Ty shrugged with a sideways grin.

"That's what I thought." Logan pushed past Ty and swerved around the corner into the room.

Zara was beside him. "AJ?"

She looked up at the two of them from where she sat on the hospital bed.

Relief washed over him, but he didn't know what to say or do.

Zara went to AJ while he hung back near the door. The women embraced. Zara asked, "What happened?"

"I took a tumble off the top of the fire truck." She gave Zara a goofy grin then winced.

"Careful." Zara squeezed the arm AJ was not cradling in front of herself.

AJ said, "I'll be fine. I blacked out; that's the only reason I'm here."

Ty spoke around Logan. "And to get that arm and your ribs x-rayed."

"They aren't broken."

Ty slapped Logan's back. "She's being as stubborn as ever."

Logan chuckled. Stubborn had always been a good word for AJ.

Ty said, "I should get back to the station if you are going to stay with her."

"I will. If she'll let me." Logan tentatively met AJ's gaze.

She nodded.

Ty left, but before an awkward silence could claim the air, a nurse stepped in. "How are you doing, Alice? Anything I can get you while you wait for radiology?"

AJ slowly shook her head, and the nurse disappeared.

Zara said, "Alice? The A stands for Alice? I don't think I can handle any more surprises today."

Logan and AJ both laughed.

"Anyway, if I go back to work, are you two going to kill each other?"

"I promise not to kill *him*. Logan?"

"I promise. I'll even be nice." He gave AJ a rueful smile.

"Okay. Call me if either of you need anything."

Logan nodded, and Zara left the room.

"You can come in," AJ said softly and pointed to the chair next to the bed.

He trudged farther into the room closer to her and sat.

He didn't know what to say. "I've been a jerk."

"You aren't the only one."

Silence fell. Why was it so hard to talk to his wife? He knew the answer. The weight of the last six years was too heavy.

As AJ exited the x-ray room, Logan fell in step beside her. She still couldn't believe he was here. They had hardly said anything to each other. Why did she choke on the words *I'm sorry*?

For one, *I'm sorry* would never be sufficient. And, of course, she was afraid he wouldn't listen anyway.

They walked down the hallway following the tech. They turned down another corridor, and Miles came from yet another one. His eyes widened. "Hey, Logan. AJ."

"Miles."

AJ nodded at him but the motion made her dizzy, so she grasped Logan's arm. He wrapped it around her.

Logan asked, "You okay?"

"Moved my head too fast."

"What happened?" Miles took a step closer to them.

AJ lifted her palms to the ceiling. "I fell at work. I'm fine, just a bump on the noggin." She relaxed into Logan's side. It didn't mean anything, but she appreciated the steadiness he was providing to her body, even if it was leaving her heart in turmoil.

The tech said, "Mrs. Jackson, I need to get you back to your room. I have another patient waiting for me."

AJ said, "Oh, of course. It was nice to see you, Miles. I trust you're feeling better."

"I am. Thanks. I'll see you guys around."

AJ and Logan followed the tech back to AJ's room. By themselves again, silence reigned.

She sat on the edge of the bed, and Logan took the chair.

Was she fooling herself to think things had changed the moment he came running to the hospital? Or was it the concussion?

She didn't know what to say. It seemed like every time she opened her mouth, it made things worse. Maybe simply sitting in the same room with each other was all they needed right now.

Resting her head against the bed, her eyelids began to feel heavy.

"Stay awake." Logan's voice was raspy.

She opened her eyes and looked at him.

The hardness that had been there for the last five years was still there, but was that a tiny little crack?

"I just want to rest my eyes."

"You know better."

"Yeah. Any idea how much longer I'm going to have to sit here?"

"Long enough."

"Are you talking to me again?"

He diverted his eyes and stared at something on the floor. "I don't know."

"Then why did you come?"

"I was scared."

"Why—no, I'm sorry. I won't push you to talk to me. Thanks for coming." She watched him carefully.

His eyebrows lifted briefly, but she wasn't sure how to interpret it.

Silence fell again. This time it was a little less comfortable.

So many words needed to be said, but so many had flown in the past that had no business being aired. If only she could take them back ...

Dr. Madison Baker entered. "Hey, AJ. Logan. I looked at your x-rays. Nothing is broken."

"I didn't think it was."

Madison smiled and came over to her. "I'm not surprised either. How are you feeling?"

AJ shrugged. "Killer of a headache."

"No doubt. Take acetaminophen such as Tylenol every six hours as long as the headache persists. But don't take any ibuprofen."

"Thank you."

"You're going to have to lie low for a bit. No work—limit physical activity. Nothing that requires a lot of focus mentally, including reading or TV. Give your brain a minute to heal up. Got it?"

AJ released a puff of air. "That's like telling a three-year-old to sit still. I'm going to go stir-crazy."

"Just don't let yourself become fatigued. Rest a lot."

"Yes, ma'am."

Madison looked at Logan. "Make sure she obeys."

His eyes widened. "I'll pass it along to her roommate." He twisted his hands in his lap.

Last Madison knew they were married ... well, they were still.

"Take care of yourself, AJ."

She nodded and Madison left.

Logan was sitting beside her, but it felt like he was a million miles away. She longed for him to take her hand and reassure her everything would be okay. But she was pretty sure those words weren't in his vocabulary.

After another eternity of sitting there, AJ was finally discharged and walked out with Logan by her side.

Zara drove up to the curb as they were coming out the front doors. Logan opened the passenger door for AJ, and she slid in. He got in the back.

They took her home to her and Zara's apartment above AJ's grandmother's house. She changed out of her uniform and grabbed a few things before going to her grandmother's living room and settling on the couch.

Logan and Zara left once she was comfortable. Her grandmother would do a fine job of fussing over her. Even if Granny's face was alive with questions about Logan being there. Thankfully, she kept her mouth shut for now.

Chapter Eight

Eleven and a Half Years Ago—May

Back home for the summer, AJ unpacked her last suitcase after a very lonely sophomore year. In breaking up with Logan, she'd lost her closeness with Will too since he'd stuck by Logan's side. And no matter how much she tried to connect with the girls in her dorm, it always fell short. She didn't know how to be friends with girls. They were boring and only wanted to braid each other's hair. Well, not really, but that's how it felt sometimes. Instead she dove into her studies. But she was out of gen eds now. She needed to actually pick a major.

She felt so lost. Her only ambition in life had been to be Logan's wife and stay home and raise a zillion kids. With a plop, she sat on the edge of her bed. She missed Logan sneaking in her window when Dad was asleep and crawling into bed next to her. The snuggling was the part she missed.

Jesus, I need You to be my all in all. We've grown closer this year now that Logan and I aren't sinning all the time, so why do I still miss him so much? Lord, help me to focus on You.

She laid back on her bed and picked up the stuffed panda Logan had given her for Christmas when they were only ten years old, and she hugged it tight. Everything in her room reminded her of him.

Crying was not an option. She wouldn't let herself.

Tomorrow she had to find a job. She'd work all summer and keep herself busy.

The screen door slammed. Dad must have changed the spring again.

A gentle knock sounded on her bedroom door.

"Yeah?"

"You've got company outside."

"Thanks, Daddy." Who would be here? Maybe it was Will.

She slid her tennis shoes on and strolled to the front of the house.

In the driveway, Logan sat on a motorcycle.

She ran to him but stopped short. "You got it!"

"I did. You like it?"

"It's awesome."

"I thought you'd appreciate it. Wanna go for a ride?"

She glanced at the house. Her dad leaned against the porch post at the top of the stairs.

He nodded. "Be careful."

"Yes, sir," they replied in unison.

Logan handed her a helmet. "I made sure I had a second one."

She strapped it on then slipped onto the back of the motorcycle behind Logan. After finding a spot for her feet she loosely held Logan's sides.

He revved up the bike. His nearness revved up her heart. He took off and drove around town and then out to the country roads. The longer they rode, the farther around him her arms reached, until she laid her head on his back and hugged him tight. The tears threatened again, but the rush of wind in her face dispelled them.

Logan stopped at a small waterfall off the road a bit. A place they had always enjoyed going together. He removed his helmet and, once off the motorcycle, offered his hand.

He stood frozen as if holding his breath, waiting for her to respond.

Accept or reject?

It felt like the weight of their entire futures hung on her response to that hand. What was she supposed to do?

In the last year she'd tried to go on a few dates, but that fell even flatter than her attempts to get closer to the girls in her dorm.

As far as she knew, Logan hadn't even tried dating anyone else.

She slid off the motorcycle and set her helmet on the seat. Staring at Logan's hand, she debated. The decision was hers.

Her heart pounded. It took all her willpower not to instinctively take his hand, but she needed to be certain. Was she willing to ... what was she risking? Her heart? He already had that, and she didn't want it back.

She grabbed his hand.

A gigantic smile overtook his face. He tugged her to follow him to the little footbridge that went over the stream at the bottom of the waterfall.

He let go of her hand and wrapped his arm across her shoulders. "I still love you."

"Same."

He sucked in a breath that made her own falter. "Yeah?"

She nodded.

His lips found her forehead, and she melted against him.

"We have to be better this time. Wait until we are married."

"I was thinking the same thing."

"When are we getting married?"

He laughed. "I wasn't planning on this, so I bought a motorcycle."

"I don't need a ring."

His laughter continued. "Let's give ourselves a minute to make sure we can handle being us again."

"Probably a good idea." She turned to face him and wrapped her arms around his waist.

He cupped her cheek. "I'm sorry it's taken me so long. I wanted to fight for you, but I didn't know how."

She nodded and swallowed, not knowing what to say.

His lips met hers, and she felt whole again.

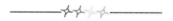

Present Day

AJ rubbed her aching head as she woke up. Where was she? Right. Granny's couch. She checked her watch. She'd been asleep for entirely too long. How was it the next morning?

Granny padded into the room carrying a tray. "Morning, Allie."

The older woman was the only person in the world who was allowed to call her by the alternate nickname.

"G'morning, Granny. Please tell me you have some painkillers on that tray."

Granny set the tray on the coffee table. "Sure do. And your favorite French toast."

"You are too good to me."

The older woman winked and took a seat in her recliner. "Now eat, and tell me how you're doing, and I don't just mean your head. That heart of yours needs to talk about the mister who brought you home last night."

AJ sat up with a groan—half from pain and half from the idea of talking about Logan. "My head hurts, but it'll heal." She flexed her sore arm and twisted her hand around. "Whoa, that still hurts too. So glad it's not broken. Again, it'll heal."

"And your heart?"

"As broken as ever, but he sorta talked to me yesterday. I still can't believe he came to the hospital."

"He still loves you."

"Doubtful. You didn't see the way he talked to me at the grocery store."

"No, but I saw how he fluffed your pillow when he put it on the couch."

AJ swallowed the pills and picked up her fork. "The bridge is gone though. He seems impossible to reach."

"Did Noah see the rain clouds before he built the ark?"

"I don't think Logan wants to live with an ark full of animals."

"Allie." Granny's rebuke of AJ's snark was full of love and humor.

"Spell it out to me, please. My head still hurts."

"Rebuild the bridge. He's your husband. As his helpmate, it's your duty to love him back to Jesus, even if he's not receptive to that love. Yet."

AJ let her fork clang against the plate. She'd drop back against the couch if it wouldn't hurt too much.

"I know that's not easy to hear, but you've never wanted me to beat around the emotion bush."

"You know me too well. I love you, Granny."

"And I you. I'm praying for you both. Like time will heal your body, it heals emotional wounds too."

"As long as they don't fester and become infected."

"You're quick. Well, we both know it's not time that does the healing; Jesus just takes the time we need."

AJ smiled and picked up her fork again.

The doorbell rang.

"Sorry, dear. The cable is down, so I called for a tech to fix it."

"That's fine. I'm going to eat. Hopefully, he's not a talker." Granny crossed the room to the front door.

AJ ate while Granny let the tech in and chatted about the problem. She led a tall man into the room.

AJ nodded a greeting with a mouthful of her breakfast.

He shot her a wide smile. A familiar smile.

"Eric?" Residual shame washed over her. Was this seriously the guy who got kicked out of their college for ruining the fountain with Kool-Aid? Somehow he'd gotten caught without her and Logan's interference, and thankfully he hadn't divulged their secret—or if he had, the powers that be decided to let it slide since they had broken up.

"Hey, AJ."

It was. And he didn't seem surprised to see her.

"I figured it was a matter of time before we ran into each other. I was pretty sure you lived in Hazel Hill still."

"Only left long enough for college."

"Is this your mom?"

Granny laughed. "If only. I'm her grandmother."

Eric winked at Granny, who ate up the attention.

Eric got to work on the cable and asked AJ, "Do you live here?" His overly friendly smile hadn't faded.

"No, well, sort of. I have an apartment over the garage." Why did she tell him that? Her concussion was probably taking her better judgment. She was tempted to add her roommate was a cop. Oh, and her husband too. But she was *not* going to explain that complication.

She focused on eating her breakfast and answered his twenty billion questions in the shortest, simplest way possible.

He seemed liked the same nice guy he had been in college, although maybe more mature than the prankster he was back then. "Will still lives in town too. I'm sure he'd love to see you."

"Maybe we can all get together."

He didn't ask about Logan. She wasn't going to bring it up either.

Eventually, the cable was fixed, and Eric left with a "See you around."

She simply smiled and waved. She'd be fine if they didn't run into each other ever again. Simply looking at him brought back the feelings of mortification she'd felt when he caught her and Logan in the dugout. She never wanted to feel that again.

With him gone and Granny on the phone with one of her younger siblings, AJ wandered out to the front porch with her Bible. Reading it wasn't going to work very well because of the concussion, but a few verses could only help.

She settled in the rocking chair and opened the Scriptures to the Psalms. A few verses was all she could focus on. She closed the Bible and held it against her chest. Jesus would sustain her. He always had, even when she'd been living in sin. And she sure had done that plenty in her life.

With her eyes shut and leaning her head back against the rocker, she rested in the arms of her Savior. She didn't have words to pray, but He knew the groanings of her heart.

At least a half hour later, she heard a car horn and opened her eyes.

"Hey, AJ!" Daryl.

She half waved—grateful the banister, yard, sidewalk, and his car door were between them.

"My offer still stands. We should—"

"No, Daryl. Drive on."

"You'll come around. See you soon." He drove away.

She resumed her eyes-closed, head-back position. When would he get a hint?

Chapter Nine

At the beginning of their shift Tuesday morning, Logan walked out of the station beside Will and Zara.

Zara swatted his arm. "I'm so mad at you for not telling me about AJ being your wife."

She'd let it slide last night, even after they left AJ on the couch at her grandmother's house. But he'd known it was coming.

"I'm not a fan of talking about it."

"But your *wife*? When did that happen? And what on earth came between you?"

"Zara." Logan stopped walking. "I can't. Not right now."

"I'm sorry." She and Will stopped too.

"I get your questions, but ... I just can't." It was too much to even think about. He needed his head clear while on duty. "Later."

"Okay." She nodded.

He squeezed her arm. "Thank you." After a bid to stay safe, he went to his car and began his patrols. Hopefully, it would be a busy day. He needed to not get stuck in his head. He'd rather chase down some criminals. Maybe Daryl would do something loathsome, and Logan could arrest him. That would feel good.

Stop.

He switched the radio on to the Christian station. A song about forgiveness played. He let out a "humph." Ain't gonna happen.

Relieved that the song was over quickly, he let the music continue to play even though he didn't really listen to the words.

An hour into his shift, a call came in that a trash can had been lit on fire. Logan was close, so he responded.

He arrived at the home of Caleb and Amelia Johnson. Caleb was a paramedic, and Amelia a city detective.

Caleb stood outside, fire extinguisher in his hand. He waved to Logan. "Hey. It was a couple of kids. They ran that way. Amelia pursued."

Logan nodded and took off down the street in the direction Caleb had indicated.

He ran half a block before Amelia, a petite woman with short dark hair, came out from around another house shoving a teenage boy in cuffs.

She smiled at Logan. "I caught one of them. The other one is long gone. Perhaps this dude will give up his counterpart."

Logan took a hard look at the kid. "Are you the one who ran out of my carport the other day?"

The kid just snarled at him.

Logan took him from Amelia, and they read the kid his Miranda rights and walked back to Logan's squad. They came around to the side of the Johnson's house, and Logan pointed at the melted mess that was once a trash can. It was a good thing Caleb caught it when he did and was able to put it out. There was a small section where it was clear the flames had licked the garage. "What were you thinking?"

The kid growled.

"Dude, grow up. You are in deep trouble here. This isn't just any house; it's a cop's home. And we don't take kindly to people messing with our own."

The teen pressed his lips together.

"Fine, don't talk. It's your right, but the truth will come out. It always does."

Amelia said, "I'm going to check on my kids, then I'll meet you at the station. Is that okay?"

"Absolutely." Logan put the teen in the back of his squad car.

He had the kid booked and passed off by the time Amelia arrived.

"Thanks, Logan."

"Of course. Any idea why they would set your trash can on fire?"

She shook her head. "I'm really not sure. I don't think I've seen either of them before."

"Weird."

"But you've seen him?"

"Some kid about the same height and build was poking around my house the other day. Didn't seem to have taken or messed with anything, but maybe I got home in time."

"Hmm ... worth noting, especially if something else happens."

"Let me know if you need more from me."

"Will do. Stay safe, Logan."

He went back to his patrols. At least that had distracted him for a moment, but as he drove, his mind wandered back to AJ and wondering how she felt today. He did hope she was fine, but he couldn't afford to let his heart worry about her. She'd made her choices.

AJ took her dinner dishes to the sink and rinsed them. She reached for Granny's plate.

"Are you sure you're up to dishes?"

"Yes, ma'am. It's the least I can do. One day, and I'm already stir-crazy." AJ took the plate from her grandmother.

"Seems like the perfect opportunity to pray."

"I'm not to tax myself, but I have prayed every moment my head will let me."

"Good thing the good Lord knows our hearts."

AJ scrubbed the frying pan while Granny wiped the counters.

"Granny, how do I do it? How do I love a man who won't even talk to me? How do I build that bridge? I'm the one who took an ax to it in the first place."

Granny stopped her cleaning and stood quietly for a moment. "Your grandfather and I didn't always have the happiest of marriages. But by God's grace, we made it the sixty-five years we did. Most people don't know this, but when we'd been married about twenty years, he had an affair."

"Oh, Granny."

She turned to AJ and leaned back against the counter. "It was a very brief thing. But I struggled to forgive him for a long time. The one thing he did that helped win me back was he stayed around. He didn't say anything, but even though we weren't sleeping in the same room any more, he'd be sure to eat meals near me or sit in the same room while I read or sewed. He wouldn't talk, wouldn't push, but eventually, I started talking to him again."

"How can I be around him? We don't even live in the same house. He avoids me at all costs."

"Have you tried the quiet part while around him?"

AJ turned off the water and slumped against the sink. "No."

"Your friends are dating. Get them on board."

AJ nodded. "I have the sneaky suspicion they expect us to be in their wedding party, so I bet they want us to at least be amicable."

Granny smiled.

They finished cleaning up the kitchen, and AJ went and rested on the couch. She sent Zara a text letting her in on the plan. She'd conspire with Will; AJ could count on it.

Her phone binged. But it wasn't Zara.

> You are so beautiful. Like the flowers in the field. Text me back. Let's chat.

A shudder pulsed down her spine.

What on earth? She started to delete it and then thought better. If this person was going to continue to harass her, maybe she should have a record. But she also didn't want it sitting on her phone. They'd be able to pull it up on phone records if necessary, right?

It didn't matter. It wouldn't continue because she'd block them. She blocked and deleted the text. She didn't need to worry about it.

A few minutes later another text came through, but this one was Zara.

> I'm down. Maybe Will can convince him to watch a movie at our apartment.

> That might not be the best place. I could come to Will's house. That'd be neutral ground.

> I like it. I'll let you know. And I'll drive—you are not to drive.

> Fine.

A friend. AJ actually had a female friend. Who knew that could happen?

Saturday night Logan poured the salsa into a bowl at Will's house. His friend had invited Logan and a bunch of friends over to hang out and play some board games, card games, something like that.

He couldn't believe Eric was there. Will didn't know what Eric had seen the night that got him kicked out of school. Will knew a lot, but not that.

Zara came into the room. "Hey, partner. I brought the chips to go with that salsa."

"Good. Guac too?"

"Of course." She removed them from the grocery sack and opened the bag and container.

Logan took a chip and dipped it in the guac before popping it in his mouth. Around the food he said, "You got the right one this time."

"I had help."

Logan looked over his shoulder. AJ stood in the doorway between the dining room and kitchen.

She waved. "Hi."

"How's your head?" Was he actually talking to her? But he had to know she was okay.

"Getting better."

"Good." He diverted his eyes and went back to fussing with the food. He returned the giant container of salsa to the fridge and arranged the dips and chips.

Zara and AJ left the room, and he let himself breathe.

"Hey, man."

Logan turned around at the only slightly familiar voice. "Miles. What's up?"

They shook hands.

Miles leaned back against the counter, propping his hands on either side of him. "So how's AJ doing? I was surprised to see you together at the hospital."

"She said she's feeling a bit better. But you'd have to ask her for more."

"Did I catch the tech call you Mr. and Mrs.? Why didn't you tell me the other day? I would never have suggested what I did if I had known."

"We ... we are, but we're separated. Have been for quite a while."

"Then why haven't you divorced her?"

Logan shook his head. Miles wouldn't understand. Divorce wasn't an option in Logan's book—sure he'd thought about it, even talked to a lawyer, but that's as far as he got. It wasn't like he would remarry. AJ was his one and only. If that was over completely, he was done.

"No need for a ball and chain without all the benefits."

Logan let out a dry chuckle. "You wouldn't understand."

"Try me."

Logan shook his head.

"No worries." Miles held up his hands. "I will not get in the way there. She's off limits; I get it." He closed the space and slapped Logan on the shoulder. "I'm excited to reconnect. Glad Will invited me."

"Me too." Even if that conversation had been awkward ... and Logan would rather just hang out with AJ.

No, no he wouldn't.

Logan followed Miles back to the living room. Megan, Jenna, and Brennan also joined and the nine of them played a round of Apples to Apples that left everyone in stitches.

Logan struggled to keep his eyes off AJ. It had been so long since they actually both came to the same thing. More often in the last five years their friend group had been split. And if both of them happened to be invited to something, one of them would bow out. With Will and Zara not only dating but talking about marriage, it was going to be impossible not to be in the same place occasionally.

After that game concluded, they split into two groups to play board games that required smaller numbers. Logan waited to see which game AJ would pick and then chose the opposite. Although he found having her in the room didn't bother him as much as he would have expected.

"Logan." Will's voice snapped Logan out of his thoughts. "Pick your color."

The four other people at the table were staring at him.

He snatched the bag of black items and dumped them in front of him. He'd simply pretend AJ wasn't sitting across the room.

Yeah, that didn't work. He lost the game miserably because he kept making stupid blunders for lack of focus.

Will barely contained his laughter, but Logan caught it. He shot a dagger of a look at his friend. Will feigned innocence, mouthing, *what?*

Logan shook his head and helped clean up the game. Everyone stood around chatting, but AJ sat to the side and listened. Eric tried to engage her in conversation. She didn't seem interested in talking to him, though she was polite.

Why was Logan paying attention to what she was doing?

He re-engaged with the story Jenna was telling.

Eventually, everyone called it a night. Logan cut out as soon as the first person was ready to leave. He felt bad. He was Will's closest friend, helping clean up would be the appropriate thing to do. And maybe he would have if AJ had left quickly, but she didn't.

Logan revved his motorcycle and zoomed home. All he could think about was pouring a glass or three of whiskey and washing down the mixed emotions he didn't want to process.

And that's exactly what he did. Once inside his lonely house, he emptied his pockets on the table and laid his Glock, holster and all, beside his keys and wallet.

A glass from the dishwasher. The whiskey bottle from where he'd hidden it behind the flour so judgy eyes like Will's wouldn't see it.

He poured it, sank into the chair, and downed the entire thing. And another.

It didn't act fast enough. AJ consumed his mind. He wanted to push her as far away as possible, but he couldn't. This was supposed to be *their* house, yet he was here by himself. How'd they gotten to where they were? He'd lost her. She was gone. It didn't matter how much he missed her. It was over.

One more glass of whiskey.

Chapter Ten

After leaving Will's house, AJ followed Zara into their shared apartment over Granny's garage and let out a gust of air.

Zara flipped on the light. "How do you think that went?"

"Better than I had feared. He didn't leave as soon as he saw me there."

Zara chuckled. "True. You know, he couldn't stop looking at you."

"Like boring holes in my head with his laser vision?"

"Not at all. I don't think he knew what to make of being in the same room."

AJ shook her head. "I have to say, I get that. Oh well."

"Friendly reminder—you haven't told me the rest of the story yet."

AJ walked to the couch and flopped down. "I know. It's not easy to talk about."

Zara sat at the other end of the couch facing AJ and simply waited.

"We were on again/off again in high school and college—"

Zara's phone rang. "Sorry." She silenced it. "Oh, I should take this. It's the station. Probably following up on—"

"Just take it."

Zara answered the phone and went to her room.

AJ shoved herself off the couch and wandered to the kitchen. She searched the cabinets. Was she hungry? She'd eaten so much at Will's.

Maybe a cup of tea was what she needed, even if it was still eighty-something degrees at ten o'clock at night.

Her phone buzzed that she'd received a text message. Pulling the device from her pocket, she swiped it open and clicked on the new message.

> I'm glad you're able to stay in your own home. Hope that means you are feeling better. You look beautiful tonight.

The phone dropped from her hands and clanged on the counter. Who on earth? She'd blocked that last number. Was this someone different? Or the same creep?

She picked her phone back up and blocked the number, deleting the message. This was ridiculous.

After sliding her phone in her pocket, she went to the window by the door and peeked between the blinds. Was someone watching her?

Nothing out of place.

"AJ?"

She jumped and turned.

"Didn't mean to startle you. Everything okay?"

"Yeah, I'm fine. I think I just need to get to bed. Do you think it'd be too much if I started going to second service with you and Will?"

"And Logan?"

AJ nodded.

Zara shrugged. "Only one way to find out. Try it. Then I'll have Will figure out if it bothered him too much."

"I like that idea. And I haven't forgotten … I just can't right now."

"Go to bed. There'll be another time."

AJ told Zara good night and got ready for bed, but cautiously entered her bedroom, checking her closet and under her bed. She was acting paranoid, but someone was sending those creepy texts, and she didn't trust they weren't from Daryl. And more than anything, she didn't trust Daryl not to take extreme measures to get what he wanted.

At church the next morning, Logan sat in a chair in the center of the row halfway down the middle section. He set his Bible over two chairs to save a spot for Will and Zara.

Will came in and handed Logan his Bible. "You survived being in the same room as AJ last night. Good job, friend."

Logan shook his head and winced.

"You okay?" Will took his seat.

"A headache, no big deal."

"You've been having those a lot lately."

Logan shrugged. He wasn't about to tell his friend the headaches were a result of his increased whiskey consumption. The more he saw AJ, the more he wanted to drink. It was the easiest way to not have to think about all he had lost.

The band came on the stage, and the guys stood as the music started. As the worship leader welcomed everyone, Zara slipped in next to Will and gave him a hug. She waved at Logan.

He returned the gesture with a smile.

AJ joined Zara. Logan tried to keep his smile but looked away in case it faltered. He shouldn't be rude, even if he wished she wasn't here. For years, they'd managed to avoid each other, even while still attending the same church. He knew she went to first service, so why was she at second today?

She had the freedom to come to whichever service she wanted. It only made sense that she'd go with her roommate, but ... he growled internally.

He'd sing and ignore her. He'd be fine. At least he tried to tell himself he would be. But he wasn't.

After worship, the pastor got up and started his sermon. Logan opened his Bible and followed along as the pastor taught out of the book of 1 John. He talked about how if we claim to love God but hate a brother or sister we are liars and murderers.

Logan was antsy. When would the service be over?

But when the pastor said, "Loving means forgiving," Logan could barely stay in his seat.

He closed his Bible. It was over and done; did forgiveness really matter now?

He bided his time by thinking about that kid who had set Amelia and Caleb's trash can on fire. She had gotten him to crack and reveal his friend's identity. The two of them had been charged with a misdemeanor and released to their parents pending the hearing. The kid never did admit to going anywhere near Logan's house, so he didn't tell them what he was doing there. It would remain a mystery for now.

During the last song, Logan felt the Holy Spirit trying to nudge him. *I just can't. I don't know how, and frankly, I don't know that I want to.*

He didn't want to deny the Holy Spirit. But it felt easier to ignore Him for now. *Let's deal with it later.* He should pray for a softened heart, but that would require more of him than he could give up right now.

When the pastor bade them all a good week, Logan turned to Will and Zara and said, "I'll see you guys later."

Logan darted away as fast as possible, which was a snail's pace as everyone slowly exited their seats.

Amelia and Caleb stopped him and chatted for a few minutes. At least it wasn't AJ. When they were done talking, Logan glanced over his shoulder. No sign of AJ.

He breathed a little easier. Walking out the front door, he considered what he should do this afternoon. It was too early to start drinking, though tempting. He didn't want to become an alcoholic, but where was that line anyway? He wasn't there yet. Surely, not.

AJ stood in the shadow of a tree close to the church. Miles stopped and said *hi* to her.

Logan halted and contemplated turning back into the church, but he felt frozen in place. How'd he missed Miles inside? If only Logan hadn't seen AJ.

She didn't engage, so Miles went and got in his rental car parked nearby.

Logan should go back inside. Surely she'd leave soon. No, he should walk by and let it be.

AJ drew her phone from her bag and read something. She fumbled the device, nearly dropping it, then darted her gaze from side to side.

What was wrong?

Her eyes caught his. The panic was more intense than her behavior seemed. It was as if her eyes screamed at him to help.

This was *his* AJ. Why wouldn't he help her?

He took two slow steps toward her. She came to him.

"What's wrong?" It came out flatter than he wanted.

Her jaw quivered as she stared at him. Was she trying to decide if she could trust him with what had her scared?

"Where are Zara and Will?"

"Inside talking to the pastor."

He took a deep breath and intentionally softened his demeanor. "What has Miss I'm-scared-of-nothing rattled?"

She smiled at the tease. He'd given her a hard time about having zero fear when they were young. "I keep getting these texts. I block the number, but then I get a new one." She opened her phone and turned it to him.

A single text message.

> You went to a different service this morning. But I waited to see you. Gorgeous as always. Wish you'd come hangout with me instead of going to that place. Next time.

If the phone was in his hand he might have thrown it on the ground. "Why would you show me this?" His arm twitched as he balled his fist.

"Because it's not what you're thinking. I'm scared, Logan."

"Trying to rip open old wounds? Salt or lemon juice?"

She sucked in a shaky breath. "It's not like that." The fear in her eyes increased. She was afraid of him now too. He didn't want that—but maybe he did.

"It feels like that." He barely opened his mouth to shoot those arrow-like words at her.

She shoved her phone back in her bag. Tears pooled in her eyes.

He was being a jerk again. Why did he do this? The terror that shook her body was real, like it had been at the grocery store. He needed to stop playing the donkey.

"Will you hang up the past for a second? I need help. Someone is watching me, and it's freaking me out. Forget it, I should just tell Zara and Will." She spun away from him.

"AJ."

Slowly she turned back.

"What can I do?"

"Honestly, I don't even know."

"How many creepy texts have you received?"

"I think this makes four. But I blocked the numbers. And I deleted them—I didn't want you to see them and get the wrong idea."

Yet that's what he did when she showed him willingly. The words *I'm sorry* would probably be appropriate, but he couldn't get his voice to speak them.

Her phone dinged. She retrieved it and handed it to Logan. Another text came through from the same number.

> I didn't mean to scare you. Come to me, not him.

They both looked around, but Logan didn't see anyone watching them.

He wanted to kill the man tormenting AJ. "Do you have an idea who it could be?"

She shrugged. "Part of me wonders if ..." She looked at him and hesitated. "I guess it could be Daryl." She cringed like she expected Logan to explode.

Despite wanting to, he kept it contained. He didn't understand why she'd be upset if Daryl was making advances again, but how did he ask that without being a jerk? "That's completely over?"

She looked at the ground. "Yes, you know that." She sniffed. "I regret what happened more than anything. I've told you I'm sorry, and I still am. He didn't like that I broke things off so quickly, but in five years he hasn't given me trouble until I ran into him at the grocery store that night."

Logan nodded. He hated that he had asked. She'd tried to reconcile their marriage. But she'd broken her vows.

Had he driven her to it?

"Hey, you two are talking?" Will's voice drew Logan out of his mind.

He and AJ turned to find Will and Zara.

Zara tilted her head. "What's wrong? I guess the two of you are talking, so that alone could explain—" Zara covered her mouth.

Logan glanced at AJ. The look on AJ's face must have been what cut Zara off. He almost wanted to laugh, but it all weighed too much to let any levity erase the tension.

Logan said, "You haven't told her about the texts?"

AJ shook her head.

"Why not? She's a cop, and your roommate."

"And you're my husband, at least you were."

"Technically, I still am." He drew in a breath. "Let's get to the bottom of this. We may be separated, but I won't stand for someone bothering you."

Chapter Eleven

Now that was the Logan she remembered. For as long as AJ had known Logan, he'd always been a protector. It was nice to see that side of him come out again.

"Maybe Amelia or Adam is still here." Logan put his arm out behind AJ to guide her inside but didn't make contact.

How she longed for his strong hands to touch her again. She missed him so much it hurt.

Amelia emerged from the children's ministry area with her one-and-a-half-year-old on her hip, Caleb and the two other children followed.

Logan waved them over. "Can we steal you for a moment, Amelia?"

"Sure." She handed the baby to Caleb and said to him, "I'll meet you at the van."

Will and Zara waited to be filled in, and as soon as the kids were out of earshot, AJ told them all about the texts she'd been receiving. "Also, Daryl drove by Granny's house the other day while I was sitting on the porch and attempted to ask me to hang out. I told him to get lost, and he drove on."

Amelia sighed. "We may be able to retrieve those deleted texts, assuming you haven't filled up your phone storage since then. Then we'd have a record of them. I can open a case, but it's not much to go on right now. With permission to search your phone records, I can see if I can find out where they are coming from. If he bought the SIM cards with his own name, we'll know who it is pretty quick."

AJ grimaced. "I doubt someone who intentionally got multiple phone numbers would do so under his own name. I didn't figure there was anything you could do."

Logan set his hand on her shoulder. "It's not nothing. If he keeps harassing you, we'll get him."

"Do I need to tell him to stop rather than ignoring it?"

Logan removed his hand, and she ached for it to return. "Ummm." He handed her the phone. "I may have already taken the liberty."

She swiped it open. Logan had sent the creep a text.

> Leave her alone.

Her heart swelled. She couldn't be mad at him for doing that. In fact, she loved him a bit more for it. But she knew better than to hope it meant more.

Amelia said, "Why don't you stop at the station in the morning, and we can get the ball rolling. If anything more happens or he sends a threat, you call me. Got it?"

AJ nodded.

"You have my cell number?"

"I do. Thank you."

"Of course. Stay safe." Amelia left.

AJ didn't know what to do. She wanted Logan to stay close, but only if his normally icy demeanor remained far away. It was too much to ask of him. She'd already invaded his space enough for the last two days. Coming to second service might have been too much, but she was so glad he'd been the one she'd found when she received those texts.

If only he could understand how much she still needed him, wanted him, desired him.

Zara spoke up as the silence lingered. "Let's eat back at our place. You too, Logan."

AJ held her breath. Would he?

"I don't know." He met AJ's eyes. What did she see in there? It wasn't the malice she expected. So much hurt.

She swallowed. "You are welcome but don't feel obligated."

"I guess I could come eat."

Will clapped his hands. "Good. Let's go."

AJ smiled. "We'll see you guys there." She wove her hand around Zara's elbow, and the women walked to the car arm in arm.

Outside, Zara said, "Are you okay?"

She let out a squeak. "Maybe."

They settled in the car, and AJ said, "Here's the stupid-quick version: five years ago, Logan and I hit a rough patch, and I had an affair with Daryl. It was only like a few times, but it's what happened. I came clean with Logan, and he kicked me out of the house."

"Oh, AJ."

"It was dumb on my part. But despite my repentance, he hasn't been able to forgive me."

"What happened between the two of you to lead to that?"

"I can't handle that story too right now, but let's just say the hardest year of our lives. We didn't handle it well."

AJ leaned back against the headrest. Tears pooled in her eyes. If she didn't stop talking about it all, she'd be a blubbering mess before they got to the apartment.

Chapter Twelve

Nearly Twelve Years Ago—Thanksgiving Weekend

Thursday morning, twenty-one-year-old Logan ran up the front steps of AJ's dad's house. They had a couple of hours to hang out before they were expected at her grandmother's for dinner prep. He knocked on the door.

No answer. Was AJ still in bed? She hadn't been feeling super great the last week or so.

He glanced around the side of the house. Her dad's car wasn't there. Logan tried the knob. It was unlocked.

He let himself in. "AJ?"

"In here."

He turned down the hallway. She sat on the floor outside of the bathroom, forearms resting on her knees.

"Are you feeling okay?" He squatted down in front of her.

She shrugged. "I'm late, Logan. Like a week late."

The implications of her words slammed into him.

They'd been stupid again. Despite their grandiose plans to wait until they were married this time around, they hadn't even made it a month of being back together before they'd slipped into old habits.

He couldn't figure out how he felt ... well, other than the guilt.

"A baby." The words slipped out softly.

"I think so. The test is sitting on the counter in there. I'm scared to look."

"But a baby." Joy surged through him. He cupped the side of her face. "We can face whatever it says. Either way, we should get married."

"I'm gonna get kicked out of school if it's positive."

"Not if we're married."

"Are you crazy? I'll be showing before summer."

"Why should we wait until summer?"

She released a rueful laugh. "Let's check the test first."

He stood and offered his hands. She took them, and he pulled her up and against his chest. Kissing her head, he hugged her close. "I love you."

"Same." She stepped back and tugged him into the little bathroom.

His heart sped up like a motorcycle on an open country road. From behind, he wrapped his arms around her waist.

She lifted the test, and they looked together.

Two bright pink lines.

They were going to have a baby. He shifted his hand to rest on her lower abdomen. Inside her womb, a little life grew. The product of their love for one another. And their inability to follow God's law.

The dichotomy of joy and guilt was unbearable. He felt like he was going to explode and implode at the same time.

She spun in his arms. Tears brimmed in her eyes. "A baby."

"A baby. Our baby."

A giggle overcame her, and a matching one burst from his heart. They had spent hours talking about having a family one day, and the day was coming much sooner than they had planned.

AJ wrapped her arms around his neck, and he lifted her off the ground and spun her around. A baby.

He couldn't get his mind around it, but his heart was all in. He was going to be a dad. One day he'd have to get a motorcycle with a side car, and they could go on all kinds of adventures together.

Setting AJ back on her feet, he gazed into her eyes. "Will you marry me?"

"This is how you ask? In a bathroom and not even on one knee?" She chuckled.

She didn't care about those kinds of things, but she was right, this was a horrible proposal. "Fine, this isn't the real proposal. I have to talk to your dad after all."

Somberness overtook them both. He was not going to be impressed.

Logan asked, "Do you know when he'll be home?"

She shrugged. "Probably not for another hour. Let's get some breakfast. I need to eat."

After AJ hid the pregnancy test in her room, they went and made some pancakes, and while they were finishing eating, her dad arrived home.

He came into the dining room and kissed AJ on top of her head. He greeted them both and settled in the living room with the newspaper.

Logan met AJ's eyes. "I'm going to talk to him."

She nodded. "I'll clean this up."

Logan shuffled to the next room. *God, I know we did this backwards, but please help us make it right. Help me find favor in Mr. Jacobson's eyes. And please forgive AJ and me for our disobedience.*

"Logan?"

He snapped out of his prayer and realized he was standing right in front of AJ's dad. "Hi."

Mr. Jacobson folded up his newspaper and set it on the coffee table in front of him. "What's going on?" He leaned forward, resting his forearms on his knees.

"I have a question to ask you. Do you have a moment?"

"I take it that wasn't the question." He gave Logan a crooked smile.

He relaxed a little. "I suppose I have more than one question then."

"Sit, son, before you hurt yourself."

Logan grabbed a wooden chair and pulled it a little closer, so he could look more directly at AJ's dad. He fiddled with his hands.

"Ask the question, Logan. I promise not to bite your head off."

He nodded. "As you know, I love your daughter with all my heart. I am committed to her, and I would like to marry her. So my question is: may I have her hand in marriage?" Logan felt out of breath.

Mr. Jacobson sat back with a serious expression Logan couldn't read. He glanced past Logan to the kitchen. "Alice Jane, come in here."

Logan's heart refused to beat normally. His chest was too constricted.

AJ came in the room and slid her hand onto Logan's shoulder. "Yes, Daddy?"

"I think you should be part of this conversation. No doubt you know what Logan asked me."

She nodded.

Mr. Jacobson met Logan's eyes. "Is she pregnant?"

Logan froze. While they'd made breakfast, they had talked about waiting to tell her dad or anyone. Logan looked at AJ.

Her dad said, "You don't need permission from her to answer the question I already know the answer to. I could see it in her face and gait when you guys got here yesterday from school."

"Yes, sir. We're gonna have a baby. I'm prepared to take her as my wife and be her one and only 'til death do us part."

"The two of you are done with your fickleness and are committed to each other?"

They both nodded. Logan said, "Yes, sir."

"Marriage isn't easy, and you will face things that will threaten to tear you apart. Seek Jesus in the good times and bad times. Seek Him individually and together. Then, and only then, can you face the challenges ahead. You two should have gotten married before now, but you are where you are. You have my blessing. When's the wedding?"

AJ's hand gripped Logan's shoulder. "Needs to be soon enough that I don't get kicked out of school."

Mr. Jacobson nodded. "The week after exams, right before Christmas?"

Logan sat up a little taller. "Three weeks from now?"

AJ smiled. "Let's do it. I never wanted anything too fancy anyway."

Logan wrapped his arm around her waist. He was going to finally marry his best friend. "We'll make it perfect."

Three Weeks Later

AJ held the trash can on her lap as Granny did her hair. In the last three weeks her morning sickness had gotten worse. She was afraid she was going to be walking down the aisle with the trash can instead of her bouquet.

"You look beautiful, Allie."

"Thanks, Granny. But I feel awful. I'm going to ruin everything by throwing up all over the pastor."

"You'll be fine. I remember thinking my morning sickness was going to keep me from everything, but I managed to do what I needed to without losing my breakfast. You'll be distracted enough by that handsome young man."

AJ hadn't told Granny why she didn't feel good. "Did Daddy tell you?"

"No, dear, I figured it out. When I heard you were planning the wedding so quickly, I was going to take you aside and encourage you to not get pregnant right away, but then I saw the way Logan looked at you. That boy is in love—has been for a long time—but it only grows like that when it's been multiplied by a new life."

"Yeah? You think we'll do okay? Like you and Grandpa? Married forever?"

A shadow crossed Granny's eyes for a split second. "I pray the two of you have an even more blessed marriage. I know you two have had a challenge keeping your eyes on Jesus, but you must learn to do so. Just because you have the freedom to express your love physically now, doesn't mean all your challenges will be gone. New ones will rise, especially as you are starting off on the wrong foot."

"Yes, ma'am."

A knock sounded on the door. Granny went and cracked it open. "You can't come in here."

Logan's chuckle came from the other side of the door. "I know. But I would like to pray with my future wife before we say our vows. I promise I won't peek."

"I guess I can't argue with that."

Granny left, and AJ went to the door and found Logan's hand coming from the other side of the door.

She hid on the opposite side of the wall and grasped his fingers. "I love you."

He said, "I love you too. Pray with me?"

"Yes."

He prayed for them. Repented of their sin, and implored God for His mercy to abound in their marriage. He prayed for protection and God's help in navigating the next stages of life. He prayed for blessing and grace above all.

When he said *amen*, AJ added, "Ditto and amen."

Logan chuckled. "Are you ready?"

"Mentally, yes. Physically, no. Send Granny back in."

"Will do. See you soon." His hand slipped from hers, and it was all she could do not to burst from the room and embrace the man who would soon be her husband.

An hour later, the front room of Granny's old Victorian-style home was filled with all their guests: AJ's mom and brother and grandpa; Logan's parents, siblings, and grandparents; Will and his entire family.

AJ descended the stairs on Daddy's arm and searched for Logan at the end of the tiny aisle. He beamed with joy and love. In three short weeks, despite exams, they had pulled off the perfect little wedding. They had tried for a church, but none were available. When Granny and Grandpa offered their home, all the pieces had fallen into place. Very little was needed in the way of decorations because Granny had a beautiful knack for Christmas decorating. Everything was perfect. AJ's nausea was even at bay as her dad gave her hand to Logan.

The ceremony was beautiful too. Not that AJ could focus on any of it as she kept her eyes fixed with Logan's.

The pastor led them in their vows. They pledged themselves to one another. Promised to walk through life together, no matter what. In the sight of God and man, they voiced the commitments their hearts had already made to one another.

The pastor then said, "I pronounce you husband and wife. Logan, kiss your bride."

Logan let go of one of her hands and slid it behind her neck and drew her close. Tenderness and passion entangled their lips. She slipped her hands around his shoulders. His other hand took the small of her back and drew her as close as possible, dipping her back slightly.

Finally. They were married. Man and wife. One. United in soul and body. God had brought them together. Even if they'd stumbled their way into this union, AJ knew God had made them for each other. They fit, maybe a little bit too much like gasoline and fire sometimes, but they encouraged each other and were always ready to be what the other needed.

Logan drew out of the kiss first and placed a peck on her forehead when he steadied her upright again.

"I present Mr. and Mrs. Logan Jackson."

Mrs. AJ Jackson. She liked it. And she'd perfected that signature when she was ten, so she was ready.

Eight Months Later—August

Logan paced the living room in the apartment above AJ's grandmother's garage. She was letting them live there rent free for the summer between their junior and senior years of college. He stopped in front of the bathroom door again. AJ had been having contractions for the last five hours. Surely it would be time to go to the hospital soon.

"I'm fine, Logan."

"Are they closer?"

The door opened. "Yes, and it's probably time to go, but it's not a rush. We're not on TV. This girl isn't coming quite yet. If I'm lucky, it'll be today."

Logan looked at his watch. It wasn't even noon yet. He hoped she wouldn't be in labor that long. Not only did he hate seeing her in pain, but he wanted to hold his little girl.

AJ set down her phone and turned to Logan. "Dance with me. The swaying helps."

He raised his hands to her and ran them along the sides of her swollen abdomen to her back, drawing her as close as was possible.

He'd never seen a more beautiful sight than the woman he loved with their child growing inside.

He hummed as they swayed back and forth. With her against him, he felt the contraction begin and seize her entire body.

"Breathe. In. Out. Deep breaths. That's it. You've got this."

They continued to sway as AJ breathed through the contraction.

When it eased, she said, "It's time to go."

"Yeah? You sure?"

"Yeah, that one hurt different."

"Okay, I'll get our bags."

In less than thirty minutes, they were settled in their hospital room. He turned on the music AJ wanted and made sure she had her water bottle and pillow.

"What else do you want me to do?"

She took his hand. "Hold my hand. You got me into this mess." She winked at him.

He laughed until another even harder contraction hit.

Surely it wouldn't be much longer. Watching AJ work through the contractions was torture. He wanted to take it away, ease her pain, but he couldn't.

Three hours later, after spending entirely too much time pushing, a baby's cry cut through the air. "It's a girl."

The doctor laid a messy baby on AJ's chest. The nurses wiped her off. She was perfect. Golden peach fuzz covered her squishy little head. He was in love.

"Logan!" He met AJ's eyes. "We did it."

"You did it." He leaned down and kissed his wife. "I'm so proud of you."

The nurses whisked the baby away to measure and clean her up more.

He stroked AJ's damp hair from her face. "What shall we name her?" They'd narrowed it down to two names but still hadn't decided.

"Bree. Breana Joy. What do you think?"

"I fully agree."

The nurse came back with a tiny bundle. "Daddy?"

His heart soared. He reached out and took the baby. "Hi, Bree. Welcome to the world."

She cooed softly, wrapping him firmly around her itty-bitty finger. He kissed her forehead before holding her close to his chest.

Chapter Thirteen

Present Day

Logan slapped some mayonnaise on his slice of bread. This apartment brought back so many memories. Ones he wished he could go back to and stay in. Little of the furniture was the same, and AJ must have put on a fresh coat of paint when she moved back in. But these walls had held them for a bit of their life together. Where they'd brought Bree home.

"Logan?"

He snapped his head toward AJ.

"Are you done with the mayo?"

"Yeah, sorry." He handed her the knife. Their skin brushed. The warmth of her touch was magnetic. Maybe coming for lunch was a bad idea.

He let the other three own the conversation while they ate. Occasionally he'd contribute, but he didn't have much to say. Being near AJ and in the apartment was pushing his sanity.

After they ate, the women cleaned up and told the guys to pick out a game. It was stupid hot outside, so being in the air conditioning was preferable. He wasn't sure he had any desire to stick around and play. He wanted to down a bottle of whiskey, but he'd settle for a nap before four days of working the night shift, which started at ten o'clock tonight.

He wandered across the room with Will to the bookshelf that had a few games, along with AJ's ever-growing library. On the shelf sat a photo frame. Without thinking, he picked it up and stared at a picture of Bree from a few weeks before her third birthday.

Zara came up beside him. "I've been meaning to ask AJ who that is."

He didn't look up at Zara; he kept his eyes on Bree's face. "Our daughter."

Zara took in a quick, sharp breath. "What?"

"Her name was Bree. She was three in this picture." He held the photograph to his chest. Moisture blurred his vision. He missed his little girl.

He set the photo down and wiped the moisture from his eyes. Turning back, he caught AJ's gaze. They simply stared at each other.

Logan finally found his voice. "I should go take a nap before night shift starts. Stay safe, AJ. Let me know if I need to beat anyone up, okay?"

She nodded. "I will. Thanks for coming over."

He darted out before his emotions got the better of him. As he strapped on his helmet, he could barely get his lungs to work.

Granny came out the back door and waved to him. He wasn't sure he could handle talking right now, but it was Granny, and one didn't *not* talk to Granny.

She walked right to him. "It's good to see you, Logan." She squeezed his arm and continued on her course toward her backyard.

Instead of driving away, he turned off his bike, removed his helmet, and followed AJ's grandmother. She sat at the little wrought-iron table and chairs.

"Granny?"

"Yes, Logan? Join me."

He sat, not sure what he wanted to say.

"What is it? What's on your mind?"

"Everything, and nothing. I'm not sure."

"Heavy heart?"

He nodded.

"You came to me, and you know I say it like it is. Are you ready to hear it?"

He shrugged.

She chuckled. "Oh, dear boy. You have always been full of passion and love. But when you suppress that love under unforgiveness, it sours and festers like a cut that didn't get cleaned out."

"I can't forgive. What happened with AJ and Daryl ... I just can't."

"You will never be happy if you live under that lie. Do you believe Jesus forgave the two of you for your impropriety before you got married?"

"Yes."

"How is this different?"

"She betrayed me. That's a whole different level."

"Sin is sin."

Thor's hammer to the chest might have felt better. Logan stood. "Pray for me?"

"Every day, Logan. You're my grandson by marriage. And I love you. Always have."

"Love you too, Granny." He leaned down and kissed her cheek before leaving.

His entire body shook as he remounted his bike. Helmet back on, he peeled out before the words he didn't want to hear, but needed to, sank in.

Without Zara's music playing, the apartment was quiet while AJ got ready for her day Monday morning. She went to the bookshelf and picked up the picture of Bree Logan had held yesterday. How one person could look so much like both of her parents was a mystery.

She kissed the frame. "I miss you, baby girl." Grief was a strange thing. Some days felt impossible, other days were numb. Then, on occasion, AJ felt normal. Today seemed somewhere between normal and numb.

Setting the frame back on the shelf, she went to the kitchen. Coffee would help her wake up. Of course, in the process of waking up she may fall into the impossible. Waking up to the reality that she needed to pursue her husband and mend that relationship made her feel overwhelmed more often than not lately.

She popped a K-Cup into the coffeemaker and let it gurgle.

"Jesus..." She didn't have the words. But He knew her heart, and she rested in that.

She grabbed the steaming cup of joe and added stevia and half-and-half. "I need you, Lord. Soften Logan's heart. Give me words—the right ones. Heal our hearts."

Leaning back against the counter, she took a slurpy sip of the hot coffee.

A knock.

She nearly dropped her mug. Gah! She was not normally this jumpy.

She glanced through the blinds. A grocery delivery? She didn't order groceries. Maybe Zara did, knowing AJ would be home. She checked her phone and the spot where they left each other notes. Nothing.

"Be right there." She ran to her room and grabbed Harry from her nightstand. Holding the Smith & Wesson behind her back, she cracked the door open and snagged the groceries from the landing. They looked like things she would order.

"Hey," she called after the delivery guy. "I didn't order groceries."

He turned and came back to the bottom of the stairs. "Are you"—he pulled it up on his phone—"AJ Jackson?"

"I am."

"Well, they're yours regardless of who sent them. I can't take them back."

"Okay. Thanks."

She took half the groceries inside and set the bags and the pistol on the kitchen table before retrieving the rest.

She unloaded them on the table. Every single item was something she normally bought, or had bought last week. What on earth? In fact, these were the exact groceries she bought last Sunday when she ran into Logan. Had he ... no, he wouldn't.

It didn't make any sense, and it felt off. Surely, she didn't order them in her sleep last night.

She checked her watch. It was nearly nine o'clock. If Amelia wasn't already at the station, she would be soon. This would be worth mentioning.

After tossing the frozen and refrigerated items where they belonged, she went to her bedroom to get dressed.

Her phone dinged with a new text. It was from *him*.

> I noticed you didn't make it to the store yes-
> terday so figured you'd need a few things.

The message concluded with a kissy-face emoji.

A shudder rippled through her body. Should she throw those groceries away? Now she really needed to talk to Amelia.

AJ hustled to finish making herself presentable and dashed out the door as soon as possible.

Chapter Fourteen

After a night shift that went a little longer than normal, Logan changed out of his uniform and headed upstairs to the detectives' squad room. He hoped to catch Amelia and see if she'd talked to AJ yet about the text messages. He may be at odds with his wife, but he couldn't knock the feeling that something terrible was afoot.

And after all, she was still his wife. He couldn't forgive her, but he still loved her. Always had, always would.

He hit the top stair into the lobby of the police station, and the front door opened. AJ walked in.

The animosity he'd grown accustomed to feeling at the very sight of her was MIA. The lack of that emotion left him not sure how to respond.

She scanned the space and locked eyes with him. She almost seemed to smile.

"Hey." His voice was raspier than he expected.

She walked toward him. "G'morning. How was your shift?"

He shrugged. "Nothing out of the ordinary."

"In your line of work, that's a good thing, I think." Her soft chuckle tugged on his heart.

"Here to talk to Amelia?"

AJ nodded and glanced toward the squad room before looking back at him with furrowed brows. "You didn't send me groceries, right?"

"No." Time for his brows to furrow. "What happened?"

"Mind coming with me, so I can tell you and Amelia at the same time?"

"It's why I came up. Of course I didn't know you'd arrive right now."

A mischievous glint flashed through her eyes. "What? Not keeping tabs on me like my stalker?" But her face fell at that last word. "I have a stalker, don't I?"

"It's beginning to sound like it. Let's go talk to the detectives." He motioned to the door, yearning to reach out and touch AJ's back as they walked but equally repulsed by the idea.

He scanned his ID and held the door for her.

Amelia sat at her desk by the window and waved them over. She had only lived in Hazel Hill for three years or so and likely didn't know their history, probably didn't even know they were married. She greeted them and told them to sit. Logan let AJ have the chair beside Amelia's desk and snatched a second one from nearby.

AJ told them about the groceries she'd received that morning and the text that had come shortly after. "They were exactly the groceries I got last week."

"When you saw Daryl? And me?"

AJ nodded.

"Did you talk to Daryl before you saw him at the register?"

"Yeah, he cornered me in the aisle right after I talked to you."

Amelia asked, "So he could have seen the items in your cart?"

"I was carrying a basket, and I doubt it. It was all a little haphazard in there."

Logan chuckled. "She's not a put-everything-in-neat-rows kind of person."

"He's not wrong," AJ said.

Amelia smiled. "Talk to me about Daryl. You've mentioned him a few times. You said he drove by last week. And you had a run-in with him at the grocery store. Tell me how these things are significant."

Logan swallowed. Maybe he should leave. "Do you want me to go?"

AJ's head snapped toward him. The pain in her eyes was unmistakable. "No. You can stay. I appreciate having you here."

He nodded. "Okay." Not that he was sure he could stomach talking about this again.

Adam Jamison, Amelia's partner, joined them. Logan stood and shook his hand.

Adam said, "It's good to see you guys. Are you ...?" He pointed back and forth between AJ and Logan.

"No, we're not back together. I'm here to ..." He honestly didn't know why he was here.

AJ finished the thought. "Because he's the protective type and doesn't like that someone is harassing a person he once loved." She then looked at Amelia. "Logan and I are married, though separated. I had a brief affair five years ago with Daryl." She sat back with a puff of air.

Logan cringed. As much as he hated hearing the words, he also hated hearing the pain in her voice.

Amelia said, "I'm sorry. Have you had any contact with Daryl in the last five years?"

AJ shook her head. "No. I mean, I see him around on occasion, but I've gotten pretty good at avoiding him."

"I hate that I have to ask some of these questions, but it'll help. Who broke off the affair?"

"I did. I hated it. I didn't want it. But I had been stupid and lost myself for a moment. Your next question will probably be about his response. It wasn't good. When I told him it was over and I wanted to be with my husband, he kind of blew up. Threw a few things—not at me—and called me some nasty things, but that was that. I haven't really talked to him since. But at both of the recent run-ins he suggested we 'reconnect.'" She shuddered.

Logan rolled his shoulder. This conversation was terribly uncomfortable. He wanted to find Daryl and put a bullet in him for ever touching his wife, but Logan wouldn't do that. However, if that man ever *did* touch her without her wanting him to, Logan might have a change of tune.

Adam sat back in his chair and gave Logan a look like he knew exactly what went through Logan's mind. Adam shook his head disapprovingly.

Logan shrugged.

Adam sat forward and clasped his hands together. "Sounds like we have a solid suspect. Let's dig into things a little bit. Amelia filled me in earlier. May I see your phone to try and recover the deleted texts?"

"Sure." AJ pulled her phone out of her pocket and handed it to Adam.

Amelia took some information from AJ to access her phone records. Adam and Amelia would dig into finding the identity of the texter. If it was Daryl, they would go have a talk with him.

Logan said, "I still can't figure out how he knew what groceries to buy. Even if Daryl saw your basket. I saw it, and the items were piled on top of each other. Wait, did you use your store card?"

"I did. I want the sale prices. Thinking maybe he hacked it?"

Logan nodded.

Adam said, "It's possible. We'll look into that too."

Logan and AJ thanked the detectives and left together. He yawned as they walked into the lobby.

"Long night, huh?" AJ asked.

"I didn't get as good a nap yesterday as I had hoped."

They stopped walking near the door.

AJ turned to him. She wanted to say something; he could see it in her eyes. So he waited. He needed to stop and listen for once.

"Thanks for being beside me in this. You have no idea how much it means to me."

He kept his eyes locked on her deep blues.

"Does this mean we're talking again?"

He looked down at their feet. "For now, I guess."

"I really am sorry for everything. I hate what I did."

He met her gaze again. "I know. At least I'm starting to realize that. But I don't know if I can ever trust you again."

"I don't know what I can do to prove myself to you. I've changed, Logan."

"Can people ever really change?"

"By the power of Christ, yes. Added bonus if they have the love and support of family and friends."

They hadn't been able to change their behavior before they were married, and as soon as times got tough, she fell into the same old sin. But had she changed?

"Have you been with anyone else?"

"No." The definitiveness of the word caught him off guard. "I may have messed up with Daryl, but I promise you I will never be with another man except you, if you are ever willing to have me back."

He just stared at her. She wanted to come back to him? Even after he was so nasty when he kicked her out of the house?

She reached out and gripped his upper arm. "I still love you and always will." She let her hand drop. Turning, she walked away until she reached the door. Before pushing it open, she looked back at him and smiled.

He stood there like a blubbering fool, watching her walk away. She was an enigma. She'd betrayed him so completely, but somehow he now felt like he was the one who had betrayed her. Had he?

Was he just as guilty? Had he driven her into another man's arms? Was his unforgiveness a betrayal to his vows?

Half an hour after leaving Logan gawking in the lobby, AJ wandered into the fire station. She couldn't go home; she was restless after a week of sitting around. She needed to do something. She was supposed to be working today, so she might as well come in and putz around some.

"What are you doing here?" Seth's tone was playful.

"I'm bored." AJ still wasn't sure what to think about the new guy. He was young, cocky, and good looking, and he knew it. Eventually, life would catch up with him and cut him down a notch. But as far as she knew, he'd had a very blessed childhood. His dad was pastor of a big church in Winston-Salem, and his parents were the picture of a beautiful marriage.

Seth laughed. "I believe it. I'm sure Ty will let you clean the toilets."

She shot Seth an annoyed look, which increased his laughter.

She went into the living area and found Ty in his office. "Please give me something productive to do. You know research says getting back to work is important to healing from a concussion."

Ty looked up from his desk and set his pen down. "I distinctly remember telling you to take two weeks off, and *then* we would get you back into work."

"I'm feeling so much better. No headache today, and I can focus on things now. A week was enough." She didn't want to tell him being home might make her an easier target for her apparent stalker.

"Fine. Only fifty percent of normal station tasks that don't involve a ladder or climbing on anything. No calls. Nothing strenuous or taxing."

"Yes, sir." She gave him a sloppy salute.

"And no overnight. Daytime hours only. You need rest—solid sleep to heal."

She nodded. Not that she relished the idea of sleeping in an empty apartment while Zara worked the night shift. The more she thought about it, the more those groceries coming into her house felt like a violation of her space.

After leaving Ty's office, she went to the checklist they kept on the wall by the kitchen—routine tasks that needed to be done. Seth wasn't joking about the bathroom. It must have been quiet this morning.

She cleaned the bathroom, then helped with lunch prep. A call came in, so she completed lunch on her own while everyone else went out.

An hour later, the crew came back and collapsed at the table set with lunch.

She sat with them. "Tell me what happened, so I can live vicariously through you all."

Brennan said, "Another cop's house got hit with arson."

"Another? There have been others?"

"Yeah, Caleb said their trash can got lit up last Tuesday. Then Sergeant Fain's house was hit on Thursday, again started in a trash can, but the side of the house caught because no one was home. It was out before too much damage was caused. Then today's call was at Officer Wells' house."

AJ asked, "Trash can again?"

"Yep, but it was too close to his car, and that lit up."

"What is going on?" She crossed her arms. Was Logan in danger? Will? Zara?

Don, a firefighter ten years her elder, said, "That's the question. It's supposedly a bunch of teens, but why? Amelia caught one of them, but he didn't talk other than giving up his partner in crime."

"Has anyone gotten hurt?"

Emily said, "Thankfully, no. But if this continues, someone is going to end up hurt or worse."

AJ's stomach flopped. Cops being targeted. The three people in the world she cared about most were officers. *Protect them, Lord.*

Chapter Fifteen

Tuesday afternoon, Logan woke up to the sound of his phone ringing. Sleeping during the day between night shifts never allotted enough time for sufficient rest. He rubbed his eyes and looked at the caller ID. Adam Jamison. Was AJ okay?

"Hello."

"Hey, Logan. It's Adam. AJ asked me to call you and fill you in on where we are on her case."

"So she's okay? Nothing more happened?"

"She's fine. We ran into a dead end with the phone numbers. Whoever this guy is bought up a batch of SIM cards or burner phones and is cycling through them. Never sends more than a few texts per phone. He must have anticipated she would block the number. Records show he tried to call her from the first number, probably to test if she blocked him."

"Does it even lead you to where he bought them?"

"Yes, a store in town. On the same day AJ received the first text."

"Surveillance? How'd he pay?"

"If you'd let me, I'll answer all these questions. Cash, and their cameras are pathetic. I'm texting you the best shot."

"Sorry." He waited for the text.

"No worries. You know I understand."

The text came through. It was a grainy black-and-white photo of the top of a guy's baseball cap. The man was wearing the most generic clothes possible. Average height, average build. Could easily be Daryl; could easily not be.

Adam continued. "The cashier remembered the transaction but said the guy hardly spoke and wore dark sunglasses."

"I appreciate y'all taking this seriously and investigating."

"Of course. Stalkers are no joke, and this guy is not taking a hint. I wish there was more we could do."

"Any news on the grocery thing?"

"Nothing. Looks like he hacked into her account and used a gift card to pay. Again, we couldn't trace it to anything helpful."

"Thanks, Adam."

"Sure thing. AJ said to keep you updated, so I'll let you know if anything happens."

The guys hung up, and Logan leaned forward where he sat on the side of the bed. Resting his elbow on his knees he ran his fingers into his hair. How he wished this had incriminated Daryl! But it didn't. They needed to get this guy to leave AJ alone.

Maybe Logan needed to suck it up and spend more time with her. He couldn't protect her from a distance. But the idea hurt.

She'd been the one to give Daryl the impression she would choose him since she did before.

But did he have that all wrong? He questioned all of his thoughts these days.

By ten-thirty that evening, as he walked out of the station ready to begin his patrols, Logan had worked his mind into an even more confused state. He couldn't sort anything out. He knew he shouldn't hate his enemies, but at the moment he was pretty certain he hated Daryl Turpin. That was the clearest thought he had. His thoughts about AJ were much less straightforward.

It didn't matter right now anyway. He had a long night of driving around the city waiting for something to happen. Hopefully his biggest challenge would be staying awake.

He took a sip of his coffee and drove.

Not even thirty minutes later, a call came in for another trash can fire. Dispatch relayed the address.

"That's Will's house!" And he wasn't far away. He flipped on his lights and siren and raced toward his best friend's home.

When he arrived two minutes later, Logan drove onto the grass. A neighbor was trying to put out the fire with his garden hose, but the flames were licking the side of the house.

Logan ran straight to the front door and unlocked it with his spare key. From the kitchen he grabbed the large fire extinguisher Will kept under the sink.

By the time Logan ran back outside, another neighbor had joined the firefight with a tiny extinguisher. It helped, but when Logan released the fire suppressant from the large canister, the flames faltered and flickered out. The neighbor's quick action had saved Will's house.

Will and Zara both pulled up from opposite directions. The relief on each of their faces was significant. They hugged, then came to Logan.

"Good thing I had a key on me."

Will clapped his friend's shoulder. "For sure. Thank you so much. But I noticed you left them in the door."

Logan laughed. "I figured getting the extinguisher was more important at the moment."

He took his keys from the door and went over to the neighbor with the hose. "Thank you for your help. Are you the one who called it in?"

"Yes. Well, my wife did. I came out here right away."

"Did you see anyone?"

"What looked like a couple of teenagers ran past our house about a minute before I noticed the flames. I can't say for sure if they did it, but it seemed too coincidental."

More teenagers. What happened to TPing someone's house? This was over the line. And again, a member of the Hazel Hill Police Department was hit.

Chapter Sixteen

Six Years Ago—August

Logan ran through the house, five-year-old Bree tearing after him with shouts of "I'm going to get you, Daddy." Logan collapsed on the couch, and Bree launched herself, diving right into him. He caught her, holding her close, tickling and nuzzling her neck. She exploded in giggles.

"Now who's got whom?" He couldn't control his own laughing. He lifted her petite body up into the air.

She wiggled and giggled. "Put me down, Daddy."

He lowered her to the floor, and she took off running. "Catch me!"

"You're so fast I don't know if I can." He shoved off the couch and pursued her around the kitchen table of their little house. He and AJ had managed to buy the little three-bedroom ranch two years ago because Granny had saved all their rent money and given it back to them for a downpayment. God had been so good. They'd both finished college, even with a newborn. He'd gotten a job at the police station right out of school, and they were doing fine for themselves. One of these days, they'd give Bree some siblings to play with too.

In their chase around the table, Logan pretended not to be able to catch Bree, but she just laughed harder, which slowed her down.

When she could barely move for her laughter, he scooped her up and snuggled her. "I love you, little girl."

AJ came from down the hall. "What is all this ruckus?"

He looked at Bree. "Let's get Mommy!" He set Bree down, and she squealed and darted toward AJ.

"Oh no!" AJ bounded over the back of the couch.

But Bree darted the other way and cornered AJ in the middle of the living room. Logan went over the couch. They had her.

Bree ran at AJ and jumped into her open arms. The little girl tried to tickle her mom.

But her little fingers weren't very effective. Logan joined them. With his arms securely around the ladies he loved, he made certain to have a hold on Bree. He tickled AJ, who collapsed against him in her own fit of giggles.

They all fell onto the floor and laughed until not one of them could catch their breath.

Logan laid back with his arms out to each side. AJ snuggled up against him and Bree sat on his chest. So much for breathing. She only weighed thirty-five pounds, which didn't seem like much until that weight was on top of him.

But he didn't care. He was with his girls.

Thank you, Lord!

Logan's heart was full to the point of bursting. Only a week ago, Bree had come to them and said she wanted to give her life to Jesus. She loved Him so much and wanted to live for Him forever. He and AJ had the privilege of praying with their little girl and welcoming her into the family of God. Wherever they went, she told everyone she met how much Jesus loved them. She was going to make a big impact on this world.

Present Day

At four o'clock on Thursday afternoon, AJ drove into the cemetery and parked in her usual spot. Trying not to think about her actions, she grabbed the bouquet of black-eyed Susans from the front seat, tossed her bag over her shoulder, and walked robotically down the path that led her through the perfectly manicured lawn.

At the junction of another path, she looked up and met Logan's eyes.

In the last five years since they'd split, they had never ended up here together. Occasionally, she'd spotted his bike and come back later or noticed he drove away because she was there, but she hadn't seen him today.

"I'm sorry. I'll come back." She was about to turn away when Logan stretched out his hand to her.

"Today isn't about us. It's about our daughter. She'd want us to be here together."

AJ nodded and took Logan's hand. Together they walked toward Bree's grave.

How had it been six years to the day since they'd lost her? They'd been so happy. She'd given her life to Jesus. She hadn't even been five for a month. Then she was gone.

AJ stopped. "I can't do this."

Logan didn't let go but turned toward her.

She gripped his hand tighter. "It hurts so much. I miss her."

He nodded. His eyes were red and glistened with moisture. He'd always been a man of big feelings. Passion emanated from him in all he did. The pain in his heart was equal to hers.

She wiped at her nose with her sleeve, not willing to let go of the flowers or Logan's hand. But he let go and wrapped his arms around her, drawing her close to his chest.

The air was gone from her lungs as sobs racked her entire being. He held her, she held him, and they both cried. Together. For the first time in nearly six years.

After a few minutes—maybe it was longer, she didn't really know or care—they walked the remaining distance to Bree's tombstone. AJ set the flowers into the vase that was part of the stone's design. Taking the water bottle out of the bag, she filled the vase.

"She loved black-eyed Susans." Logan stuffed his hands in the pockets of his shorts.

"She really did." AJ took a blanket out of her bag and laid it on the ground.

Logan helped her straighten it, and they sat close but not touching. Silence settled between them.

AJ thought back to that dreadful day. They'd gone to the river for a fun afternoon with some people from church. Bree had been learning to swim and was doing a great job. She'd gotten too confident and gone in by herself when they'd turned their backs briefly.

AJ had never seen Logan run so fast. He'd caught Bree not very far down the river, pulled her out, and they had tried to revive her, but it had been too late. She was gone.

Logan broke into her thoughts. "I love how she always wiggled her nose at broccoli."

AJ chuckled and tears splashed out of her eyes. "She couldn't decide if she liked it or not. She was so silly."

Logan nodded.

AJ needed her husband. Why didn't he see that? He hadn't seen it in the months after Bree's death. He'd retreated into himself, not realizing he needed his wife too. AJ risked contact and rested her head on his shoulder.

He didn't move. Not toward her but not away. "I hate that I failed to save her."

"You didn't fail. It wasn't your fault. It wasn't anyone's fault. It was an accident."

"I should have saved her."

AJ lifted her head and wrapped her hands around Logan's elbow. "Logan, please hear me. It is not your fault. Have you blamed yourself all these years?"

"I'm her dad. I should have protected her."

"You couldn't have. It was an accident."

"But ..." He met AJ's eyes.

"No buts, Logan."

Emotion distorted his face and racked his body.

She tucked her feet under her and wrapped her arms around his shoulders. He leaned into her as six years of pent-up emotion spilled out.

She held him and cried with him for at least twenty minutes before Logan found his voice again.

"I can't forgive myself."

She grabbed a box of tissues from her bag and offered him one. He plucked it out.

She snatched one too and twisted it in her hands. "Logan, I know two things. One, there's no need for forgiveness in this because there is no sin. You need to let it go and not hold onto false guilt. And two, Jesus is the one who forgives sin. He's also the one you need to surrender everything to. All of it. Bree's death. The fact we weren't able to save her, even as first responders. The ways I hurt you. The grief. The pain."

He took another tissue. "Yeah."

Lord, help him.

Chapter Seventeen

Nearly Six Years Ago—January—Four Months after Bree's Death

AJ walked to the front door after a twenty-four-hour shift at the fire station. She'd slept all of three hours when a three-alarm warehouse fire woke her at two in the morning. She needed sleep, but the adrenaline was still running too hot.

Logan's bike in the carport told her he'd gotten home from his overnight shift too.

She unlocked the door and pushed it open. "Logan?" She needed a hug even more than sleep.

Logan sat slumped over the end of the kitchen table, tumbler glass in his hand, a bottle of whiskey nearby.

She called his name again.

He lifted his head. "Hey."

She ditched her coat and shoes and walked to him. "Rough night?"

"It was a night."

"What's with the whiskey then?"

"Just needed a glass." He stood and shifted away from her.

He had hardly touched her in two months.

Setting his glass in the sink, he turned toward the hallway.

She reached out to him. "Logan."

He stopped and looked at her. "I'm headed to bed. I'm tired." He walked away.

How could he not see she needed him? She hated having to chase him down for any affection or comfort. Sure, he was hurting, but so was she. They needed to walk through this together.

She followed him. "I need you."

He stopped but didn't turn. "I have nothing to give. I don't know what you want from me."

"You. I need you. Nothing more. You don't need to give me anything except an iota of your attention."

His shoulders sagged. "I'm exhausted."

She let him get ready for bed, and she did the same.

They were both exhausted. And not from working nights. They were empty casings. Grief had stripped them of themselves, of joy, of true rest. And of sleep. AJ didn't remember the last time she'd slept through the night. She could sleep for twelve hours but never straight through. Too many times she woke up thinking she heard Bree crying for her from across the hall. But Bree wasn't there. Never would be again.

AJ crawled into bed beside Logan. He laid on his back and let her snuggle up against him, but he didn't wrap his arm around her and hold her like he used to.

Hot tears poured out of her eyes and soaked his shirt, but he said nothing and didn't move. Once again, she cried herself to sleep.

Present Day

After leaving the cemetery, Logan bought food for dinner, including some broccoli, before heading home. As he rode, he tried to sort out his feelings about being at the gravesite with AJ today, but his emotions were still all discombobulated. It had been cathartic to cry. He was man enough to admit it, at least to himself. He hadn't cried like that since he'd held Bree's lifeless body against his chest—once everyone forced him to face the fact she was gone. Maybe bottling up his emotions for so long hadn't been wise.

But hearing AJ's words had not only uncorked it but busted the bottle open. It was going to take a while to process and let the words sink in. Was he really not at fault for Bree's death?

AJ's voice repeated in his head. *"It was an accident."*

He pulled into the driveway and parked his motorcycle in the carport.

His trash can and recycle bin caught his eye. Maybe he shouldn't keep those in the carport with all the crazy fires those teens had been starting. For whatever reason, it was clear they were targeting law enforcement. He didn't want his house to be the next casualty.

He rolled them onto the driveway, clear of the carport and a nearby tree. Good thing he wasn't in an HOA, but even if he was, he wouldn't care.

A car slowed in front of his house. The window rolled down and Miles waved. "Hey, Logan. How's it going?"

"Not horribly." He walked to the vehicle and leaned his forearms on the door. "Still driving the rental? Any hope for your car after the accident?"

"Unfortunately, it's needed more repairs than they thought. Had to order something I guess."

"I'm surprised the insurance didn't total it and give you the cash to get a new one."

"It was close. I really like that car though. Oh well." Miles shrugged. "You got big plans for this Thursday evening?"

"A date with a bottle of whiskey."

Miles laughed. "My kind of night. Let me know if you ever want a drinking buddy."

It was Logan's turn to laugh. "I was about to throw some brats on the grill. Want dinner?"

"That sounds great. You sure you want the company?"

"Beats hanging out by myself." Logan patted Miles's car and moved out of the way so his friend could park in the driveway.

Logan grabbed the bag of groceries from his motorcycle and welcomed Miles into his home.

"Glass of whiskey?" Logan asked.

"That'd be great."

Logan dug two glasses and the bottle of alcohol out of the back of the cabinet.

"Who are you scared will find that?"

"I'm not sure I'd hear the end of it from Will. He's always afraid I'm going to go off the deep end." Like he nearly had after losing Bree and then again after losing AJ.

"He's a good friend. You two have stayed close since we were kids, huh?"

Logan nodded. "You keep in touch with anyone from high school?"

"Not really," Miles said. "Ran into Kristen not that long ago. She's married with three kids."

Once Logan had the brats ready, the men went out back and chatted about work and sports while getting the grill fired up. While they cooked, Logan ran in to use the restroom. When he came back out, Miles was watching a video on his phone.

"Hey, Logan, look at this video. Isn't that Will's house?"

He walked over, and Miles handed his phone to Logan.

The video showed two teenagers setting a fire in Will's trash can. "It is. Can you send this to me?"

"Are you on social media?" Miles asked.

"Not really. Just text me the link if you can."

"Sure. Looks like this is a social-media dare. There's a hashtag." Miles clicked on the hashtag, and it took them to a list of videos from all over the country of teens setting trash cans on fire.

"That's Amelia's house."

"Whose?"

"One of the detectives. We caught that kid. Didn't know he recorded himself. That won't help his court case."

"I'll send you that one too," Miles said.

"Thanks, man. We've got to put a stop to this. Someone is going to end up hurt."

"It's amazing no one has been yet."

Logan nodded. He got the brats off the grill, then brought the bottle of whiskey out with the broccoli and condiments. They ate on the back deck and drank a few more glasses. Probably too many. Logan did anyway.

He stopped when he realized he was going to start talking about AJ. The whole point of drinking was to numb himself, not to loosen his tongue.

Miles must have caught the drift. "I really should head out now. Mind if I leave my car? You may have served me a bit too much to be safe behind the wheel."

"Probably shouldn't drive home from a cop's house inebriated."

"The fact that you can pull that word up after so much to drink is something."

"Eh, I use that word at least once a week at work."

"Ha. Well, I'm out. Thanks for dinner."

Logan showed him out the front door then collapsed on the couch. He needed to find out which detective was on the trash-can-fires case.

He called Adam's number.

"Jamison."

"Hey, it's Logan. I found some very interesting information this evening regarding the trash-can fires."

"Are you home?"

"I am."

"I'll swing by. I'm out walking Rusty. As long as you don't mind the dog."

"Not at all."

"I'm only a block away." Adam and his wife, Ella, lived about a mile from Logan.

They hung up, and Adam was knocking before Logan even made it to the door.

Adam shook his hand, and Logan invited him and the dog in. The men sat on the couch, and Logan gave the golden retriever a good rub-down.

Logan showed Adam the videos and sent him the links. They chatted about the case for a few minutes.

Adam said, "I'll pass these on. Can't believe it's a stupid so-cial-media dare. I will never understand why teens do these things when they should know better."

"We were all young and dumb once."

"Speaking of which ..." Adam ran his palms on his pant legs. "You've been drinking."

Logan slumped back against the couch. "I had a friend over. It's nothing."

"It's not nothing on the anniversary of your daughter's death."

That one hit square in the heart.

"At least I wasn't drinking by myself."

"Which is what you would have done if your friend hadn't come by?"

Logan nodded.

"Man, it's not worth it. And I know you know that. I've been down that road, especially when the woman you love, that isn't quite yours anymore, is in danger."

Logan nodded again. He knew Adam's story.

"Now, I suggest you run that bottle down the drain before my wife finds it."

Logan chuckled. "Ella poured yours out?"

"Yep. And I haven't had a drop since. You have to lean on Christ in the midst of the hard stuff. The bottle isn't actually numbing anything except your ability to hear His voice. Don't let that happen. Take it to Him. He can handle it."

Why did everyone have to butt in? He appreciated Adam's advice, and he knew he was right, but it wasn't as easy as Adam made it sound.

He nodded, wanting Adam to think he was letting it soak in. In one sense he was, but it felt like Adam had taken a meat tenderizer to his tough heart.

Adam stood. "Let me know if you need anything. I'm just down the street. Seriously, even if it's simply to sit on the back deck and toss a ball with Rusty here instead of drinking. Got it?"

"Will do. Thank you." He shook Adam's hand and gave Rusty another rub.

They left and Logan turned back to the kitchen table. He contemplated the bottle. He'd already had too much, but he wasn't ready to pour it down the drain.

After putting the whiskey away in the cabinet, he went to the hallway and stopped in front of Bree's closed door. He'd kept her room like it had been. He went in and cleaned it regularly, but he couldn't remove any of the things without AJ. It wouldn't be right.

He opened the door and let the light from the hall be enough. He walked in and picked up her stuffed hippo from the bed, then sat down.

Adam was right. The alcohol didn't affect the emotions Logan had hoped to kill.

"I'm sorry, baby girl. I'm sorry I keep trying to smother the feeling of missing you."

Chapter Eighteen

AJ walked up the stairs to her apartment. She'd had dinner with her dad after leaving the cemetery. It had been a wonderful time talking to him about Bree, going through photographs he had, and reminiscing. She told him about her time with Logan at Bree's grave. Before she left, her dad had prayed for her and for Logan.

She made plenty of noise unlocking the door since she knew Will was over based on his truck in the driveway. Pushing the door open, she said, "Hey, guys."

Zara and Will were in the kitchen cleaning up from their dinner.

Zara set down her towel and strode to AJ, drawing her into a hug. "Will told me what today was."

AJ fell into Zara's arms, soaking in the hug from this woman who had become her best friend in the last two months.

Will came over and wrapped his arms around both of them.

AJ leaned her head into him. A fresh wave of grief overcame her. She hadn't even been able to tell them about the day yet.

Her baby was gone—had been gone longer than she'd been on earth. And her husband had rejected her. But God was still good. He'd provided friends. A daddy who loved her and still took care of his little girl. God had given her a glimmer of hope today too. Maybe, just maybe, Logan's heart was beginning to soften. Maybe reconciliation was possible. Maybe.

She stepped out of the hug and wiped her face. "Sorry."

Zara handed her a tissue. "You're allowed to cry." Zara swiped her own eyes too.

AJ met Will's eyes. "You'll never believe what happened today. Logan let me hold him while *he* cried." She told them about what happened at the cemetery.

"Wow. I'm really glad he heard you say that. I've been trying to tell him that for years, but I think he really thought you blamed him."

"Never."

"I know." Will squeezed her shoulder. "Should I go check on him?"

Sheepishly she glanced at the floor. "I drove by on my way home. Miles's rental was in the driveway, and Adam was walking out the front door."

Will smiled. "I'm glad to hear about Adam. Miles... I'm not sure how helpful he'd be."

AJ said, "Agreed."

"Either way, I'm going to get out of here and let you two ladies have your evening and girl talk." Will opened his arms to AJ.

She embraced her oldest friend. "Thanks, Will."

"Praying for you. And Logan too, of course."

"You will never know how much I appreciate that."

He winked at her and turned to his girlfriend.

AJ excused herself to the living room to give them a minute to kiss without her awkwardly gawking at them.

Will hollered goodnight as he walked out the door.

Zara went to the freezer. "Rocky Road or chocolate chip cookie dough?"

"Oh, you are too good to me. Cookie dough."

"Big bowl or little bowl?"

AJ laughed and walked back into the kitchen. "Just hand me the carton."

Zara held the carton back. "No, I want some too."

They fixed two big bowls then settled in the living room.

Zara dove into her ice cream, giving AJ the space she needed to decide what she needed to talk about.

After a few bites, AJ said, "So Will filled you in on what happened to Bree?"

Zara nodded.

"Remember on Sunday when I told you I had an affair after the worst year of our lives?"

Dawning lit in Zara's eyes. "Yes. Losing Bree."

"We were a giant mess of grief. Looking back, I can see what was happening. Now I know Logan was blaming himself. He thought I blamed him too. So he kept me at arm's length. I needed my husband, but he didn't know how to be there for me. And I didn't know how to be what he needed either."

"Grief is tricky."

"I ran into Daryl at the gas station he owns. He asked how I was doing and was nice, sweet even. After months of Logan's negativity and on-and-off drinking, it was refreshing to talk to someone who cared about how *I* felt. I made a point to go in the store more regularly, then one day Daryl invited me over to his house for coffee. That's all it was, but it didn't stay that for very long. Coffee across the table one day turned into coffee on the couch the next day—to no coffee and a back rub—to hands wandering."

"I've told you bits of my past. You know I understand how that goes."

AJ nodded. "I should have gone to my husband. I should have pursued him and taken the time to figure out what he needed from me in his grief—not be self-consumed with what I needed. But I didn't. I should never have spent time with Daryl. I was vulnerable, and Daryl took advantage of that."

Zara's eyes narrowed. "AJ, did Daryl force you? Did you feel like you couldn't get away?"

"No. Did he take advantage of the situation? Yes, but I was a willing participant. I could have walked away plenty of times, and I sure didn't have to go back like I did."

"How long did the affair last?"

"A month. I hated myself for it. I was ready to break it off one day when I went to his house, but he suggested I leave Logan instead. I ran out and didn't look back. However, it took me two months to tell Logan the truth."

"Bet that didn't go well."

"Not even close. He kicked me out right away. And that was that. I've tried a few times to talk to him, but most of those times ended up like last week at the grocery store."

Zara released a whoosh of air. "I'm so sorry, friend."

"Thanks. You okay with watching a movie or something? I need a distraction."

They picked a funny movie, and AJ fell asleep before Buttercup swam with the screeching eels.

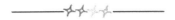

Despite his splitting headache Friday morning, Logan jumped on his motorcycle to meet up with some of the firefighters and cops for a round of basketball. They normally played in the evenings, but occasionally someone threw out a morning time. Five thirty was way too early, but he went anyway.

He walked into the gym, and Will, without comment, tossed him a bottle of ibuprofen. How did he know? It wasn't a reaction to a grimace or rubbing his forehead. Yet Will had been ready with bottle in hand.

Logan walked up to Adam, who sat in the bleachers tying his shoes. "Did you tell Will about last night?"

"Didn't even tell Ella, though I was tempted on that one. I will if you need someone to help you."

Logan shook his head and tossed his gym bag on the bleachers, then sat and changed his shoes.

They played a hard game. Will and Adam didn't let Logan take it easy at all. They pushed him the entire game to keep up. Every time they passed to him, he'd be sure to pass it to one of the other guys, so he didn't have to take a shot. The three he took in the first half of the game totally missed.

Caleb Johnson came over to him while they were taking a mid-game water break. "You okay today, Jackson?"

Caleb worked as a paramedic out of the same station as AJ, so he likely knew what yesterday was. Maybe.

"Just off today. I'll be fine."

Caleb held Logan's gaze, apparently not believing his lie.

"You know what yesterday was?"

Caleb nodded. "Praying for you. Let us know if you need anything."

"Thanks."

Caleb slapped him on the shoulder.

Logan knelt on one knee and adjusted a shoelace that didn't need it until the game resumed. As much as he wanted to be irritated by Caleb, he wasn't. The opposite in fact. There were people around him who not only cared but also prayed for him. They'd been around when Bree died too, but he'd been too self-consumed to realize it in the moment. Maybe if he had accepted a little more support, it wouldn't have felt so unbearable.

They resumed their game. The meds must have kicked in, and Logan actually made a few decent plays and even a handful of baskets.

On his way home from the gym, Logan drove toward AJ's. He shouldn't take the long way to get home, but he felt drawn to her. He needed to scope out the area and make sure no one was lurking around.

He turned down her street. A cable-company van was parked outside the neighbor's house. Why was a cable guy already out at seven in the morning?

Logan slowed. The worker was at the utility pole, but it looked like he was staring at AJ's apartment. Wait, was that Eric?

Logan stopped in front of the van and took off his helmet. "Eric?"

The man jumped and spun around, eyes wide. "Logan." His gaze darted back and forth.

"Didn't mean to scare you."

"Oh, umm ... I ... uh. It—it's ... It's okay." He shifted his feet.

"Are you sure?"

"Yeah, totally. I just didn't hear you coming."

Logan wanted to laugh. His motorcycle wasn't a Harley, but it wasn't quiet either.

"Just getting some work done on this line. Got to keep the cable running, people have to have their internet."

"Sure. But I find it interesting that you're keeping an eye on my wife's apartment while you're working."

"Wife? What wife?"

Eric had missed the memo? True, until last Saturday, Logan hadn't seen or talked to Eric since before he and AJ got married.

"AJ. We got married during junior year."

"Then why did you two hardly interact at Will's last week?"

"It's a long story, but she's still my wife. Why are you loitering here?"

"Dude, I'm working." Eric's voice cracked a bit.

There wasn't anything more Logan could say, but he'd drive around for a bit. If Eric was still here in an hour, he'd call it in.

Chapter Nineteen

As AJ walked to the front door, she rolled her shoulders. Hopefully, it wasn't too soon after her concussion for a run, but she needed it. She'd let herself sleep until eight, but thirty minutes later she was feeling completely restless. She would work her first full twenty-four-hour shift starting tomorrow morning. And she was ready, even if it was likely that Ty wouldn't let her go out on calls.

She opened the front door. A card-sized envelope and tiny, stuffed dalmatian dressed up as a firefighter with a sign around his neck that said "Hero" sat on the wooden railing. Backing up, she let the screen door slam.

"Zara? Zara!" AJ stared at the items.

"What's wrong?" Zara came out of her bedroom, pulling her hair back in a ponytail.

AJ pointed at the items.

"Oh, dear. Call Adam."

AJ nodded and dialed the number.

"Jamison."

"It's AJ. The stalker is back. It's an envelope and little stuffed toy. I can throw them in a Ziplock and bring them by later."

"Not ideal, but we're on another call right now. Is Zara there?"

"Yes. I'll put you on speaker." She clicked the button on her phone.

Adam said, "Take pictures and bag it without touching it. AJ, any chance you have a doorbell camera or such?"

"No. I've thought about it but never got one."

"That's all right. Call me immediately if there is anything else."

"Thanks, Adam."

They hung up, and Zara took care of photographing and bagging the items.

AJ wanted to know what the card said, but she knew better than to touch it without gloves. It would have to wait.

Zara set the bagged items on the kitchen table.

"Now I want to run five miles instead of two."

"Oh no, you don't. You aren't leaving here by yourself. He may be a romantic stalker, but that doesn't mean he won't turn violent. No way I'm letting you go on your own."

"Then lace up, because we're going running."

Zara shot her a fine-but-I'm-not-happy look. "Give me five."

Seven minutes later, their feet were hitting pavement as they ran down the street toward the walking path. Having been married to a cop, AJ knew to vary her path, but she'd only ended up with five different routes she cycled through. Zara followed AJ's lead.

The women didn't talk—just ran, easily keeping pace with one another.

AJ was able to direct her thoughts to prayer and processing life. She ended up praying for Logan for nearly five minutes straight. The more she prayed for him, the more her heart yearned for him. She missed him in her life. Missed his hugs. Missed laughing with him. She even missed fighting with him. They were supposed to be living their happily ever after, but it was so far from that. She'd take ever after with him even if they couldn't have the happy, because life without him was lonelier than she could have fathomed.

AJ was deep in her head when Zara grabbed her arm and yanked her to a stop.

"What?"

Zara pointed at the ground.

There on the asphalt, in sidewalk chalk, her name was written in three-foot letters.

"What on earth?"

Zara didn't let go of her arm but led her to follow chalk arrows pointing away from her name. Down the path a little farther, they found a second message, also in sidewalk chalk.

Come away with me and let's have the adventure you've always dreamed of.

Next to the message he'd drawn a heart with a good-sized rock set in the center. Under the rock was a couple of brochures. The top one was for whitewater rafting.

AJ pulled out her phone and instinctively stepped closer to Zara, who had her right hand under her t-shirt, no doubt on her concealed firearm. Her left hand let go of AJ's arm and rested on her back. "Call A—"

"Already on it."

He answered. "Jamison. This is too soon."

"I know you are on another call, but we can't bag and tag this. I need you guys."

"We'll be there. Want me to call Logan?"

"Not yet. Zara's still with me."

She gave Adam her location and hung up.

Zara said, "Are you sure you don't want Logan here?"

AJ dropped her shoulders. "Of course I want him here, but we aren't there ... yet."

"Exactly. Yet." Zara pulled AJ into a hug.

126

AJ received the comfort from her friend while keeping her eyes peeled for anyone suspicious.

When they let go, they both continued to search the area.

Adam and Amelia showed up in less than ten minutes.

"He knew exactly where I run."

Adam scrunched his face as he stared at the chalk message. "I would have thought you knew to vary your path."

"I do. But most of my routes come through this way."

He walked over to the heart. With gloves on, he moved the rock and picked up the brochures. The second one was for a bed-and-breakfast. "This tells me he doesn't know you very well, or is incredibly insensitive."

"When I was in high school and college, I dreamed of going on a whitewater rafting trip. It was a bucket list item before Bree died."

Adam nodded. "That's interesting."

Zara flung her hand into the air. "Wouldn't Daryl know you erased that one from your list?"

"You would think, but he's not the most sensitive man. And like Adam said ..."

They all stared at each other. Regardless of insensitivities or not, her stalker knew she loved adventure and had once upon a time had grand dreams of whitewater rafting.

Was he watching her now? He'd obviously been watching her, following her. How did she not know? Not sense that someone was keeping an eye on her?

It unnerved her. She thought she was good at having situational awareness. If so, why didn't she realize someone was keeping tabs on her?

She hugged herself.

Amelia came up beside her. "Are you okay?"

"A little shaken up at the realization that I really do have a stalker. It was one thing for him to know I went to church and which service. That's not too hard to figure out, but this is too much. I don't want anything to do with him, so why won't he go away? I mean, I know the answer; he's delusional and a stalker, but ..." She shivered despite the warmth of the September morning.

"I'm sure your adrenaline is screaming to run, but let us take you home."

AJ nodded. CSU had arrived and was processing the evidence, so AJ and Zara left with the detectives.

Back at the apartment, all four of them went up so AJ could show the detectives the gift left that morning. On the landing in front of the door lay a bouquet of carnations. Her stomach flipped.

Adam stopped her and picked them up with a gloved hand. A card stuck out of the top.

Please consider my offer. You and me. Together. We'd be great.

AJ snatched the flowers from Adam's hand. "Want the card for evidence?"

"Yes." He snatched it out. "What are you doing?"

"Sending a message." She chucked the flowers over the side of the railing, and they dispersed across the driveway. She shouted, "Get the hint and leave me alone."

Running down the stairs, she skirted Amelia and Zara. AJ went to the flowers and stomped on them, grinding several into the ground.

She looked around, watching to see if anyone was there. Was he watching her even now? She kind of hoped so.

Spinning, she bounded back up the stairs and through the door Zara held open for her.

Once inside AJ had to work to calm herself. The adrenaline and frustration coursed through her like a semi with broken brakes headed down a mountain pass. With a shaky hand, she gave Amelia the bag of evidence. "I'd love to know what the card says, if possible."

"Let's find out." Amelia snapped on a pair of gloves from her pocket. She removed the envelope from the bag and carefully extracted out the card. She held it so everyone else, especially AJ, could see it.

The front was a painting of a dalmatian, no words. Apparently he had a theme for this gift. On the inside was a typed note.

You and I would make a great couple. I'm not sure why you keep ignoring my messages. Text me back or better yet, call me. Let's meet up and spend some time together. You are a hero. Be my hero and save my aching heart.

"Blech. He's so creepy." AJ shuddered.

Zara said, "Never heard of a not-creepy stalker."

AJ laughed, a smidge of tension releasing from her body.

Amelia closed the card and slid it all back into the plastic bag.

"What do I do?" The next steps were lost on AJ. "How crazy is this guy? Is it Daryl? Is it someone else? He obviously knows where I live, but who doesn't? Am I safe here?"

Amelia took AJ's shoulders. "Hey, first breathe, second pray, third we'll figure it out. One step at a time." She took a chair from the table and with a motherly glare told AJ to sit.

All four of them sat.

AJ set her phone—which she'd been gripping—on the table.

It buzzed.

AJ jumped. She felt like a fool. It's not like this guy had threatened her, but still ...

She looked at the text message. "It's him."

Amelia squeezed AJ's forearm. "What does it say?"
She read it aloud:

> Why would you smash such beautiful flowers? I thought you would love them. And what's with the cops? Don't you want to go rafting? We would have so much fun. Please choose to give me a chance.

She slammed her fist down on the table. Then typed a reply.

> I'm married. I choose my husband. Please leave me alone.

She hit send before anyone could tell her not to. But they didn't. "I'm so over this. Should I ask him who he is? I shouldn't have typed that. We could have lured him in or something, couldn't we have? But now he'd know it's a trap. I didn't think."

Adam rested his arms on the table, leaning forward. "No. Telling him to leave you alone is totally legit. The fact that you've made it so clear makes it that much worse for him if he continues."

"But if we can't figure out who it is, what difference does it make?"

"Two things are going to happen now: he will either make himself known eventually, or he will actually get a clue and leave you alone. If he really wants to win you over, he's got to realize he can't do that without revealing himself. Has Daryl made any more advances?"

"No, I haven't seen him."

Adam nodded.

AJ slouched onto the table. *God, reveal who this is so I know if I should be really concerned or not. I don't feel like I'm in danger as much as I'm angry and feel like my space has been violated. Please help.*

130

Five Years Ago—October

Logan was fuming while doing the dishes. He almost wished AJ hadn't told him about Daryl. Because now the very thought of touching his own wife repulsed him. The ultimate betrayal.

The last year had been absolute torture after losing Bree. He was finally figuring out how to breathe without his little girl. But this was the kick in the stomach he couldn't take.

When AJ had turned off the TV earlier, he could tell she had something on her mind. Then she'd said those dreadful words: "We need to talk."

He thought it'd be something like she wanted to move or wanted to see a counselor or something. He'd never anticipated she'd had sex with another man. She'd been vague about it initially, but he asked her straight out. At least she didn't lie.

Dishes clanged against the sink and each other. He didn't even try to control himself. He was livid.

They had sat on the couch after she said the words. And he bled out. What little life he had left in him was now gone.

He had the mind to go march right to Daryl's door and ... and ... he didn't actually want to think about what he wanted to do to the man. He'd thought for a split second that maybe Daryl had raped her, and then Logan would do something. But she went back. Did it again. Nope, she was to blame.

After ten minutes of silence, he told her she needed to leave. Pack up all her stuff and leave. Move out. It was over.

Occasionally, over the din of his dishwashing, he could hear her sobbing down the hall as she packed.

It killed him. He hated it. He didn't want her to leave. But he couldn't have her stay either. He could never trust her again. He could never be intimate with her again. She was the only one he had ever shared himself with.

Once the dishwasher was loaded, he moved on to the counters and table. By the time she came down the hall with her suitcase, he had shifted to scrubbing the outside of the cabinets. By the time she'd filled her car, he'd cleaned the oven and the floor too.

On her final trip, she stopped by the front door, hugging her pillow. "Logan?"

He stood and crossed the room. "Goodbye, AJ. Come back and get anything else while I'm at work."

The twenty-some years flashed before his eyes. From the little girl he'd been enamored with when she dressed as Robin Hood, and he was Little John, and they rid Sherwood Forest—aka Will's backyard—of thieving squirrels. To that first kiss in the asylum. To the first time they'd made love. To on and off again. To finding out Bree was coming. To marrying the girl of his dreams. To having the family he could only hope for.

It all crashed to the floor. They'd lost it all. Their little girl. Trust. Love. It was all dead and gone.

AJ's eyes pleaded with him. "If you decide to talk it out and work through this, call me. I love you. Forever and always."

He stared at her, unable to say anything.

Tears streaming down her face, she turned and walked out of the house. Their house. The one they were supposed to grow old together in. But that would never happen now.

Logan walked to the door, closed it, and locked it.

He stalked across to the kitchen and pulled out the whiskey and a glass. He'd been doing better, not drinking nearly as often as he had last winter. But he needed it tonight.

He downed one glass, then another. Then a third.

The love of his life was gone. Chose to betray him. And now she was out. It was over.

Logan couldn't breathe. The anger surging through his veins felt like fire.

He chucked the glass across the room. It slammed into the wall and shattered. Like his heart and his life.

Chapter Twenty

Present Day

Saturday afternoon, the fire truck rolled back into the station after responding to a small kitchen fire. Ty had actually let AJ go out on the call, though she'd been under strict assignment. But it was a simple call since the fire was contained to the oven and the owners handled it properly.

She jumped out of her seat, and they all set their gear back up for the next call. Once everything was set, AJ went to the kitchen to get a snack.

"Hey, AJ." Brennan nodded toward the window.

Logan stopped in front of the station and took off his helmet.

"What's he doing here?"

Brennan quirked an eyebrow. "I was going to ask you that. Want me to tell him to get lost?"

"No!"

Brennan laughed. "That's what I thought, but I remember ..."

"I know. Thanks." She squeezed his arm and darted out the door, slowing as she approached Logan.

He smiled tentatively at her.

"What are you doing here?"

"Just driving by, and I thought I'd check and make sure everything is all right."

"I'm fine."

"Adam called me and told me about yesterday." Logan got off his bike and shoved his hands in his pockets.

She pressed her lips together.

"Are you scared this guy will get violent?"

She shrugged. "If I knew who it was, maybe."

"Still think it's Daryl?"

Another shrug, this time she hoped it covered her squirm at Logan mentioning Daryl's name. "The rafting idea doesn't feel like him. But he can be quite the jerk, so maybe it is."

Logan shifted his feet. "Do you have to get back inside or are you free to talk for a few minutes?"

"We just returned from a call, so I have a few down minutes. What's up?" They really were talking again, weren't they? She tried to keep her excitement subdued, especially since she had no idea what he might want to talk about. "Something in particular you're thinking?"

It was his turn to shrug. "Not really. Thanks for Thursday. It was good to be there with you."

"Same." Was it too soon to tell him she missed him? Probably.

They stood there, silent. Why was it so hard to talk to him, especially when that was all she wanted to do?

"How are you really doing, Logan?"

"Fine, I guess. Surviving."

How she longed for him to thrive in life not just survive, but she understood. "I get that. You still love being a cop?"

He smiled. "I do."

She wanted to dive into deeper conversation, but she wasn't sure how.

"I've been thinking about taking the sergeant's exam."

"You'd be a great sergeant."

Color rose in his cheeks. "Thanks. I've hesitated because nothing ever seems to go right. What if my past wrongs come back to bite me again?"

"What do you mean?"

"Well, seeing Eric made me think about the fact we knew what happened and never reported it. Didn't help that I read the verse in Leviticus the other day that said we were just as responsible."

"We definitely were in the wrong, but what would that have to do with your job?"

"Hard not to put two and two together that God punished us for our ... indiscretions by taking our daughter."

AJ felt slammed with Logan's words. "No. That's not how that works. We confessed that sin, and Christ paid the price. Sin doesn't need to be paid for more than once. Christ's sacrifice was sufficient."

"But consequences ..."

"Are not punishments for sin, they are the natural workings. Bree died because she ventured too far and the water caught her. She died because we live in a fallen world."

"I don't need a sermon right now."

She reached out and touched his arm. "I'm sorry. I'm not trying to preach. But I've just wrestled with these very same thoughts."

He did not rip his arm away like she thought he might. He looked down at her hand. "I want to believe what you're saying."

"You have to wrestle through it. Talk to Him about it." She moved her hand from Logan's arm and pointed heavenward.

He shifted around uncomfortably. AJ guessed he and God weren't on the best of speaking terms right now. *Jesus, take hold of Logan's heart and help him work through this. Help him find forgiveness from You and extend it to me.*

"If you're so spiritually enlightened, answer me this: If God is sovereign, why'd our little girl die?"

"I don't know. I can't possibly know the answer to that. But I know He is sovereign, and I know nothing happens without His oversight. That doesn't mean He orchestrated her death for anything. But I know He will work all things together for our good and His glory. No matter how much it sucks. He can use it to draw us closer to Him."

Gah. She was preaching again. But Logan clearly needed to hear it.

"I'm sorry. I don't mean to get heated. But I'm super passionate about this."

He snorted a dry laugh. "I can tell."

She shot him a cheesy grin. Silence fell between them.

"Too bad you came to all of this after you cheated on me."

An arrow hit her heart. "That's not fair."

"Love and war."

"No."

"Why'd you run off and have sex with another guy then?"

She took a deep breath. "How many times do I have to apologize?"

"Until I understand."

"No, until you forgive me. I've forgiven you."

"Forgiven me? For what? You're the one who—"

"For being a crappy husband. News flash, Logan, I was grieving too. I know I was an awful wife. I didn't know how to help you through your grief because you wouldn't talk to me. I needed you to be there occasionally, not burying your face in a stupid glass of whiskey. I needed a hug, Logan, a hug."

He took a step back. "I couldn't. Every time I looked at you all I could see was Bree."

"Same. Every time I looked in your eyes it was hers staring back at me. But I was willing to face that. I needed to face it. And so did you."

"She's gone. And then so were you."

"Only because you kicked me out and refused to work through any of it. The affair was long over, yet you couldn't even look at me. Still all you do is look at me and think about that one act of indiscretion. I love you, Logan, not him. I was wrong. And I've owned up to it. Please, I beg you to forgive me. Let it go. See Bree in me again."

He spun around and hopped back on his bike.

"Logan, please don't leave."

He started the motorcycle and peeled away.

AJ collapsed to the ground. What had just happened?

Logan sped the whole way home and whipped into his driveway, barely stopping soon enough in the carport not to hit the planters stacked in the back.

He kicked a random stone, then the stupid trash can, which was still a decent distance from the house. The bin was empty after this morning's pickup and fell over.

A car drove by. "You all right, Logan?"

Miles. "I'm fine."

"You sure?"

"Not in the mood, Miles. I'll talk to you later." Logan went straight for the front door and didn't look back. AJ's words were swimming in his head, and Miles wouldn't understand the faith aspects he was wrestling with. If he wanted to talk, he needed to go to someone like Will or Caleb. Miles was a decent friend, but drinking was too tempting as it was.

He closed the door, locked it, then leaned back against it, sinking to the floor.

"Why, God? Why did you let all this happen? If it wasn't to punish us, then why? I don't get it. I know I'm not going to, but I want to. No, I want my little girl back. She'd practically be a young lady by now. But she's not."

Bree was gone.

AJ was gone.

"And AJ. I can't get out of my head that that filthy excuse for a man put his hands on her, and she let him. How can I get over that?"

He shoved himself off the ground, snatched a pillow from the couch, and chucked it at the floor. He had so much pent-up energy. He wasn't sure if he was more mad at AJ, God, or himself.

Crappy husband.

Had he actually driven her into Daryl's arms? He leaned forward, resting his hands on his knees, sick to his stomach. He'd closed off to her so much. He'd been so afraid she blamed him for Bree's death that he couldn't look her in the face.

He felt so guilty that he couldn't hold her, couldn't think straight, couldn't do anything but put one foot ahead. And at times that had felt like too much.

"God, is AJ right? Does my guilt not lie in letting my daughter drown, but in being a lousy husband, a selfish jerk?"

He righted himself and plodded to the kitchen.

The bottle of whiskey still sat on the kitchen table. He wanted to down the entire thing. Too bad it was already half gone.

Logan snatched a glass from the drain board and set it next to the bottle.

Rubbing his face, he yanked out a chair and plopped down.

"God, I'm here. Finally talking to her ... and You. What do I do?"

AJ's words echoed again. *Forgive me.*

"I don't know how. What does it mean to actually forgive her? Pretend like it never happened? But she betrayed me. How do I forgive that? I don't know how."

He seized the whiskey and removed the lid. He poured the glass full.

Staring at the amber liquid, he swished it around, careful not to spill it on his hand. Drinking wasn't the answer. But he wanted to continue to ignore the pain, the reality, the truth.

He needed to seek God.

He needed to pursue his wife.

He needed to accept Christ's forgiveness and AJ's.

He needed to forgive AJ.

More of her words bombarded his mind.

I needed you to be there occasionally, not burying your face in a stupid glass of whiskey.

He stopped the motion of the glass. No, he was done with this. If he kept drinking, nothing would change.

He stood and whipped the glass across the room, whiskey and all.

Chapter Twenty-One

AJ tossed the playing cards on the table. Brennan had found her crying on the lawn in front of the station, dragged her inside, and made her play a round of Go Fish with him before they got back to duty.

She laughed. "You beat me fair and square. I'm going to get back to work now. And thanks."

He winked at her. "I expect the same if I need it one day."

"You will."

His cheeks reddened. Brennan was growing ever closer to Megan, but the situation with her ex-boyfriend was sticky at best, making her very hesitant to get involved with Brennan.

AJ chuckled as she went to check the chore list. Someone still needed to clean the bathrooms. Seriously? Again? Might as well.

She wanted to keep her mind off of Logan as much as possible. But she knew she was too distracted to focus on one of the continuing-education videos she needed to watch, so she moseyed to the bathrooms.

She was mid-toilet-scrubbing when the alarm sounded and announced a residential fire.

With the brush back in its holder, she removed the cleaning gloves off and draped them on the caddy.

In the normal firefighter mode that resisted raising unnecessary adrenaline, she walked quickly toward the truck bay and her gear. The display read the address and the crossroads closest to the fire.

She froze. She knew that address.

Logan.

She ran to the bay.

Seth grasped her arm as she flung off her shoes and nearly fell over as she rushed into her turnout pants and boots.

"Chill."

"You don't understand." She looked at Don. "That's Logan's house. My house."

"Let's go!" Don shouted; the panic she felt came through in his voice.

She jumped in the back of the truck with Seth. Don and Ty in the front.

She couldn't breathe. Was Logan okay? What had happened?

As Ty pulled the truck out and turned on the siren, AJ fought against the worst-case scenario wanting to play out in her head. Logan had to be okay. He probably wasn't even home. He'd been so upset. Surely he went for a long ride. But what if he was inside.

"Do we know who called it in?" AJ asked.

Don looked at the screen. "Says a neighbor. AJ, focus on what we know. While that's not much, don't let your mind play what we don't know."

She nodded, but it felt impossible. Her legs bounced uncontrollably. They couldn't get there fast enough.

They turned onto the street. She could see smoke rising above the trees. "Oh Lord."

Pulling up in front of the house, AJ put her helmet on and slid out of the truck, diving into the job. The living room and kitchen half was nearly engulfed in flames.

Was Logan home? His motorcycle was in the carport. "No!"

She ran to the truck and reached for her oxygen tank and mask. Ty put his hand on hers, preventing her from putting on the tank. "You are not going in."

"Ty, I have to. My husband is in there. I have to save him."

"Even if you didn't have a concussion—"

Seth cut Ty off. "I'll go in. I'll find him, AJ."

"Thank you."

AJ helped Ty with the hose and Brennan joined them. The flames were starting to lick the carport.

"Wait, the motorcycle."

"AJ, leave it. It's not worth it."

"Unless it has a full tank. We don't want it to ignite."

Ty nodded. "Get it."

AJ ran to the carport. The heat from the fire was intense. It singed the small bit of bare skin she had. Flipping up the kickstand she pushed the bike away from the house, past the garbage cans, and close to the road.

Garbage cans. This fire hadn't started in the garbage can?

Seth had been inside for a long time now. Did he find Logan? What if he was dead?

She stumbled backward and ran into someone. Strong hands steadied her. She spun. Adam.

Taking off her helmet, she stared into the detective's eyes. "I don't know if he's in there."

Adam squeezed her shoulder. "Praying."

"Thank you. Would you call Will?" Not waiting for his answer, she turned away and tried to focus on doing her job.

Seth exited the front door, but he was by himself. He shook his head.

Where was Logan?

"I didn't find anyone."

She wasn't sure if she should be relieved or more scared. The house wasn't that big, but if he was at the point of origin, maybe Seth couldn't get close enough to find him.

She froze and stared at the house. The house she and Logan were supposed to grow old in together. Now that would never happen for even more reasons. Everything had burned to ashes. Their family. Their marriage. And now their house.

Someone took her helmet from her hand. She turned to find Adam again. He pointed down the sidewalk.

Logan.

He was alive.

She ran. She threw off her turnout jacket and sprinted with abandon.

He darted to her. They met in an embrace that nearly knocked the wind out of her.

"You're alive!"

"Yes." The word was breathless in her ear as his arms held her tighter than they had in what seemed like an eternity.

She held him, wanting to never let go.

Chapter Twenty-Two

Logan held AJ as close as possible, every curve of her body fitting against him.

"I was so afraid I'd lost you."

"I'm here. Finally."

Her body heaved against him as a sob rocked her. He wrapped his arms a bit tighter around her, and they wept together.

"I'm sorry." He could barely hear himself say it over the roar of the fire and the hissing of the water meeting the flames. But she heard him.

She melted into him. He never wanted to let go again. How had he been so stupid to let her walk away regardless of what had happened?

"AJ!" Don called.

She slid back from Logan, cupping his face with her hands. "I need to ..."

He nodded and reluctantly let go.

Adam helped her slide her jacket back on and set her helmet on her head. Logan went to him and watched AJ do everything with her team to help stop the fire.

She was graceful and determined. Strong and agile.

Adam's hand rested on his shoulder. "You still love her." There was no question in his voice, but Logan still nodded.

"I guess I never stopped."

"I know. Will and Zara are on their way, not knowing if you are alive or not."

Logan twisted his hands. "Surely there is something we can do to help. The cop in me can't just stand here and watch my house burn."

Adam pointed. "There's a crowd gathering over there, let's go see if they saw anything."

Before they even got to the bystanders, Will and Zara drove up in Will's truck.

Zara ran to Logan, Will a few steps behind. "You're okay!"

"I'm alive anyway." He hugged her, then Will.

"Your house ..." Will's voice trailed off.

Logan finally really looked at it. Too much of it was gone. The firefighters seemed to have the fire under control now, but the living room and kitchen area were gone. The bedrooms no doubt had smoke and water damage if not worse. His house was gone.

Other cops on the scene were talking to the bystanders, and Adam had joined them. So Logan stood with his friends, waiting for a clue of what to do next.

Will kept his arm across Logan's shoulders. "Those teenagers took it too far this time."

"Yeah, so much for keeping my trash cans away from the house."

"Really?"

"Yeah, they're over there." Logan pointed to the unburnt receptacle.

"Logan!" Miles called from the police line closest to his house.

Logan walked over with Will and Zara.

"Are you okay?" Shock covered Miles's expression. "What happened?"

"I really don't know."

"You weren't home?"

"No, not long after I saw you, I decided to go for a walk to blow off steam. Glad I decided not to drink. If I had, I might have been passed out inside when the fire started."

Will slapped him on the back. "I'm proud of you, man."

Logan loosed a wry laugh. "I poured the glass ..."

"But you walked away." The pride on Will's face almost made Logan laugh.

About twenty minutes later, AJ walked over to where the four of them were still standing. "It's out. Still too hot to go in and see if anything is salvageable, but the fire is out."

She looked exhausted, helmet hanging from her hand, soot streaking her damp face.

Yet she'd never looked more beautiful. She held his gaze, longing in her eyes.

He lifted his hands. He wanted to hug her but wasn't a hundred percent sure she'd be okay with that.

She smacked her helmet into Will's abdomen and, as soon as he took it, stepped toward Logan.

He closed the space and pulled her to him.

She encircled his waist with her arms, laying her head against his chest.

It felt so good to hold her, his wife, again.

He wiped away the hair plastered to her face. "Are you okay?"

She lifted her head. "As can be, but all of your things ..."

He shrugged. "It's just stuff. I'm ready to talk, like really talk."

Her eyes lit up. "Good."

"AJ." Ty called her.

Her countenance fell. "I guess I have to go back to work."

"Until tomorrow morning?"

She nodded and let go of him.

Ty came over to them. "AJ, take the rest of the shift off. Be with Logan. I'll call someone else in. Be with your husband."

"Thank you, Ty. I need to get my shoes."

Logan said, "I'll take you. Thanks to whoever saved my motorcycle."

Ty nodded toward AJ. "It was all AJ." He took her helmet from Will.

She removed her turnout jacket and handed it to Ty. "Take this back too?"

"Of course."

"It was my turn to make dinner."

"Stop." Ty pointed at her. "You are excused from firehouse duties."

"Yes, sir."

Ty put his hand out to Logan. "I'm sorry about your house."

Logan shook his hand. "Thank you for getting the fire out."

Ty turned and left.

Logan glanced around. Miles was gone. That made this less awkward. "Will, can I stay at your house?"

"You don't have to ask. What do you need right away? While you take AJ to the station, Zara and I can swing by the store and get you the necessities."

Logan rotated and stared at what was left of the house. The reality hit him. He didn't even have a toothbrush. Nothing. Shorts to sleep in. Underwear. Deodorant. Let alone ... pictures of Bree. Her favorite hippo.

He couldn't breathe.

It was all gone.

"Hey." AJ's hand rested on his chest.

But he couldn't peel his eyes away, not until she put her hand on his cheek and directed his vision to her.

"It'll be okay."

"But ... Bree ..."

"We'll go through it tomorrow."

He nodded and let her lead him away and to his motorcycle. With a promise to meet Will and Zara at Walmart, Logan and AJ climbed onto his bike.

Her hands around his waist was the support he needed to keep himself steady as they rode away from the wreckage of their past.

Chapter
Twenty-Three

Two hours later, Logan sank back onto Will's couch. Going to Walmart and buying a few essentials had been sobering. Thinking about all that was gone was overwhelming, but he also didn't want to assume the worst. It was possible that some things back in the bedrooms would be able to be cleaned and restored, but not much.

AJ came into the room. "Dinner's ready." They had bought some frozen pizzas while at the store.

"Okay." But he didn't move.

She came and sat down beside him. "Not hungry?"

He shrugged. "I probably should eat."

Her hands rested on her knees, but he wondered how much she was resisting reaching out to touch him. He helped make the decision and took her hand.

She squeezed his.

He didn't know what to say. So many thoughts flew through his head. He needed to say *I'm sorry*. He needed to say *I forgive you*.

He needed to say *I love you*. But he couldn't find his voice to say any of the words.

"Let's go eat." She stood and pulled his hand.

He tugged back. "Wait. I need to say a few things."

She sat again, close enough that her knee brushed his, sending warmth through his leg.

He stared at her hand in his. It had aged—not in a bad way—but while it looked like he remembered, a few fine lines had appeared.

"What is it, Logan? Don't feel like now—"

"If I've learned anything, it's that I haven't learned as much as I should have, but today has taught me a lot. After we fought earlier, I realized I was wrong. So wrong for so long. I'm ... I'm sorry, AJ. I have been a terrible husband. I believe 'selfish jerk' are the proper words."

She chuckled ruefully.

"I've always loved you, at least as far as my emotions go, but I haven't loved you like Christ loves the church."

Her hand tightened around his.

"I forgive you. I want to trust you again. It may take me a while—and heavens knows it'll take me a minute to learn how to love you right—but I want to try. If you'll give me a chance."

"That's a big change from earlier today."

"I know. But even before the fire, I realized I was the one who needed to change. As I was walking, I had a good, long talk with God, and He made it clear I need to put some work into this. So if you are willing, I'd like a chance to start over."

"We can't start over."

The words knocked the wind out of him like he'd run into a brick wall.

"The past is part of who we are. It's there and can't go anywhere. But we can start fresh."

Air rushed back into his lungs. "Yeah?"

"Yes." She rested her other hand on their joined hands. "It's not going to be a magic switch; I'm not that naive. But I've wanted us my entire life."

"Even after I've been such a jerk? I feel like a gigantic dolt because I didn't even realize how much of a jerk I was being."

Her snicker mostly came through her nose, but it also shook her shoulders. "Oh, honey."

He reached up and traced the side of her face with his fingers. "Do I need to win your heart again?"

"My heart is yours, you know that. But we need to rebuild, not only our home, but our marriage."

"I don't know what that looks like."

She shrugged. "Me neither, but I think we start with spending more time together and talking."

He nodded. "Let's start with dinner with our friends?"

"Please."

They stood, staying hand in hand, and joined Will and Zara in the kitchen.

Sunday afternoon, AJ walked beside Logan to the burnt remains of their house. After church, the four friends had had a quiet lunch, Logan and AJ waiting for the call from the arson inspector. He'd agreed to let them tag along since they worked for the police and fire departments.

The inspector met them at the front of the house. The older man with a classic firefighter mustache that curled up on the ends extended his hand to each of them. "I'm so sorry for the loss of your home."

AJ said, "Thanks for letting us come over during your inspection, Leroy."

"Of course. I think I'm getting a good picture of what happened, but I have a few more sections to inspect. But it can be incredibly dangerous in there. Wear these masks and gloves."

They both took what he offered and put them on. AJ had known to wear work boots, long sleeves, and pants, despite the eighty-degree weather, And told Logan to do the same.

Leroy added, "Other than passing through, I want you to stay out of the living room and kitchen. Pretty much everything in there is a loss. Go to the bedrooms and see what if anything can be salvaged and if it's worth calling a restoration team. You already talked to your insurance company?"

"I called them last night."

"Good. Let's go in. Be careful. The floorboards in the entryway are soft."

Masks and gloves on, they entered through the front door.

No amount of firefighting experience could have prepared AJ for entering her own burned-down home, one she hadn't lived in for the last five years. But so many memories were packed into this place. And it was gone.

She couldn't tell if her heart stopped or pounded harder.

Logan offered her a hand across a rafter that had fallen during the fire. She took it and refused to let go as they walked into the short hallway. The first door on the right led to the extra room. When she had lived here, they used it partly for storage and partly for an office-type space. The door was open, and the room was gone.

She went in, reluctantly letting go of Logan's hand. "Did you still keep the fireproof box in here?"

"Yeah. Careful, I'll get it." He passed her.

The roof was mostly intact, but the ceiling was falling in. The flames had clearly made it into this room. The window was busted, but they hadn't had to vent the roof.

Logan found the fireproof box that contained all of their legal documents and set it outside the front window.

AJ looked around. She couldn't tell much of what Logan had once had in the room. A few books were still on the shelf. She reached for one, but the spine crumbled as she took hold of it. The rest of the book was intact but was a lost cause. Too much of it had been destroyed to be saved.

They didn't bother to check the bathroom.

She couldn't stomach the closed door, so she went into the open master bedroom.

Much of it was gone too. AJ went to the chest at the foot of the bed and lifted the lid with care. "Looks like these blankets could be worth saving."

From the closet, Logan said, "Not everything in here is a complete loss. I'll call a restoration team. Even if we save a few things, I think it's worth it. The insurance will help."

"Oh good." The walls at this end of the house were still intact despite the damage from the heat and smoke.

She went to the window at the back and inspected the yard. The tree branches had curled back in response to the intense heat.

"AJ?"

She turned to Logan, who stood by the door. "Yeah?"

"We need to check Bree's room."

She remained motionless. "It was still her room?"

"I couldn't remove anything without you."

She stared at him. She couldn't get her feet to work and shook her head instead.

He closed the distance. "We have to."

"I can't." She swallowed. "If it's all gone, then she's gone forever."

He took her shoulders in his hands. "Look at me." He waited until she met his eyes. "She's here"—he touched AJ's chest with the tips of his fingers—"and here"—he transferred his hand to his own chest. "If we lost every last picture and keepsake, we'd still have her. But you're the firefighter; tell me what you've told me about closed doors before."

"The fire is much less likely to spread to a room with a closed door."

"Okay then, let's go see." He lifted one arm toward Bree's room and rested the other on AJ's back.

She stepped forward. Logan was right there with her.

At the door, AJ extended her arm but stopped short.

Logan reached around her and directed her hand to the knob. Together they turned it. They pushed the door open, but AJ closed her eyes. She couldn't hope for as favorable an outcome as she had seen in house fires over the years.

"AJ." The breathlessness in Logan's voice forced her to open her eyes.

The painted pink room was still there. Purple bedspread, Bree's favorite hippo, her doll house. Her Mary Janes and itty-bitty Converse were still tucked under the edge of the bed.

AJ's knees gave out on her, and if Logan hadn't caught her, she would have collapsed to the floor. She turned and gripped Logan. "It's okay."

"Isn't this why you teach people to close their bedroom doors while they sleep?"

"But to see it so tangibly ... Logan, it's all okay."

"I know." Tears streamed down his face and traced the edge of his mask. He drew her to his chest.

That's when she realized tears were falling from her eyes as well.

They stood there holding each other for a few minutes. Almost everything in the room would be worth restoring. All of it was no doubt smoke-damaged, but not so much it couldn't be washed out.

Once the restoration company completed cleaning Bree's belongings, AJ would sit with Logan, and they could sort out what to keep and what to pass on to someone in need. She wasn't looking forward to that, but it was so much better than having to shovel it all into the trash.

Thank you, Jesus, for this. You are so good.

Chapter Twenty-Four

Logan led AJ out of the house. He couldn't quite comprehend how most of Bree's things had been saved from the raging fire. If he hadn't kept that door closed ... For once his difficulty facing his grief had been of some benefit.

Once out front, they found the arson investigator with police detectives Doug Ramirez and Wyatt Remington. They exchanged greetings.

Leroy said, "I've been over it several times. This was not at all like those trash-can fires. Those were made with paper and lighter fluid. This was entirely different. I've found evidence of a canister of camping fuel at the point of origin."

Logan crossed his arms. "I don't own any of that. These teenagers are stepping up their game. That's not good."

Doug shook his head. "I'm not so sure about that. We've been monitoring the hashtag and have yet to see your house lit up. Doesn't mean it won't show or the kids were scared enough to not post, but this feels different."

"The point of origin is the kitchen sink." Leroy lifted his finger in the air. "But I can say one thing for certain, this fire was no accident. It wasn't because you neglected to clean your dryer vent or because a dog lit the pizza box with the gas stove. This was deliberate—whether a teenage prank or something more sinister. Someone intentionally burned your house. This was arson."

Logan's heart ramped up. Whoever did this needed to pay.

AJ's hand wrapped around Logan's elbow, bringing him down a notch. He wanted to explore the thought of why in twenty-four hours he'd gone from so angry at her to settled by her presence, but that would have to wait.

"I don't understand why anyone would target me. I haven't arrested any arsonists."

With a soft voice barely loud enough for Logan to hear, AJ said, "As if dealing with me having a stalker wasn't enough."

He rested his hand on hers, which still held his arm.

The three investigators promised to do all they could to find the culprit or culprits and left.

Logan went to the window and picked up the fireproof box.

AJ followed him. "I don't understand who would have done this."

"How much do you think Daryl is your stalker?"

"Fifty-fifty. I mean, plenty of things point to him, but too many give me pause. Do you think he would do this?"

"I don't know. I guess I was going to ask you that."

She shrugged. "Maybe it was a teenager who took it too far."

"It shouldn't be ruled out yet. But let's let the detectives do their job. For now. We should take this somewhere and make sure we have the most important items."

She nodded. "We can go back to the apartment."

Will and Zara already had plans with his family for dinner. They had suggested canceling, but Logan told Will it would be good to have some alone time with AJ. Like she said, spending time together was the most important step for them to take after five years of being estranged.

Logan put the box in the trunk of AJ's car. He sat in the front seat and stared at the house. Disbelief still ruled his emotions when looking at the remnants. What would they do now? He could live with Will for a while, but he and Zara were getting married, and then Logan would need to move out.

Would he and AJ eventually live with one another again? He'd been the barrier from them being together this entire time. He didn't need to guess as to what she desired. She'd made it clear. But how did he feel about it?

They were married. But how long would it take to rebuild their relationship? As long as it took to rebuild their house?

"Logan? You okay?"

He nodded. "Should we rebuild it?"

"I don't know. I assume you're talking about the house itself?" A slight smirk quirked her lips.

"Yes. I know the answer about our marriage. Even if I don't know how to rebuild it, we will."

A breath audibly caught in her throat.

It was his turn to smile. He was no longer assaulted by what she had done every time he looked at her. It wasn't like he had forgotten, but did forgiveness really make that big a difference that fast?

Trust would take longer to build, but for the first time in five years, he actually thought maybe one day he could learn to trust her again.

"It's getting close to dinner time. Should we get some takeout?"

"I'd like that." One step at a time. One meal at a time.

Curled up on the couch, AJ stuffed a load of chow mein from the carton into her mouth and listened to Logan tell her a cop story from earlier in the year. She loved it when he told stories from work. The dumb-criminal ones were always the best, but this one was about how he'd saved a raccoon from a chimney.

She swallowed. "Sounds a lot like a firefighter's job."

He laughed. "Hey, I can save animals too." He leaned over and took a chopstick full of chow mein from the carton she held.

While he was close, she nabbed some of his fried rice. It was like they hadn't lost the last five years.

They continued to chat and finished eating. Then they went to the kitchen table and opened the fireproof box.

Logan said, "I put a few other important things in here too." He pulled out a Ziplock bag with a clipping of blond curls.

AJ took the baggie and fingered the curls through the plastic. Her baby girl's first and only haircut.

Next he produced a folder of papers. Bree's drawings, or at least the best ones. The girl loved to draw and color, so they had made a point to keep their favorites and her favorites, but not all of them because that could have filled an entire room. And she was only five.

"Oh, Logan, thank you."

"I have these in here too." He removed a jewelry box and opened it.

Three white-gold rings. The day he had kicked AJ out he had made her give him her rings.

"I took all three and put them in here. I assumed they would stay there until the day I died, but here we are. I don't know if we're ready for them, but I'm glad they are safe."

She ran her finger along the bands and diamond. "If you didn't think we'd ever pull them out again, why didn't you sell them or get rid of them in one way or another?"

"Because I wanted them on our fingers."

She stepped closer to him, putting herself fully into his personal space. How did she voice her deepest question without offending him?

His eyes narrowed.

The seriousness of her thought must have written itself in her expression.

"I promise to not blow up."

She bit her lip and searched for the right words. "We wasted so much time."

"And for that I'm sorry." He raked his hand into her hair and leaned closer.

"Me too." She spun out of his touch but made a full rotation and met his eyes again.

Confusion toyed with his eyebrows, but he took a confident step toward her and took her hand. He twirled her around, but she danced away.

She was teasing him, but he appeared to fancy the flirting.

"Playing hard to get has never been your game."

She stopped shy of the wall and said, "True." Desire for her husband ignited in her. She had missed this man with more intensity than dynamite.

Grabbing his arm she tugged him toward her. And he came willingly.

"Now that's the girl I remember."

She giggled as he slid one hand around her waist and the other along her jaw to the back of her head.

His face came close. She ran her hands up his chest to his jaw.

"Logan." She loved saying his name. "I've missed you so much."

He nodded and moisture filled his eyes.

She ran her thumb along his jawline.

His lips lingered so close to hers. Should she wait for him to come to her? Should she make the final move? *No, let him.*

Eyes searching hers, he waited. For what she didn't know, but she'd led him here; it was his turn.

He pressed his lips to hers, tugged her body closer, and then stepped her back against the wall. Passion surged.

When the Bible talked of two becoming one flesh, it wasn't exaggerating. With this kiss, AJ felt like half of her had returned. This was the man she'd given herself to so long ago. They weren't ready to go there now, but every fiber of her being felt alive.

His tender lips danced with hers, leading her, loving her.

She never wanted to leave this moment, but she knew them. If they didn't step out of the kiss now, they'd be running to her bedroom ... *her* bedroom. Not theirs.

With reluctance she drew out of the kiss. His warm heavy breaths told her he was hungry for more, as was she.

Even if he wasn't pressing her against the wall, she wouldn't be able to move away from him. She didn't want to.

Words finally came from him. "We need to wait."

She nodded.

"It's always been easy for us to fall into the physical relationship, but I want more than that."

"So do I."

"We aren't ready to ..."

She put her finger on his lips.

He leaned his forehead against hers.

This time she closed the micro-chasm. Wrapping her arms around his neck, they met lip to lip with a gentle, controlled passion.

Her phone dinged across the room.

Logan broke the kiss. "You should check that."

"Pretty sure there is no one in this world who should separate me from you."

He tapped her on the nose. "Touché. But still." He stepped away, giving her space to go to her phone.

She picked it up and checked the text message. Maybe it was Zara checking for clearance to enter.

It wasn't.

It was *him*.

> STOP. STOP. STOP. What is happening here? He didn't want you. I want you. You're supposed to be with me.

AJ dropped her phone on the table. How did her stalker know about Logan?

Chapter Twenty-Five

Logan picked up AJ's phone from the table. "What is it?" He tucked her under his arm as he looked at the screen.

Another text message dinged.

> Let go of her, Logan. You neglected her. Let someone who will care about her have her. You had your chance and ruined it.

Logan set the phone on the table and wrapped his other arm around AJ too. In her ear he whispered, "I wonder how he knows I'm holding you."

She shuddered in his embrace. "He must be watching us."

Logan glanced at the windows. The blinds were closed. It was overcast, so he hadn't thought to open them when they arrived with dinner. Were there cameras in the apartment? As much as he hated the idea, it was the next logical thought.

"I'm calling Will." He didn't let go of AJ while he dialed Will's number. When he answered, Logan said, "Are you guys headed back to the ladies' apartment soon? More eyes would be helpful. We need to play hide and seek."

"We're on our way already; should be there in about five. You suspect there is something hiding in there?"

"Yep. I'll explain when you get here."

"I say call Adam too."

Logan hung up with Will and called Adam. He remained vague, but Adam didn't ask any more questions.

Logan held AJ until the door opened.

AJ jumped but remained tucked against him.

Zara walked in followed by Will and Adam.

She said, "That's a sight for sore eyes. Not that I'm okay if the creep scared you again, but I knew you two would make a cute couple."

Logan shook his head. "We were the cutest couple ever."

"Are. We're still married, remember."

He loved that AJ could still have a sense of humor even when she was scared out of her mind.

Everyone gathered around, and Logan released AJ with one arm and turned to their friends. "I believe there is at least one camera in this apartment. We were hugging and AJ got these texts." He showed them the phone.

Will raised an eyebrow. "Hugging? Just hugging?"

"Shut it. The point is: the blinds are closed. Only way I can think of him knowing this is by watching us. But if there is no way to see in from the outside, he must be watching from inside."

Adam nodded. "Seems reasonable. I say we spread out and search everything. Probably should check outside too. But whatever you do, don't touch anything directly. Maybe, just maybe he used his bare hands to plant them."

"I have a box of gloves." Zara disappeared for a moment and came back.

They all donned gloves and began searching. Adam out front, Logan in the kitchen, Will the living room, and the women looked through each other's bedrooms.

It wasn't long before each of them shouted, "Found one."

Adam came back in saying he found two. One that covered the driveway, another that covered the stairs and door to the apartment.

Zara came out of AJ's room. "I found two in there."

Adam asked, "Has anyone checked the bathroom?"

AJ shook her head. Logan followed her to check.

She walked into the small room. "I think I'm going to throw up if there is one in here."

"I might have to kill this guy if there is."

"Zara said two were in my room. I don't always change in the bedroom, but I do on a regular basis."

Logan's blood ran hot. Whoever this jerk was, he had gone too far. And if there was a camera in the bathroom too ...

Logan and AJ looked through the bathroom but didn't find anything obvious. Not that any of them had been obvious. The tiny little cameras operated on a battery and sent out the signal wirelessly. There was one place he hadn't checked yet.

"Do you have a step stool?"

"I'll get it." AJ disappeared for a moment and then arrived back and handed him the stool.

After unfolding it, he climbed the first step and popped the cover off the exhaust fan.

Inside was another tiny camera. It took all his willpower not to crush the vile little device.

AJ wrapped her arms around her waist. "So, not only did he come into my home, but he's been watching me? How long?"

Logan shook his head. "There's no way of knowing. I mean we can find out what the battery life is on these things and that will give us a slight idea, but ..."

They went out to the living room, and Logan handed Adam the camera from the bathroom.

Will's face turned bright red. "Oh, you have got to be kidding me!"

AJ said, "Unfortunately, no."

Will clenched his fist in front of him. "If I get my hands on this guy—"

AJ touched his arm and nodded to Zara, who had gone pale. Will turned to her and drew her to his chest.

AJ spun to Logan. The anger and fear that mixed together in her eyes was a force he was glad he wasn't the target of.

He rested his hand on her shoulder. "We'll get him. I will do everything in my power to."

Was he going to be able to protect her? This stalker had taken things from a "romantic" level to one driven by much more carnal desires, and from there it wouldn't be a leap to violence.

But Logan couldn't be with AJ all the time.

And Zara. After all she had been through recently, she looked like she was going to crumble. Even if she wasn't directly being targeted, her space had been violated, again.

They needed to get to the bottom of this before anything worse happened.

Beep. Beep. Beep.

AJ hit the stop button on Granny's timer before removing the chicken and rice casserole from the oven. After finding all the cameras in her apartment last night, she refused to be there alone, so she'd asked Granny if she'd like some company for the evening while Logan and Zara both worked second shift.

"I think it's ready, Granny."

The older woman shuffled into the kitchen. "It smells amazing." She came up beside AJ. "And it looks beautiful too. I'll get the salad out."

They fixed the salad and their plates, then sat at the dining room table.

The casserole was entirely too hot to eat. After Granny prayed, she said, "Tell me about what's changed with you and Logan. Because I happened to look out the window yesterday afternoon and saw him coming back to the apartment with you. I want all the particulars."

AJ chuckled and poked at the too-hot casserole while telling Granny all the details from the last four days. She knew about the fire, but AJ hadn't had the opportunity to tell her everything.

"You know I want more than the facts, dear. How do you feel about it all?"

Warmth flooded AJ's cheeks. "I'm cautiously excited. He changed so fast, I feel like I'm suffering from whiplash."

"I think that means he has truly forgiven you. That boy had a brick wall of unforgiveness fortified around his heart. But when he released his grip on it, the wall collapsed. Sounds like he also let Jesus in immediately to sweep it away."

AJ nodded. "Thank you for all your prayers."

"Prayer is a powerful thing. That wall may be gone, but you two have a lot to rebuild. I will continue praying. You are praying for him too?"

"I try. I have been. I wish I was more consistent praying for him every day."

"It takes discipline. But it is of utmost importance. I noticed the biggest difference in my marriage when I was consistently praying for your grandpa. And it wasn't only about God working in his heart. By praying for him, God worked in my heart too."

AJ nodded. "I believe that, have felt that. I wish I knew what to do to rebuild our marriage."

"Keep following Jesus. If Logan is pursuing Jesus too, you'll naturally grow closer. Praying for him and encouraging him in his walk is the best way to do that."

The casserole had finally cooled enough, so silence fell between the women as they ate.

She hadn't told Granny much about the stalker or how scared she was because she didn't want to worry her. They had a nice dinner and decided to watch a Cary Grant movie together afterward.

But the entire time, AJ felt like she needed to watch over her shoulder. She closed all the curtains much sooner than Granny would normally, but she didn't protest. Granny was astute enough that despite AJ's lack of forthrightness about the stalker, the older woman would understand what was going on.

Chapter Twenty-Six

Logan drove his patrols around the city. He'd thought about taking time off. His sergeant had even suggested it, but being out on the streets helped keep his mind distracted from all that had happened. Although being with AJ would have been nice.

He was thankful he kept his uniforms in his locker at the station—except for when one needed to go to the cleaners—so the fire hadn't claimed them. As long as he didn't think about it all too often, he was holding together fine. Even more than wanting to find the person who lit his house on fire, he wanted to find AJ's stalker and bring the full extent of the law down on his head. They had several charges to put on him, if only they knew who it was and were able to link all of the evidence to him. Though that wasn't looking promising.

Before his shift, Logan had talked to Adam and Amelia and, so far, the cameras weren't leading to much. They had a lot more work to do with them, and the tech guy was doing his job to see if he could trace the signal. But while Amelia was hopeful it would lead to something, Logan hadn't missed the skepticism on Adam's face.

Turning down a neighborhood street near Lincoln Elementary, Logan kept an eye peeled for any hooligans up to no good.

Down another street, his headlights caught two shadowy figures dart across the road. In the driveway across the street, a trash can blazed.

Logan flipped on his lights, and over the loud speaker, commanded the teens to stop.

They turned and his headlights caught their faces. He'd seen these two around and knew their parents. "Zach and Brandon."

Realizing they'd been busted, both boys' shoulders slumped.

Logan got out of his squad car. "Put your hands on the hood."

Zach said, "Yes, sir."

Both boys obeyed, and Logan radioed it in. Officer Stillwater, the owner of the house with the fire, came out with an extinguisher.

"Thanks, Jackson. You caught them?"

"Sure did. You got the fire?"

He gave the affirmative.

Logan grabbed a second set of cuffs from his car. He hated having to cuff these boys, both of whom were only fifteen, but they'd put themselves in this situation.

He told them to sit on the curb. "Now I need some information from you boys, and if you talk to me I might be willing to help you out a little. You're still in trouble, but maybe less if you are forthright with me."

They both nodded.

"What is the deal with this dare?"

Brandon shrugged. "It's just a stupid social media thing."

"Then why do it? You aren't stupid. What does it get you that makes it worth risking your futures?"

Zach said, "If the video goes viral, we'll get a bunch of followers."

"To what end?"

Zach shrugged.

"You do realize the number of these videos out there now reduces your chance to go viral?"

Brandon deflated even further. "I guess it was stupid."

"Yeah. What if someone had gotten hurt?"

Brandon sat back up. "But nobody has. It's just some trash cans."

"Guess you didn't hear my house burned down on Saturday." Logan crossed his arms.

Zach said, "I heard about that. Everyone at the skate park today was talking about it. Nobody knows who did it."

"Is everyone owning up to the other fires?"

"Yes, sir," Zach said. "But no one knows about your house. Jeremiah was mad because whoever did it broke the rules of the dare."

This was confirmation of the suspicion that someone other than a teenager targeted Logan.

Stillwater walked over and glared at the boys. "You two. Still sore about my telling you not to skate around the library where signs are posted telling you not to?"

The boys looked at the ground.

Logan said, "Is that why you picked Officer Stillwater's trash can?"

The boys nodded.

Logan turned to Stillwater. "They've been informative about this stupid dare that's floating around on social media."

Stillwater crossed his arms. "Good. You two should be glad I was able to put it out easily."

Brandon said, "We made sure we pulled it away from the house, so it wouldn't damage anything else. Unlike the guys who got Cooper's house."

Logan glanced at Stillwater. "Did we get those kids?"

"Sure did. Arrested them at school on Friday." He looked at the boys. "I *thought* that would convince you all to stop this nonsense."

The sheepish expressions on the boys' faces made Logan want to laugh.

Zach said, "They were in lockup all night."

Logan nodded. "That can be arranged for the two of you too."

Brandon pleaded, "But we didn't catch the house on fire."

"Yeah, but it's still arson. You set a fire on purpose with the intention of destroying property." Logan stepped toward the boys and lifted Zach to his feet. "To the station with you two."

Stillwater took Brandon and, once both teens were secured in Logan's squad car, motioned for him.

Logan stepped out of earshot of the boys and joined Stillwater, who said, "I'm fine if you just call their parents and don't book them or anything, especially if they were helpful."

"I can do that. I'll give them a stern warning too."

"Please. This has got to stop."

"Agreed."

Logan took the boys to the station and pretended to book them, putting them in holding while he went to call their parents.

Once they were on the way, Logan went to the boys and sat on the bench across from them in the holding cell.

"Now here's the deal, guys: we're gonna let you go. Your parents are coming to get you, but if you *ever* do something like this again, you're going to be in more trouble than a skateboarder face-planting on a cactus."

They both delivered a sincere yes, sir.

"And one more thing. Can you two do me a favor?"

Brandon jumped on it. "Whatever you want."

"Let me know if you find out anything about other kids involved in these pranks, especially if you ever hear anything about my house. And encourage your friends to cut it out."

"Yes, sir." This one was more emphatic than the last.

Logan led them out to the lobby where their parents met them. He didn't envy those boys tonight. The likelihood they'd be at the skate park any time soon was slim.

AJ sat up from where she'd been dozing on Granny's couch. She'd heard something, although she had no idea what. She reached in her bag for Harry, but the cold polymer did not meet her hand. She didn't have the pistol. Because she didn't have her concealed carry license, she couldn't carry it out and about, so she'd left it in her apartment.

She listened but didn't hear anything more.

It was only eleven o'clock. She had another hour before Zara even got off duty. Granny had gone to bed a while ago. With a shift starting tomorrow morning at seven, AJ needed to get some sleep, but she wasn't about to go into her apartment on her own. Logan and Will were going to come home with Zara to secure it before the women went to bed.

Lying back down, she tugged the blanket up under her chin but couldn't go back to sleep. Her mind spun with the idea that someone was out there hunting. Okay, maybe they weren't hunting her but wasn't that the next level of escalation this guy would likely take?

Adam had been very straightforward with AJ about the typical progression of stalking. He'd also told her he made a point to talk to Daryl this morning. Though Adam said he'd kept it casual and non-threatening, he'd been ready to slap Daryl in cuffs and bring him in if necessary.

But it hadn't been. Daryl had denied any involvement other than the comments at the grocery store and out the car window. And he had shown Adam surveillance from his convenience store to corroborate he couldn't possibly be the one who'd delivered the gifts on Friday.

Despite her doubts the stalker was Daryl, AJ didn't know who else it could be. No one else had shown interest in her. And why would anyone? She wasn't trying to be self-defeating, but it didn't compute.

At least she was strong and had a clue about defending herself. Thinking about what maneuvers she would do if someone snuck up behind her, she finally dozed again.

She was dreaming about kicking a masked figure in the gut when her phone rang an hour and a half later. It was Logan.

He'd called her. Her heart sped up even faster than the pounding after being woken up from a crazy dream.

She answered, "Hey."

"We're about to pull into the driveway."

"Thanks for the warning. I don't have Harry with me, but if I did I wouldn't want him to say hi to you."

"Umm ... Harry?" The unease in his voice was blatant.

"Oh right, you haven't met my Smith & Wesson."

His sigh echoed over the phone. She tried not to laugh out loud. "I'll meet you outside."

They hung up, and she slung her bag over her shoulder. She exited the house through the back door, making sure to lock it behind her.

Waving to her friends and husband, she walked toward them but stopped.

Something was wrong.

She spun around. No one was there. But she had the distinct feeling of being watched.

Logan came up beside her. "What's wrong?"

"I felt like someone was over there." She pointed toward the darkness that hid Granny's garden.

Will came over and shined a flashlight on the area. "I don't see anything, but I'll check if there is any evidence of someone traipsing about."

"Thanks, Will." AJ turned to Logan. "Work was okay?"

He nodded.

She wanted to greet him with a kiss, but she wasn't sure she should. They hadn't kissed good night or goodbye when they saw each other that morning. Just those intense ones in the kitchen yesterday.

Zara came over to them. "Staring at each other is cute and all, but I'd love to go to bed."

AJ's face warmed, and she looked away. "Same. Let's get upstairs."

Will came back. "I didn't find anything. But I got a weird feeling, so let's be on guard while we go up. I'll go first."

Zara looked at AJ. "Do you have Harry?"

AJ shook her head.

"Okay. Logan can take the rear."

The four of them went up the stairs. The door didn't show any signs of tampering, but it hadn't when the cameras were installed either.

Zara unlocked the door, and Will and Logan went inside, sidearms drawn, ready to engage. Will flipped on the light.

Both men gasped as the women came in behind them.

The apartment had been trashed.

Logan said, "You two wait here. We'll make sure no one is inside."

As the guys cleared all the rooms, AJ took in the space. Two cartons of ice cream were turned over on the kitchen table, oozing everywhere. The cushions were off the couch and oddly dispersed throughout the room. Every last one of her books were now upside down on the bookshelf.

"All clear," Logan called. "AJ, come here."

She carefully stepped around the random things strewn across the floor and found Logan on the threshold to her bedroom. "What?"

Her room was backward. The creep had not only been in her bedroom, but he had rearranged all of her furniture. Her bed was on the opposite wall from where it had been, as were her dresser and desk.

And all of her underwear and socks had been dumped on the bed.

But as violating as that was, it wasn't even the most shocking part. On the wall, written in oozy red, were the words: *I still see you.*

A shudder rippled through her body.

"I think it's ketchup." Logan opened the closet door. "He messed with this too."

All of her hangers had been turned around, plus the clothes had been switched to the opposite order from what they had been in.

Her skin felt like it was going to crawl right off her body. Some creep had touched all of her things. "What on earth?" AJ wrapped her arms around her middle.

Logan shook his head. "This is the strangest thing I've ever seen. I have no idea what he was thinking." Logan walked over to her, and she accepted his embrace.

She was so grateful for his strength and comfort. And glad she wasn't having to cope with this alone. A dreadful thought burst into her head. "Oh no."

"What?"

She let go of Logan, ran to her nightstand, and opened the drawer. Her StopBox was missing. "No!"

"Again, what?"

"Harry's gone."

"He stole your gun?"

She nodded.

"Hey, guys?" Will called.

AJ and Logan left her room and found Will standing outside the bathroom.

He said, "Look at this." He stepped aside, giving them a clear view of the bathroom floor. It was covered in ... shampoo, soap, conditioner, shaving gel. It was as if he had opened every bottle and emptied them onto the floor. In fact, that was exactly what happened.

Zara came up beside AJ. "How do we even clean that up? And I don't know about you, but I'm not sure I can sleep here knowing some creep has been messing with our stuff."

"How bad was your room?"

"Eh. A few things put in random places, but nothing like yours. However, the kitchen is a hot mess."

It was all too much. AJ gripped Logan's arm to steady herself.

Will said, "I have an idea. Take pictures and call Adam or Amelia."

AJ snapped photos with her phone while Logan called Adam.

Will went to the kitchen and came back with several large spoons, spatulas, and cups, then started scooping up the puddles of soap. "I'd leave it, but it could damage the floorboards."

AJ grabbed some towels and, once Will cleared the area in front of the door, she laid down the towel so he could go farther in. Eventually, Zara and Logan joined Will, and AJ went to let in Adam and the CSU team.

She walked them through what had happened, including the missing firearm, and the team collected evidence. About an hour later, CSU finished and left, leaving Adam behind with AJ and her friends.

They all worked to clean up the mess, and it was in decent shape by four in the morning. She needed to be at the station in three hours, but she could not sleep in the apartment.

She was flipping her books back when Will came to her. "I'm going to take Zara to my parents' house to get some sleep. Do you want to come too? You are more than welcome. You know how my mom is."

She checked her watch. "At this point, I think I'll go to the station and sleep with ear plugs in. That way I can get the most sleep possible before my shift starts. But I appreciate the offer. I can always go to my dad's too."

Will nodded and walked away.

All five of them left the apartment utterly exhausted. The emotional toll was as much as the physical. But AJ couldn't get over how much she appreciated the people God had put in her life.

AJ rolled over in the bunk at the fire station. Someone was touching her shoulder.

"Morning, sunshine." Emily. The young, cheery EMT held out a donut on a small paper plate.

AJ popped the earplugs out of her ears.

"I found your note to wake you, but Ty demanded I wait another hour. I made sure the guys saved you one of these."

"Oh, sweet dear. You are my favorite person today." AJ swung her feet off the bed, sat up, and took the donut. "Not just for the donut, but for listening to Ty and giving me more time. I'm so tired I could scream." Completely disregarding the nasty taste in her mouth, she took a generous bite of the chocolate-iced pastry.

"Been there. A fresh pot of coffee is waiting for you too."

"Definitely going to need that." AJ finished the donut and got ready for the day.

Ten minutes later, she walked into the living area.

Don said, "Look, someone actually decided to come to work today." He winked at her.

She simply shook her head, not acknowledging what he said. After getting her coffee, she mulled about, seeing what everyone else was up to for the morning. When the coffee was gone, she deposited her cup in the sink, and Brennan came around the corner and tossed her a football.

"No one will throw the ball around with me, but I need to start practicing for that Thanksgiving game if I want to be quarterback."

She chuckled. The entire department had been joking all year about having a football game for Thanksgiving, but considering the day would most likely be busy with kitchen fires, they were talking about playing the game the Saturday before.

"Fine. Let's go." AJ had never been close to her brother, but one of her favorite memories was when he taught her how to throw a football.

She and Brennan went out front, then to the side yard of the station. During their shifts they were expected to get some level of exercise in as time permitted, and this counted.

She tossed him the ball.

He caught it. "Go long."

She ran down the area where they liked throwing the ball. It was shaded from the bright sun by tall oak trees. AJ caught the ball and quickly released it back to Brennan in a perfect spiral.

The longer they tossed it back and forth, the more she felt like she was being watched. It finally distracted her enough that she missed one of Brennan's throws. The ball bounced off her hand

and rolled toward the trees that lined the side of the fire station's property.

She jogged after it. Once she'd grabbed the football, AJ glanced up.

A face stared back at her from behind a tree.

She jumped. And screamed.

"Sorry, I didn't mean to startle you."

"Eric?"

"Hey, AJ. Is this the fire station you work at?"

"Yes."

Brennan ran up beside her. "Is everything okay?"

"Yeah, this is Eric. He scared the tar out of me." She looked back at Eric. "What on earth are you doing back here?"

He pointed over his shoulder. "I'm working on the cable lines over there. I dropped a nut and it bounced. I need to find it."

"We can help you look." She stepped closer.

"No, it's fine. Oh, look, there it is." Eric leaned over and reached his hand to the ground. "Got it. We're good. Didn't mean to bother your game."

"It's no bother." AJ watched Eric hurry away. That was incredibly odd.

Brennan said, "Did you see him actually pick anything up?"

"No. Is it just me or was that strange?"

"It was more bizarre than an OMC song."

She gave him a confused glare.

"Never mind. You're too young." He jogged away, backward. "Toss it."

She released the football, and they resumed their exercise. But the disturbing notion that Eric had been watching her didn't dissipate from her mind. Was he her stalker?

Chapter Twenty-Seven

Around one o'clock Logan drove up in front of the fire station. The bay was open, and the engine was there, so he hoped that meant AJ was too.

He gripped the bouquet of flowers he'd bought. Slowly, he walked to the open bay, praying the whole way. He hoped AJ would receive his flowers well. As he had lain in bed this morning, he'd felt a nudge from the Holy Spirit that although AJ was eager to rebuild their relationship, he needed to be intentional to woo her.

Walking into the bay, he found the new guy and Brennan working on equipment.

"Hey, guys. Is AJ around?"

"Well, look who it is. Good to see you, man." Brennan came to him and shook his hand. "She's here." He pointed up.

Logan looked to the top of the firetruck. AJ stood. "You're gonna get hurt again."

The new guy, whose name he couldn't remember, said, "She isn't afraid of anything, is she?"

She came over the side of the truck. "Oh, I'm afraid of plenty, but heights isn't one of them." She bounded to the ground.

He extended the flowers. "These are for you. I wanted to bring them in person so you knew they were from me." He winked at her, hoping she'd find humor in it.

She chuckled and reached for the bouquet.

"And we're out." Brennan and the other guy left.

She took the flowers. "Thank you. They're beautiful."

"Just like you." Warmth filled his cheeks.

"Are you blushing, Mr. Jackson?"

"You bring it out of me, Mrs. Jackson."

They each stepped a little closer. With her free hand, AJ reached out and touched his abdomen.

A strand of golden hair had fallen from her ponytail, and he brushed it away from her eyes. "I was wondering ..." this should not be a hard question to ask *his wife*, but he was struggling to get the words to form. "Would you do me the honor of going on a date with me, maybe Saturday?"

Joy sparked in her eyes. "I would love that."

"Excellent. I'll plan something fun, something that fits us."

"So I can wear pants?"

"Unless you want something fancy."

Her eyebrows quirked. "You know me well enough to know that answer."

"I do. I know you well enough to know that while it's not your preference, you like it every once in a while."

"Touché. But I like the idea of having fun with you, relaxed and not hoity-toity. Save that for a different occasion."

"Sounds like a plan. I suppose I should head to work."

"Probably. Maybe I'll see you, but calls that require both of us tend to be more serious than I want either of us to have to deal with tonight."

"Very true." He cupped the side of her face and kissed her forehead. "If I don't see you tonight, I'll see you tomorrow."

"Yeah? When?"

"Call me when you get off."

"I could do that. I really don't know where to go. I don't want to put Granny in danger."

"I know. We'll figure it out."

She closed the distance between them and wrapped her arms around him.

He embraced her, hugging her close. How he'd missed holding her!

In her ear he whispered, "I love you."

She melted against him and released a slight noise of contentedness. "I love you too."

"I know. Thanks for taking me back."

She lifted her head and looked him in the eye. "Same."

Again touching her face, desire flooded his mind.

She nodded slightly.

He leaned over and covered her lips with his own in a sweet, gentle kiss. He'd be in trouble if he didn't keep it there. Releasing her, he stepped back. "More of that soon enough."

She fluttered her eyebrows.

He laughed. How he loved her!

Somberness clouded her face.

"What's wrong?"

"I almost forgot to tell you with all this kissy talk. I saw Eric today. He was supposedly fixing some cable lines over there"—she pointed to the side of the station—"but it seemed like he was watching Brennan and me while we were tossing the football around."

"That's weird. I also caught him outside your house on Friday morning. I mean, he said he was working on cable lines."

"It is his job, but it felt really strange."

He stepped back to her. "Be careful."

"I will. Is it crazy to be suspicious of Eric?"

"I don't think it's crazy to be suspicious of anyone right now."

He kissed her cheek and said goodbye with another admonition to be careful.

As he drove to the police station, he tossed around the idea that Eric could be AJ's stalker.

Chapter Twenty-Eight

The next morning, AJ finished up her end-of-shift chores. The night had been fairly quiet. A small car accident had brought both Logan and AJ to the same scene, but thankfully, everyone involved was okay. Having Logan smile at her while they both worked was a delightful change from a few weeks ago. The rest of the night had seen a few calls, but nothing tragic, and she'd been able to sleep a sufficient amount.

She checked off the items she had taken care of and went to the kitchen to wait for the others to be ready to leave. The next shift had already arrived and was beginning their tasks.

Seth walked into the kitchen with his backpack over one shoulder. "I'll walk out with you if you're ready."

"I'd appreciate that." Maybe this guy wasn't so bad. A little too altruistic at times—was that actually a thing?—but she appreciated his thoughtfulness. And she hadn't forgotten that he'd run in to look for Logan. She'd be forever grateful for that.

They left the kitchen, and Emily and Brennan joined them to walk out. Laughter floated among them as Brennan made a few jokes, but at the sight of AJ's car, they all stopped.

On the hood, a stuffed bear was duct taped down. They walked closer. It was actually hogtied with zip ties. And it wasn't just any bear. It had pink and blue plaid lining in its ears and a matching skirt. It was the bear Logan had won for her at the county fair when they were sixteen. It had been in her apartment. Had this creep taken anything else that belonged to her?

Emily pointed. "There's a paper underneath it."

"Not that this guy has left a single fingerprint on anything, but I probably shouldn't touch it until the cops get here."

Brennan said, "You call Logan; I'll call it in."

"Reach out to Adam directly," AJ said.

Brennan nodded and called Adam.

AJ dialed Logan's number, and he answered right away. "Good morning."

"If only."

"AJ?" The concern in his voice comforted her a bit.

She told him what she had found.

"I'll be there as fast as I can."

Within ten minutes, Adam, Logan, and two CSU techs arrived. Adam held the note so AJ could read it too.

Don't think you can hide from me or that I'm not closer than you think. You need to leave Logan and come be with me. I can help you get divorce papers, and you can make it legal if you must. He hasn't treated you well, you need someone who will treat you like a princess. You will be my princess, even if I have to hogtie you like this stupid bear. You will be mine.

AJ's entire body shook and made her queasy. This was a step farther than anything he had done so far. It was a direct threat. She wasn't safe.

Logan massaged the back of her shoulder and directed her closer to him. He'd read the note too.

She leaned into him, praying this threat would at least hold a tiny bit of evidence and lead to exactly who this was before he could make good on his threats.

This guy saw Logan as an obstacle to making her his own. Was he going to hurt Logan? Was this stalker the one who set their house on fire?

Anger surged through her veins like molten lava. Threatening her was one thing, but if this stalker so much as threw a rock at Logan, she'd do worse than he could imagine.

She wrapped her arm around Logan's waist and held him a little closer. They had a lot of wasted time to make up for, and no one man—especially a stalker—was going to stand in the way of their marriage.

Chapter Twenty-Nine

Logan and AJ went back to Will's house to decompress and simply spend time together. AJ had been sure to tell Adam about Eric too, and Adam said he'd do some investigating. It seemed a little too coincidental that he was around yesterday right before this threat was delivered. The fire station also had a camera on the parking lot, so Adam would check it to see if the stalker could be identified on the video. Regardless of how careful they were not to get caught, most criminals messed up at some point. It was a matter of time before they figured out this guy's identity. Logan hoped and prayed it wouldn't be too late.

With two mugs of coffee, he walked into the living room where AJ sat on the couch. "I hope you take it the same way you used to."

"Some things never change." She accepted the mug he offered.

He settled close to her on the couch, and she turned toward him, pulling her feet to where her knees brushed his leg. Electricity coursed through him. It wasn't the same kind of jolt he'd gotten as a teenager when they were newly in love, but it was as electrifying.

"I was thinking about something, and it might sound kind of strange."

He settled on the couch and draped his arm across the back. "Strange has never scared me."

"I recognize I have to rebuild your trust in me. And one way I'd like to do that is by setting some guidelines or boundaries for myself when it comes to time with other men. I thought of this last night after I had been tossing the football with Brennan. I want to set up the fence even beyond what you're comfortable with."

His heart warmed at the suggestion. "I don't have a problem with you tossing the ball around with Brennan; you two have been doing that for ages. And I really do trust him implicitly, almost as much as I trust Will."

"But even with those two, I think it's a good idea to make a rule of not riding in a car with only me and another guy."

"Unless it's an ambulance with Brennan—on a call."

"Only on a call."

Every rule had an exception.

She continued, "I won't be in a room alone with a man. Even if I'm at the station. If I'm the only one in the room and a guy comes in, I'll go find another place. I want to stay above reproach on this."

"I appreciate that, but public spaces at the station are a little different."

"Still. I'll make a point to be overly cautious. I love you and want to protect our marriage—especially as we rebuild." A soft smile graced her face.

He nodded, astounded by her proactive approach to this. Setting his mug on the coffee table, he traced the shirt seam that lay on her shoulder, then let his hand slide down her upper arm.

"What does the future look like for us?" Her voice was soft.

He gently squeezed the top of her arm, rubbing his thumb in slight circles. "I don't know. I haven't had time to dream it possible."

She chuckled softly.

"You've been the one to hold onto hope for us. What do you see?"

She shrugged, still cradling her mug. "Honestly, I had hoped to move back into the house with you at some point ... but that's as far as I would get because then I'd remember Bree wasn't there too." Her lips quivered as she took a sip of her coffee.

"As much as we had *us* before we had her, it's hard to comprehend us without her."

AJ nodded and stared into her cup. "I always wanted more children, but I'm so scared."

Logan took the mug from her hands and set it beside his. Turning back to AJ, he wrapped his arms around her, drawing her to him. "Same."

She scooted closer, bent legs resting completely on his, and nestled against his chest.

He added, "Obviously, we take it one day at a time, but I hope we can work through our grief and fear enough to trust God to give us the courage to have more kids."

"Can we go to counseling together?"

He bristled at the idea, but that was his pride. *Jesus, help me.* In humility, he said, "I think we have to. I think I need someone to help us—me—identify what we should work through. I want to buck up and be fine, but that hasn't worked."

She leaned back and met his eyes. "I noticed." The smirk and teasing glint made him shake his head.

He poked her between the ribs.

She squirmed. "That's not fair. You're not ticklish."

"Ha! I'll take that unfair advantage." Using both hands he got each of her sides.

She squealed, kicked, and draped her legs over his. "Stop it." She playfully swatted his chest.

He quit tickling her and drew her closer until his lips had captured hers.

It took a moment for her giggles to subside and relax into the kiss. But his heart swelled with the joy of holding his wife close. The kiss intensified.

This was his wife, whom he'd missed so.

He ran his hand into her hair but got stuck on her ponytail, so he pulled the hair tie out.

She ran her hands up his chest, sending his heart to supersonic speeds.

Leaning her back on the couch, he drew out of the kiss and searched her eyes. So much desire, so much hope, so much love met him.

Cupping the side of his face, fingers playing with his hair, she smiled.

Unable to resist, he lowered himself, meeting her lips again. She giggled, delight emanating from her. He broke off the kiss before he let his hands wander farther than her waist.

He slid his arm under her and laid down next to her. She snuggled into him, laying her head on his shoulder.

"I guess Will wouldn't be impressed if we re-consummated our marriage on his couch."

A giant laugh burst out of AJ. "Oh my word, he'd kill us."

Logan wrapped his arms tighter around her. "I look forward to sleeping with you in my arms again."

"But where are we going to live?"

"I don't know. Should we rebuild or look for a new place?"

She sighed. "I wish I knew the right answer."

"I don't think it's a matter of right or wrong. Rebuilding will be a process, but that's the same with our relationship. Do we jump right in or take more time?"

"Yes?"

"Either/or question, babe."

She chuckled. "We should pray about it."

Something panged inside Logan. He should be the one leading them to the cross before the bed. But he loved that she was in tune spiritually and could shove him in the right direction. She was the best helpmate any man could ask for.

"Jesus, AJ and I come to You with all of this. Our marriage, as broken as it has been, we ask You to fix it. Help us know how to love one another the way You have loved us."

They took turns praying aloud for everything from repentance to housing to future children.

Mid-prayer AJ's words trailed off. Logan craned his head to look at her face where it still rested against his chest. She'd fallen asleep.

Giant emotions overtook him. He never thought the day would come that she would fall asleep in his arms again, but it was here, with a promise of more to come.

He shifted a little and fell asleep too.

AJ woke from the most contented sleep she'd experienced in a long time. With his arms wrapped around her, Logan snored softly.

She twisted enough to look at his face. That caused him to shift, and his arm left her side and draped over his eyes. Apparently she wasn't the only one who didn't get enough sleep last night.

Quiet voices came from the kitchen. Will and Zara must have arrived. AJ was grateful they'd let them sleep, though she was quite curious what comments were made. Not that she really cared.

She looked at her watch and was surprised to find it was already after noon. They'd slept for nearly two hours. Logan's arm was bound to be asleep.

He stirred, eyes fluttering open. "Well, hello."

She giggled.

"Let's see. Where did we leave off?" His hand went to her waist and lips to her mouth.

She let him kiss her for a moment, but then pushed him away with more giggles. "We aren't alone, silly."

"Aw, shucks. Does that mean it's lunchtime?"

"Yes, siree." She booped him on the nose. Sitting up, she stretched, keenly aware of Logan watching her closely. She shook her head in amusement. Some things never change.

Once she stood, he got up too, and they wandered into the kitchen. They found Will and Zara at the table, eating sandwiches.

Zara said, "Hey, sleepyheads. Sorry we didn't wait for you, but help yourselves." She gestured to the counter where all the sandwich fixings were laid out.

"Thanks. And thanks for letting us sleep." AJ touched Zara's arm.

"It was too cute a sight to disturb." Zara shot her a cheesy grin.

AJ shook her head, and she and Logan made lunch. They sat with their friends and chatted.

Will asked, "Where are you going to stay tonight?"

"I was thinking about going to my dad's," AJ said. "I'll hang out with him this evening."

Logan paused with his sandwich halfway to his mouth, then lowered it back to the plate. "Do you think he'd be okay if I slept on the couch?"

"I think he'd like that."

Will said, "You two realize you are married and don't have to hold any level of 'propriety,' right?"

"Will!" Zara slapped his arm.

"What? It's true." In a lower, almost under-his-breath voice, he added, "It's not like propriety was ever something they were very concerned with anyway."

AJ picked up a piece of lettuce from her plate and chucked it at Will's face. She chortled, especially when the lettuce landed on his nose.

All four friends laughed. They lingered over lunch, and before long it was time for the three officers to head off to their third of four evening shifts.

Logan tugged her into another room before they left. "I want you to be careful and watch your back." He traced her hairline with his fingertips.

"Of course. You too." She rested her hands on his chest. "I'll see you at Dad's when you get off."

"You're going straight there now?"

"Yep, won't even pass GO or collect anything."

His lips covered hers for a brief moment. "I love you."

"I love you too." She hugged him extra tight. Why was it so hard to let him go? She'd see him after work.

He pulled her back and searched her face. "You okay?"

She shrugged. "God did not give us a spirit of fear. So this feeling isn't of Him. I have to trust our safety into His hands." She closed her eyes. "Jesus, keep us both safe this evening."

"Amen." Logan kissed her forehead. "You'll be okay, and I'll see you as soon as I can tonight."

She nodded and kissed and hugged him again. But anxiety sat in her stomach like curdled ice cream. As they all drove off, she continued to pray, surrendering the anxiety to God constantly.

Midnight was coming fast, but not fast enough. Logan was anxious to get back to AJ. She'd seemed worried, which was totally expected. He'd texted with her as he was able to during his shift to check on her and let her know he was fine.

Driving through downtown and approaching a green light, Logan glanced to the right. He looked left in time to see a car careening toward him.

Logan slammed on his breaks, stopping before he was even in the intersection. The other car flew through.

The light was definitely red.

Logan flipped on his lights and pursued. As he reported it in to dispatch, he came up behind the car, which was going ten miles over the speed limit, but the driver didn't slow or seem to see him at all.

Since it was late and there were homes nearby, Logan flipped on his siren for a quick burst of sound and then for another brief moment. That did the trick.

The car drove into a parking lot, and Logan stopped behind it and turned on the spotlight to illuminate the driver's door.

He approached the driver with caution. Every traffic stop came with its risks. A cop never knew how the driver would react to getting pulled over. Throughout the years, Logan had experienced everything from sobbing teenage girls to grown men threatening him, and occasionally the other way around.

The window went down. "Evening, officer."

Logan stepped into the driver's line of vision. They both groaned. "Hi, Daryl." Would this interaction prove to be why AJ felt so anxious?

"Officer Jackson. How's the missus? I heard you two are finally back together."

"It's none of your business, but we are." Logan stifled another groan. He was not in the mood to talk about life with this guy who was no longer his friend.

"No thanks to me, I know. Seriously, I'm sorry, man."

The words hit Logan square in the chest, and he nearly took a step back in shock. But was Daryl just trying to get out of the ticket coming his way?

"It's in the past." He held out his hand. "License and insurance."

Daryl sighed, leading Logan to believe his suspicions about Daryl's friendliness were spot on.

Daryl gave him the necessary paperwork.

"Sit tight while I process this. You know why I pulled you over, right?"

"Because you want to give the man who serviced your wife a hard time."

"I had no idea it was you. And like I said, it's the past. I even forgive you." A tension left Logan's body with those words. He meant it. He actually forgave the man for his part of messing up their marriage.

Daryl's eyebrows furrowed. "I suppose that light was red ..."

"*And* you were speeding. I could also add a failure to stop for an officer, but I think I'll leave that off."

"Thanks?"

Logan went back to his squad car and processed the ticket, grateful the interaction had gone much better than he could have imagined. So far.

He returned to Daryl's car, handed back his ID, and gave him the ticket. "Slow down and pay attention to the traffic signals."

"Yeah. Guess I'm just tired."

"Go home and go to bed then. Get off the road."

Daryl gave him a thumbs up and barely let Logan step back before he drove off.

Logan wished he'd been gutsy enough to ask Daryl directly if he was the one stalking AJ, but Daryl had an alibi. What if he had doctored the video? Or if the time stamp of the video was set wrong? Daryl wasn't the dumb jock he led people to believe at times.

It was worth considering. But it wasn't like Adam to miss something if there was a chance. Logan wished he knew the answer.

But more than wishing, Logan needed to pray. He resumed his patrols and did just that.

God, I need to relearn having prayer be my default. I miss those years of constant communication with You. I let myself believe it was Bree's death and AJ's betrayal that made my life feel so hollow. But that was only a fraction of it. You need to be the source for everything. Help me depend on You.

He finished his shift, and while walking out of the station with Will and Zara after midnight, he told them about pulling Daryl over.

Will said, "Sounds like you handled it well. I'm impressed. You gonna tell AJ?"

"I kind of have to. I have to learn to talk to her better than I have in the past."

Zara said, "True words. True for both of you."

Logan nodded. "I need to get to her. She said she was going to wait up for me. Are you both staying at your parents?"

Will said, "Yep. I'm too tired to drive her out there, then drive back to town."

Logan told them both *good night* and strapped on his helmet. He couldn't wait to get to AJ's dad's house, to kiss his wife, to make his anxiety rest at least for a few moments while he knew she was safe in his arms.

He left the station and headed toward the other side of town. AJ's dad lived out a little farther than Will but not nearly as far as Will's parents. It was the same route however.

Turning out of the busier area of the city, he made his way down a road that had fewer houses, spread farther apart and lined with clusters of woods.

When he and AJ had bought their house, it had been because that was what they could afford at such a young age. They'd dreamed of living out this way where they could have more land. Maybe that's what they needed to consider now. Not simply re-build what had been but build new. Even if it was only new to them.

He'd tried to be careful with his money over the years and had saved quite a bit. That, in conjunction with the insurance money, might mean they could afford a small farm now.

His mind spun with the idea as he approached a stop sign at a state road that didn't have a cross stop sign.

He rolled past the imaginary line so he could see farther around the trees.

He leaned forward over his handlebars.

Pkew.

A sharp wind hurled past his back.

Did someone shoot at him?

Chapter Thirty

Logan jumped off his motorcycle and dropped to the ground. Another shot whizzed past.

Reaching under his t-shirt, he drew his pistol.

He opened fire into the woods, the direction the shots had come from. He hated not seeing his target, but at least he knew there was a thick growth of trees there and not a house.

Logan loosed two more shots then paused. No shots returned. Maintaining his aim at the dark woods, he took his phone out and dialed 911, barely looking down.

He reported it and said, "Plain clothes officer in pursuit."

Logan grabbed his stronger flashlight from his saddle bag. After moving his bike to the side of the road, he ran into the woods, sweeping the 1300 lumen beam to and fro, gun trained in the center of the light, ready for whatever he might spot.

Inside the tree line, the beam hit a speck of blue, catching his eye. He approached.

Not seeing the shooter, he inspected the object.

A gun lay on the ground. And not just any gun. One with a robin's-egg-blue extended magazine, mag release, and trigger. Was that AJ's gun?

He squatted and held his hand near the barrel without touching it. It was warm. Someone had tried to kill him with his wife's gun. What on God's good earth was happening?

That meant—Logan jumped to his feet—AJ's stalker was ... Logan ran into the woods. "Where are you? Show yourself."

Logan kept the beam going back and forth. He had to find this guy.

A car started in the distance and squealed its tires as it drove away.

"No!" Logan kicked at the underbrush, then turned and went back to his motorcycle and the scene to wait for backup.

He walked up to his bike as Officer Stillwater arrived. Two more officers showed up before Stillwater could even shake Logan's hand.

"You okay?"

"I don't know how he missed me. Grateful nonetheless. So grateful."

"Did you see the shooter?"

Logan shook his head. "But looks like he ditched the weapon. The same one we reported stolen from my wife's nightstand two nights ago."

"Show me."

A few more officers arrived while Logan showed Stillwater the Smith & Wesson.

Stillwater squatted by the pistol. "Guess we'll find some nine millimeter bullets over there." He pointed toward a streetlamp across the road.

Logan analyzed the trajectory. "Yeah, and some more in these trees where I shot at him."

"Let's get out of here and let evidence collection work it."

As if on cue, the CSU van drove up.

The men went back to the road. Logan said, "I need to call my wife."

"My advice, for what it's worth—call someone to get her and bring her here. Don't let her drive right now, even if a stalker wasn't after her."

Logan nodded. "Good thought." He stepped away and called Will.

AJ had tried to doze, but it wasn't working. Anxiety ate at her stomach. Logan told her he was leaving on time. He should have been to her dad's already. Why wasn't he here? Maybe she should call him.

"Alice Jane, you are going to put a hole in my carpet with that pacing."

She spun toward her dad. "Sorry, but Logan should have been here by now."

"I know, but are you trusting God?"

"I'm trying. Keep laying down my anxiety, but I have an awful feeling something is wrong."

Her daddy opened his arms to her, and she walked into them. "Look, there's a headlight now."

She twisted out of her dad's embrace and darted to the door.

"AJ! You have a crazy man after you. Make sure who it is before you run out."

She stopped at the door and slid the curtain to the side.

It wasn't Logan's motorcycle. The single headlight was Will's truck. What was Will doing here?

Zara got out of the passenger side.

AJ swung the door open and burst outside and down the steps. "Where's Logan?"

Will came around the front. Neither of them looked terribly grave. Were they in shock? Something terrible had happened, hadn't it?

Zara said, "AJ, Logan's been shot—"

"What? No! I knew something—"

Zara grasped her arms. "*At,* AJ. Let me finish my sentence. Logan's been shot *at*. He's fine but wanted us to come get you."

AJ's knees gave out as relief mingled with the horror that someone had tried to kill her husband.

Zara caught her. "He's okay but wants to see you. Go put shoes on."

AJ regained her balance and nodded. Turning, she went to get her shoes. Her dad stood on the porch.

"He's okay?" Worry lines creased her dad's forehead. "Go get him and bring him home." He turned to Will. "Son, you've got a headlight out."

Once her shoes were on, she hopped in Will's truck, Zara taking the middle seat between them.

Five minutes later, Will stopped on the far side of an intersection swarming with police. AJ jumped out and—after looking both ways—darted across the road, scanning for Logan.

"AJ!"

She spotted him and ran straight to him, slowing enough to not knock the wind out of either of them. They embraced.

After a moment, she leaned back and took both sides of his face in her hands. "What happened?"

"I pulled up to the stop sign and someone opened fire from the woods." He paused.

"There's something more."

He looked to where the shooter must have fired from. A tech stood near the edge of the woods holding an evidence bag.

Logan took her hand and guided her over to the tech. "Is it bagged?"

"Sure is." The tech handed Logan the evidence bag with a gun inside.

"Harry!"

"Yeah, I'm feeling like a lucky punk today."

She chuckled, but less at the movie reference and more in astonishment at what was happening. "This proves the stalker wanted to kill you."

Logan let go of her hand and rested his on her shoulder. "That's exactly what this means."

She was going to be sick to her stomach. "Does that mean the fire was supposed to kill you?"

Logan shrugged.

"Apparently, whoever it is knows we wouldn't get a divorce."

"And you told him you wouldn't leave me for him."

"I did say that, didn't I?" She hugged herself and leaned into Logan. "What are we going to do? How are we going to catch him? What will it take? One of us ending up dead?"

"Not on my watch." He wrapped his arm across her shoulder and kissed her temple.

Resting her head on his shoulder, she sent streams of thanks to God for watching out for Logan tonight, followed with pleas to keep them both safe. What would this guy try next?

Chapter Thirty-One

They didn't get back to AJ's dad's house until pushing three o'clock in the morning. It had taken a bit of coaxing, but Logan finally got AJ to go to bed. He went to the kitchen for a glass of water before heading to the couch.

AJ's dad came into the kitchen. "I'm glad you're safe."

"Thank you, sir."

"It's Dad. We've gone over this before."

"That was a long time ago. I haven't exactly turned out to be the man you were hoping for—for your daughter."

"Son, none of us are perfect. You both made your fair share of mistakes, like her mom and I did. I'm sorry we weren't a better example for the two of you as to how to make a marriage work."

Not sure how to respond, Logan sipped his water.

"I'm proud of the both of you for not taking the easy way out."

"Ignoring each other was the easiest thing we could do."

"But you didn't get divorced because you both knew your marriage was worth fighting for, even if you didn't actually fight for it."

"I should have. I will now."

"I know, and I couldn't be prouder of the way you are coming back together."

Logan nodded. "Thank you. Means a lot to hear these things from you."

"I've always liked you, even if I wasn't impressed with how you behaved with my little girl."

"I get that more now. Though Bree was so little ..."

"She was. But even if she was still with us, she'd always be your little girl."

Logan ruefully smiled at the thought. She would have been beautiful, but oh such a handful. She was her mother's daughter through and through. He missed his baby.

"Bree would be happy to see her mom and dad back together."

"It would have broken her heart to see how we grieved."

"Here's your opportunity to make up for lost time."

"Yes, Dad."

The older man grinned and slapped Logan's shoulder. "Now, you two are married. There is no reason you need to sleep on the couch." Dad left the room and threw a *good night* over his shoulder.

"Good night." Logan shook his head, finished his glass of water, and debated what to do.

With all that was happening, he simply wanted to hold AJ, know she was close. He turned the light off and padded to her room. With as quiet a motion as possible, he opened and reclosed the door.

AJ slept with her back to him. He lifted the blanket on the double bed and slid quietly in behind her, laying close but not too close.

He rested his hand on her arm.

She startled.

"Sorry, I didn't mean to wake you."

She rolled to her back and then toward him. "What are you doing in here?"

"I wanted to be close to you, to hold you. To be sure you were safe."

Light from the waxing moon poured between the curtains illuminating the side of her face, enough that he watched a contented look cross her face.

"I expect nothing from you right now. I simply want to be near you. But if you want me to go back to the couch, I will."

Her hand shot to his chest. "No. Stay. Hold me." Her voice shook, and she sniffed.

Sliding one arm under her and wrapping the other around her waist, he tugged her close. "AJ?"

Another sniff. She slid her arm around him and snuggled her head into him. "It's okay. You're okay. I'm okay. This is exactly what I need, but I didn't know how to ask."

"Never hesitate again to tell me you need me to hold you. I'm a total dolt. You just have to tell me like it is. I'll try to be less doltish, but—"

"But you're my dolt, and I love you."

It was his turn to laugh. "Thanks. I love you too."

They snuggled close to one another. Logan's body ached to know his wife again, but he was equally exhausted, and within minutes they both fell asleep.

AJ rubbed her eyes. It was morning, but she did not want to wake up.

Movement in the bed next to her made her eyes snap open.

Logan.

He was here with her. She could hardly believe it. She had hoped for this but hadn't dared to believe it really would come about. He'd been so closed off from her for so long, was it truly possible they could be "us" again?

Careful not to wake him, she slid her arm beneath the pillow under his head. He stirred. Turning toward her, he ran his hand across her abdomen and then around her, burying his head against her head and shoulder.

He kissed her neck. "Good morning, Mrs. Jackson."

She giggled. "G'morning, my dear husband."

He faded again. She'd always been more of a morning person than he was.

She stroked his hair while she prayed for him and their safety.

Logan was her husband. She was so glad she never gave up on him, even though she hadn't exactly fought very hard. She had wondered plenty of times if one day she'd get served divorce papers, but they had never come, and she was so grateful. She knew she would never file, but he had been completely in the right to do so. Still, he hadn't.

She kissed his forehead, and he stirred again.

With eyes closed, Logan said, "You're inviting trouble, Mrs. Jackson."

"We're married. It's no trouble."

He pushed himself up on his elbow and gazed into her eyes. "Do you mean that?" His hand that had been tucked around her ran up and down her side.

She nodded ever so slightly.

"Morning breath and all?"

Her heart raced. "Since when did I care about that?"

His smile quirked with anticipation. "Are you sure you're ready?"

"I've been ready for five years."

He lowered himself until his lips met hers. Soft and sweet until passion roared like a bonfire, and they gave themselves fully to one another as husband and wife.

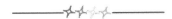

A few hours later, all ready for their day, they fixed lunch. AJ couldn't stop smiling. She felt invigorated by their renewed marriage.

Logan came up behind her and reached around her to snatch the mayonnaise.

"That closeness is completely unnecessary."

He kissed her neck. "Are you complaining?"

"Oh no. Quite the opposite."

He set the mayo down and fully encircled her waist with his arms. The stubble on his unshaved face tickled as he continued to kiss her neck.

"You're going to be late to work."

"Why would I be late to work?" His laughter made her heart sing.

She spun in his arms. "Like you don't know." She draped her arms around his neck.

He captured her mouth for a brief moment, leaving her breathless when he pulled away.

She groaned.

He laughed. "I love you."

With an exaggerated sigh, she rolled her eyes in mock annoyance.

"Something was bouncing around in my head."

His face turned serious, giving her pause. She waited for him to continue.

"I don't think you should go to work tomorrow. It's not safe. Your schedule is predictable, and he'll know right where you are."

She let go of him and stepped out of his arms. "Are *you* going to call in?"

"No."

"Then why should I?" She resumed making her sandwich.

"I'm trying to look out for you and protect you."

"What's to say he won't figure out where I am and come here?"

"Nothing is saying he won't. But I can be with you all day tomorrow."

"And what about today? If you go off to work, I'm going to be here alone until Dad gets home around four. I won't be alone at work either. Frankly, I feel safer at the station with so many around."

"I don't know, I have a bad feeling about it, and I don't think you should go."

"I'm going to work, Logan. It's not up for discussion."

"And I'm going to work today." He finished making his sandwich and turned toward the dining room.

"I'll try to swing by for dinner."

"Just don't get yourself killed or anything."

"I don't plan on it."

She covered the ham, lettuce, and cheese with another slice of whole wheat and joined Logan at the table. They ate in silence, the tension thick. Why did they both have to be so stubborn?

But she didn't know what to say. She'd missed too much work from her stupid concussion. If she didn't go in, someone else would end up pulling a double shift and have to sacrifice time with their family. And at least at the station she was surrounded by guys who would beat up anyone who tried to mess with her.

Half an hour later, Logan had to leave for work. They'd hardly said anything, and she hated it but was still at a loss for words.

She walked him to the door and handed him a set of keys. "Take my dad's old truck. You're too easy to spot on your bike."

He took the keys from her. "Good idea. Are you okay with using one of those family trackers, so we can know where the other one is? May alleviate some of our anxiety."

"That's a good idea." They both took out their phones and set up the app.

Logan slid his phone back in his pocket and cupped the side of her face.

She met his eyes. Frustration mixed with longing stared back at her.

"I love you. Stay inside and don't trust anyone who comes by."

She nodded, leaning into his hand. "You stay safe. Come home to me."

He covered her lips with his own.

And then he was gone, driving her dad's old beater of a truck down the long driveway. She closed the door and locked it.

With all the blinds shut as much as possible, she sat on the couch with a book. For the next two and a half hours she disappeared into a fantasy world where the hero rode a dragon and the danger was from urgals, not a stalker.

211

Chapter Thirty-Two

By the time Logan arrived at AJ's dad's house around midnight, he was worn ragged. The day had not turned out at all how he had hoped. Having dinner with AJ was out of the question. He'd hated to have to tell her he couldn't, but the station had been crazy. The full moon might not be until Saturday, but all the crazies had been out tonight.

Logan had been stuck at the station dealing with the influx, as his sergeant had refused to let him go out on patrols after nearly being shot the night before. Logan had argued but hadn't put in much effort because he knew AJ would appreciate it.

He drove her dad's old truck down the driveway and parked between AJ's car and the house. Logan hoped to talk AJ into at least letting him take her to work tomorrow, but he was afraid of starting another fight. Then again, maybe they could have a repeat of the fun they'd had that morning ... well, not with how early she needed to go to work. He still wished he could convince her to call in, but she'd always had a strong sense of duty, and if she said she'd be there, she would be.

But he would do what he could to keep her safe.

Inside, the house was quiet. All the lights were off except one by the door and another in the kitchen. On the wall by the hall, stuck there with a strip of painter's tape, was a note. He took it down and read it.

Logan,
I was too tired to stay awake any longer. Please come sleep beside me. I know we don't see eye to eye about going to work, but I still need to know you're safe, and I want you near me. I love you and am sorry we fought.
Love, AJ <3

He smiled and tucked the note in his backpack, which was in the living room. He'd keep that note. It might not be much, but it meant the world to him. After getting ready for bed, he snuck quietly into AJ's room.

He wished he'd gotten to talk to her, but he'd have to get up when she did in the morning and insist on taking her. He kept praying and releasing his anxiety to God, but he still had a bad feeling about tomorrow.

After putting his phone and gun on the nightstand, he slid into bed next to her and wrapped his arm around her. He kissed her temple and whispered, "I love you."

She snuggled against him but didn't really wake up.

He laid his head down and fell asleep with AJ tucked under his arm. At least she was safe right now.

AJ caught her alarm before it got too loud. She slid out of bed without disturbing Logan too much. He reached for her but remained asleep even when he didn't find her next to him any longer.

She'd been able to sleep much more soundly once he was beside her. Knowing he was safe gave her body and mind the freedom she needed to fall into a deep sleep.

After getting dressed and brushing her teeth, she grabbed a pre-made protein shake. Before she went out the door she slipped back into the bedroom and kissed Logan's temple. "I love you."

He barely stirred past a smile. He was exhausted. She hoped he'd be able to sleep for a few more hours.

At 6:40 she climbed into her car and headed toward town.

About three miles down the road, the car started making some strange noises. It wasn't exactly a new car. And when was the last time she got an oil change? Had she waited too long again? Before they split, Logan had been sure to take care of all those things. It was hard for her to remember to call and schedule it. Hopefully, Logan could take that task over again.

As she approached the edge of town, the car sputtered.

"No, no, no, no, no."

Had she run out of gas? The gauge said there was still enough in the tank, but the car was acting like it was out.

She pushed the car as far as she could. Rolling through a stop sign, she turned down another road. Will's house was only three blocks away. At least she'd feel safer there than on the edge of this country road barely wide enough for two cars.

But it didn't make it.

The car gave its last gasp and coasted to a stop.

AJ slapped the steering wheel.

Chapter Thirty-Three

Logan rolled over. Where was AJ? He had a faint memory of her kissing him.

He woke up fully.

No! She'd left. He needed to see her before work. He wasn't mad at her for going. He wanted her to know that. Plus he had an uneasy feeling he couldn't account for. She needed to understand how he felt.

He dressed in record time, grabbed the keys to his motorcycle, and took off down the road, praying he could catch up with her by the time she got to work. He wanted to steal a few moments with her before she clocked in.

✧✧✧✧

AJ groaned. Where was her cell phone? She needed to call Logan.

She dug it out of her bag, but a car drove up behind her and stopped.

Panic flashed through her. What if it was her stalker? Had he done something to her car?

She fumbled with her phone and dropped it. *Not the time to be a klutz, AJ.*

Reaching to the floor, she picked up the phone then checked her side-view mirror.

Relief washed over her. It was just Miles.

After popping the hood, she opened the door and got out, phone in hand.

"Hey, AJ!"

"Miles."

"Is everything okay?"

"My car died. Do you know cars?"

"Not really, but I can give you a ride to town."

"No, I can call Logan. Do you mind hanging out with me until he gets here? We've had some ..." She probably shouldn't say too much about her stalker; it felt weird to talk about it. "I guess you could say we've had some bad luck lately, and I'd rather not be alone while I wait for him."

She lifted her phone to dial Logan, but Miles's hand covered her phone and hand.

"You don't need to do that. I'll take care of you. Are you headed to work? I wouldn't want you to be late. Let me give you a ride, then you can call a tow truck from there. It'll be fine."

"I appreciate your desire to help, but I just need to call Logan." She stepped back.

Miles made an equal step. "Let me."

Another step back, once again matched by Miles,

"Give you." He pressed her up against her car. "A ride."

"No." Her heart sputtered before taking off at full speed. Why was Miles acting like this? "I won't ride in a car with another man. Logan and I have that agreement. Please back off and let me call my husband."

"I don't think you understand what's going on here, dear." Miles drew a knife from his pocket with his left hand.

She gasped. Her phone clattered to the ground.

He pointed the knife at her throat, then ran it down her sternum until it was aimed at her gut. With his other hand he reached up and touched the side of her face. "I've tried to woo you, but you've been so rude. Play time is over. You will be mine."

AJ trembled. *God help me.*

Chapter Thirty-Four

Logan sped down the tree-lined road on the most likely path AJ had taken. He approached a turn that would put him only three blocks from Will's house. He slowed for the stop sign. He wasn't going to stop completely, but then he spotted two cars. And two people.

Miles's car. AJ's car.

They were standing up against AJ's vehicle. Miles was close and being affectionate with her.

With Logan's wife.

Bile rose as his chest compressed.

Miles had said he'd stay away from her, that he respected Logan's choice to not file for divorce. But his friend had betrayed him.

And even worse. His wife was with the man. Letting him touch her. And after they'd had sex yesterday. Was she a complete floozy? Had she been planning to meet Miles? Was that why she'd insisted she go to work?

Miles walked AJ to the passenger's side of his car and opened the door for her. He leaned in the car over her.

Logan wanted to hurl. What was she doing? Had she lied about her commitment to him? Had it been a ruse to try and build his trust? To what end? So she could rip his heart out and smash it once more?

Miles got in the car, and when they drove off Logan whipped his bike around and rode back into the country. He wasn't going to follow her and confront her. He'd cut her off again. He was done. If she was going to step out on him again, he was going to let her. Divorce might actually be on the table this time.

Chapter Thirty-Five

Logan rode and rode. He opened up the throttle and zoomed down the country roads at speeds he knew better than to do. But what did he care if he killed himself at this point? Life wasn't worth living without AJ and Bree. He just couldn't do it.

God, I can't. I can't do this—

His phone rang through the Bluetooth set in his helmet.

He stopped on the side of the road to check who it was. Ty? What did his unfaithful wife's boss want?

He answered, "Jackson."

"Hey, where's your wife? She's never late for work. Is everything okay?"

"Why are you asking me and not her?"

"She didn't answer her phone and from what I heard you were staying together."

Logan huffed. "I don't know where she is. She left for work. I followed her because I wanted to take her, but she slipped out while I was sleeping, and she met up with a guy I thought was my friend. Don't know where they would go. Nor do I care at this point."

"Snap out of it, Jackson. Your wife loves you and would never do what you're suggesting."

"Oh really? Well, she did in the past." He had thought Ty knew that piece of information, didn't he?

"That's the past. I'm talking about today's AJ. If she went with someone, something is terribly wrong."

A sinking feeling filled Logan's stomach. Had he misread the situation back at the cars? She hadn't acted like she was under duress.

"I'll ride around and see if I can find her."

Ty said, "You might want to call it in."

"I have no evidence that it isn't exactly what it looked like."

"Logan, she's had a stalker."

Another call rang in. Adam.

"Adam is calling, so I guess I'll talk to him about it."

"Please. I'm praying."

"Thanks, Ty." He switched to the incoming call. "Jackson."

Adam skipped all niceties. "I need you and AJ to come to the station right now."

"I'll be there in fifteen minutes. But AJ can't. She was headed to work, but I saw her get in a car with Miles Blumetti."

Adam swore under his breath. "Then get in here faster."

"Adam?"

"When you get here. Drive safe."

Logan wished he hadn't ridden so far away from town, but at least he hadn't gone straight out for the last thirty minutes.

Miles wasn't her stalker, was he? If he was, he'd never be able to reconcile letting her fall into the man's hands while he watched. And not just watched but assumed the worst. He swallowed a throat full of bile.

AJ shook as Miles pushed her forward into his house through the back door. When he'd made her get in his car, he'd zip tied her hands together. He'd also tried to kiss her. He'd been mad when she turned her head, but as much as she didn't want to make the man holding a knife to her angry, she wasn't about to kiss anyone other than Logan.

They had driven around for fifteen minutes and then switched cars, leaving the one he'd been driving on the other side of town.

Miles closed and locked the back door.

"Why would you bring me here? Don't you realize this is the first place they'll look?" Not that anyone knew Miles was her stalker. They had never even suspected him, but AJ wasn't about to tell him that.

"They won't find us. This way, my dear." He shoved her through the kitchen and into a hallway. He took out a key fob and pushed a button. A series of faint mechanical sounds echoed from behind the wall, and it opened. No obvious door, just hideous wallpaper, but the wallpaper seams were actually a door. It opened up into a small room, maybe five by eight. The room contained a cot and plenty of food and water.

Miles shoved her inside and followed behind.

"We're gonna stay here for a little while. No use screaming or anything like that. These walls have studio-level sound-proofing."

He pushed her down on the cot.

Her leg bumped against the metal bar running the length of the small bed. She winced.

"Give me your hands."

She obeyed. What choice did she have?

He took a chained handcuff and attached it to her wrist, but he did not cut off the zip ties. The other end of the chain was attached to the wall, drilled into what looked like concrete. She wasn't going anywhere.

"I'll be back in a little bit. I need to take care of that pesky husband of yours before we can run off together. I can't believe how hard he has been to kill. But once he's gone, you'll be all mine."

Miles backed out of the room and closed the door.

Logan. What was Miles going to do to him? Miles had been the one to take a shot at him. Did he burn down their house too?

Chapter Thirty-Six

Logan all but ran into the detectives' squad room and to Adam's and Amelia's desks. "What's going on?"

Adam stood. "You said you saw her get in Miles's car?"

"Yeah. Why?"

"I've already put out a BOLO." Adam pointed at the chair next to his desk, but Logan didn't sit.

"Okay. Why? Do you think he's her stalker? I can't believe that."

"Sit, Logan."

He obeyed even though his body was ready to run a marathon. "Talk to me, Adam."

Adam sat back down and pulled up a video on his computer. Amelia sat across from Adam biting her lip, concern making deep creases in her forehead.

Adam said, "The boys you not-quite-arrested brought this video in this morning. Apparently, a group of kids were headed to your house to light your trash cans up, but someone had beat them to it. Watch the video."

He hit play, and Logan watched as the teens recording themselves headed toward Logan's house, but ducked behind a tree when they heard a blast from inside. Then the flames. Anger flooded Logan.

One of the kids said, "Look over there. Are you videoing? Zoom in. Who is that?"

Another kid said, "I don't know. But I think he lives down the street."

"Shhh. He'll hear you."

They all got quiet, and the camera zoomed in. A figure came from beside the house, looking to and fro. The camera caught his face.

Miles. The man in the image, despite his ball cap and black clothing, was unmistakably Miles.

Logan dropped to the back of the chair. His supposed friend had tried to kill him ...

And Logan had watched his wife get into a car with him.

Logan leaned forward, dropping his head into his hands. He'd totally read that situation wrong. He should have gone up to them and assumed the worst of Miles but not of AJ.

What was he planning to do to her?

A small hand came to rest on his back. Amelia said, "We'll find her. The warrant for his home is already in process."

He lifted his head from his hands and nodded. How had he let this happen?

"Logan." Adam waited until Logan looked at him before he continued. "Don't blame yourself; you know that doesn't get you anywhere. Think. Is there anything Miles has said to you that would indicate where he might take her?"

Logan shrugged and racked his brain. "I can't think of anything." Were there any signs? "Miles had indicated he was interested in AJ before he knew we were married. They even went to homecoming together once in high school, but when I told him to back off, he did, without complaint ... Wait. Her stalker was already sending her messages when I told him we were married."

Amelia said, "That clearly didn't de-escalate him, but might explain part of why he didn't reveal himself. Mind you, that's just speculation. I think we should check out AJ's car, the place where he took her from."

"Can I come too?" Logan stood with them, but before they could answer, Logan's phone rang. "It's Miles."

"I doubt he knows we suspect him at this point unless he's listening to the scanner and heard his car reported. So act casual. I'll trace your phone." Adam sat back and started typing on his computer.

Logan answered the phone, heart thundering in his chest. "Jackson."

"Hey, Logan. It's Miles."

"Hey, what's up?" It nearly killed him to not shout at the jerk on the other end of the line.

"I still owe you for those delicious brats. I'd love to have you over for dinner. Are you busy tonight?"

Adam indicated for Logan to keep him talking.

"Unfortunately, I'm busy this evening."

"Come on, man. I've already got a rack of ribs on the smoker. They've got your name on them."

Adam gave him a thumbs up.

"I just can't, man. Also, do you by chance know where my wife is?" Logan fought to keep his voice steady.

"Oh, that's right, AJ is married to you." The sneer in his voice was unmistakable.

"Yeah, do you know where she is?"

"Shouldn't you keep better tabs on your wife? Who knows, maybe she'll step out on you and choose another man."

Logan's hands began to shake as anger coursed through his body like a bull through the streets of Spain.

"Where's AJ?"

Click. Miles had hung up.

Logan nearly dropped his phone.

Adam stood. "Let's go. He's at his house. No need for a warrant now."

Logan grabbed Adam's arm. "If he took her with such ease, then he probably has a weapon. That's the only reason I can think of that she didn't kick his butt."

"We'll be careful, but we'll beat SWAT there."

Logan ran out with the detectives and hopped in the back of their unmarked police sedan. While Adam drove, Logan prayed.

AJ scooted back on the cot until her back was against the cold wall. She stared at the zip tie rubbing against her wrists. If she didn't have the cuffs on too, she'd be able to break free from the zip tie. It was standard, not one of the heavy-duty ones, so she knew from experience how to break it. When she, Logan, and Will were kids, they'd bought a pack of different sizes and practiced. But the chain didn't give her enough range of motion.

The door opened, and Miles came back in carrying a laptop. He sealed the door closed behind him.

"I have a feeling we're about to have company. I don't understand why Logan would think I would know where you are."

"Maybe because you do."

"Touché, my dear. But *he* has no reason to suspect it's me."

"But he does?" How had he figured it out? Some evidence must have surfaced. *Please, Lord, help Logan find me.*

"I called him to see if he wanted to have dinner, and that jerk turned me down. Then he asked me if I knew where you were."

"I'm late for work. Wasn't very smart to kidnap me when I'm supposed to be somewhere. Would have made more sense to take me after work."

"And get caught messing with your car in the fire-station parking lot? I don't think so."

"Ha. So you did sabotage my car?"

Miles glared at her.

"Tell me what else you've done. You stole my gun and tried to kill my husband. Good thing you're a bad shot."

"I'm a fine shot; the idiot moved at the last moment."

"You set the fire too, didn't you? How exactly did you expect to kill him in a house fire?"

"He was supposed to be knocked out."

"How?"

"I poisoned his whiskey."

AJ's stomach churned. That had been a very calculated maneuver. Miles could never have guessed that would be the night Logan would decide to stop drinking. *Thank you, Lord, for protecting Logan. Protect us both now.*

Miles's phone buzzed. "There they are." He opened his laptop and sat beside AJ on the cot.

She tried to put more distance between them, but there wasn't anywhere to go.

On the laptop he opened six separate camera views. One showed the front door. The others covered the back door, the hidden door to the panic room, the living room, the kitchen, and what appeared to be Miles's bedroom.

Miles was unreasonably calm. He had full confidence the room they were in was beyond detection.

Adam and Amelia came up to the front door. Logan leaned back against the unmarked police sedan.

Logan! She wished she could run to him.

But this psychotic man stood in her path. How could she get away? There had to be something she could do. She'd need to overpower Miles. The knife was in his pocket, as was the key for her handcuffs, and the key fob that opened the panic room. But how?

As she contemplated a plan, Miles watched Adam bang on the door.

The SWAT team arrived, and they surrounded the house.

Miles sat back against the wall. "They're brave. If they know I have you, coming in guns blazing could be a really bad idea. Wonder if your husband is thinking about that? Lucky for you, I want you in one piece. They won't even know we're here."

The team busted through the front and began searching the house.

AJ watched it on the screen but couldn't hear anything through the walls. And she could see they were shouting, talking, making noise, but she couldn't hear any of it.

"Told you it was soundproof."

Had Miles invaded her thoughts now too?

"If you can't hear them, they can't hear you. Didn't I do an amazing job on this space? Not exactly how I imagined using it, but it's working quite nicely if I do say so myself."

How long was she going to have to endure this man's endless arrogant prattle?

She'd come up short with how to overpower Miles. She thought about knocking the computer from his hands and then kicking him in the head when he reached for it. But what if he reacted to her before grabbing it? She had a strong sense keeping him calm was her best chance at survival.

She didn't have enough reach to slide her hand into his pocket to pull out any of the keys. If she could get the key fob and open the door then the SWAT team could find them. But it wasn't going to happen. Plus she was pretty sure the fob was in the pocket on his far side.

On the screen, she could see the team clearing the house and finding nothing. Cops she knew walked right past the hidden door with no clue she was behind it with a lunatic.

Logan came through the front door with Adam and Amelia. He looked around the living room and strode straight toward the camera. He seemed to search for a moment but found the camera quickly.

"Oh, this should be interesting." Miles maximized the feed and turned the mic on.

Logan said, "I will find you."

It was both a threat to Miles and a promise to her. Her heart swelled so much she couldn't keep a smile from creeping onto her face. She tucked the hope into her heart. If only Logan knew how close he was to them.

Lord, help him find me. Keep us both safe.

Chapter
Thirty-Seven

Logan's pulse pounded like he was driving down a rumble strip as he looked through Miles's house for any clue as to where he had taken AJ. He'd known it was too good to be true to think AJ would be there, but this was where his phone had been when he'd called Logan. So where were they now? They'd gotten here quickly, but not quick enough. Apparently Miles had been ready to leave. Logan had to find some clue.

"Hey, Logan." Adam's voice came from the other end of the house. "You might want to see this."

Logan went down the hall and turned into what must be the master bedroom. It was minimally decorated. Simple lamp on a nightstand, neutral colors everywhere.

Adam stood along a wall holding the edge of a large canvas of an abstract painting. It was strangely off center in the room.

"What is it?"

Adam tugged on the side of the picture. It came out from the wall and folded open, revealing a collage of pictures of AJ. Miles had been watching her for more than three weeks.

Pictures of AJ running through the park. Going into and out of the fire station. Coming and going from her dad's house, Granny's house, and Will's house. At church. In her apartment, including ones of her changing.

Logan's blood ran hot.

What had set Miles off? Miles had been in that car accident. Was that when he noticed her again because she'd been on the scene? Logan thought back to when that was. But it looked like he'd been taking pictures of her longer than that. However, the text messages started the day after the accident. They'd suspected Daryl because of the timing, but clearly they'd been mistaken.

Logan shook his head and reached out toward the pictures of AJ but didn't touch them. This man had violated his wife's privacy. A monster raged inside of Logan, wanting to come out and avenge AJ's honor. *Lord, keep this monster in check.*

They continued their search and left. They didn't want to talk about next steps knowing Miles had cameras in the house. They'd found a few but hadn't searched specifically enough to know if they got them all or not.

In the car, Adam and Amelia both turned to Logan. Adam asked, "Are there any locations that connect Miles and AJ?"

"We all went to high school together and were in the same friend circle. I doubt he'd take her to the high school. It's Friday, and school is in session." He thought through anything that might have been significant to Miles other than the gym where he'd gone to the dance with AJ. "The asylum. Enzweiler. We used to play Capture the Flag there all the time."

Zara. After her ordeal a month and a half ago, she'd not be ready to face the idea of Enzweiler again. But he hadn't called her or Will yet.

Amelia broke into his thoughts. "It's worth checking out. I'll get us some back up."

"I need to call Will and Zara."

Adam drove while Amelia radioed for backup.

Logan took out his phone and dialed Will's number.

Will answered with a groggy voice. "Why aren't you still sleeping?"

"Because AJ's been taken."

"What?"

"Miles is her stalker and took her this morning."

"Miles? Seriously? Mild-mannered Miles?"

"That's the one. Apparently he's a sociopath. He's been following AJ for a while."

"And he took her?"

Logan gritted his teeth. "Are you listening to anything I say?"

"Sorry. Processing."

"We're headed over to the asylum to see if he took her there."

"Have you checked your app for her phone?"

"Oh, I forgot about that. Thanks."

"I'll wake Zara up, and we'll join the search. I'll get my parents praying too. We'll all be praying. Have you called AJ's dad?"

Logan slumped back. "No."

"I'll take care of it."

"Thank you." The friends hung up, and Logan opened the family finding app. Her phone came up right away. "Take Wakefield Road instead of Brighton. That's where AJ's car broke down."

"Got it." Adam nodded. "We should get that scene processed immediately too."

Amelia radioed that in as well. The whole force was coming out to help find AJ. It reminded him of how so many people had supported them when Bree died. The entire community had surrounded them with love in the form of meals and kind words. Those first months had been a blur, but they had kept moving

233

forward only because of the community that had come out and surrounded them with support through the initial grief.

He was torn. So many places to be. He wanted to stop by the car, but he also wanted to check out any possible locations where AJ could have been taken. But teams were going to her car and the asylum. It would be okay. It had to be.

Another loss would break him completely. He'd never recover.

The Holy Spirit whispered in his soul. ***My grace is sufficient.***

Sustain me, Lord. I should have sought You in my grief and hurt, but I didn't. Forgive me. And forgive me for assuming the worst of AJ.

They stopped in front of AJ's car, taking his mind away from his prayer, but his heart stayed prostrate before the Lord. He'd tried too often to do things by himself and learned the hard way he couldn't possibly get through this on his own. Only the God of the universe, his heavenly Father, could sustain him now.

Logan got out of the car and walked toward AJ's.

A cell phone lay on the ground. She'd had her phone in her hand when Miles had approached her. Why had she gotten out of the car?

He looked at the hood. She'd popped it but hadn't opened it. Maybe that's what happened: her car died, and she had to stop.

Logan darted to the hood and lifted it.

"What is it?" Adam asked.

"I'm wondering if Miles sabotaged her car, and she stopped because it broke down."

Amelia said, "Keys are still in the ignition. Someone who left on their own wouldn't have left them there. Not that we needed that confirmation, but it's helpful."

Logan looked back at Adam, who was fiddling around under the hood.

"Yep, this has been messed with." He went on to explain what had been done. Logan's ears glazed over, not because he didn't understand what Adam was explaining, but because Miles had again invaded their space. He'd been in AJ's dad's driveway at some point in the last day and a half, and they'd missed it.

Adam grabbed his shoulder. "Hey, it's not your fault. We keep moving forward. We will find this guy if it means we grid out and search the whole city."

Logan swallowed the anxiety building in his chest and nodded. He had to keep positive, determined, for AJ's sake.

Chapter Thirty-Eight

Shotgun in hand, Logan inched down the hallway of the old Enzweiler Insane Asylum, which was slated to be demolished next month. As dangerous as it had been when they were teens, it was doubly so now.

And it wasn't worth having a place where evil men could take their victims.

Where had Miles taken AJ? Had he hurt her? Would she be able to get away and signal for help?

Logan and his team reached the end of the hallway. It was clear. No one was there.

All the teams met out front. Having ten people sweep the building had only taken ten minutes. No one was there.

"It was worth checking," someone said. Logan wasn't sure who. He was too busy trying to think of any other place Miles would go. But he didn't know Miles well enough to even guess.

He checked the time on his watch. It was almost ten o'clock. She'd been gone for three hours. What if he'd left town with her? They could be in a completely different state by now.

Logan's knees gave out, and he leaned on the trunk of the nearest squad car, then sank onto the bumper. The weight of possible loss was unbearable. *God, sustain me. Keep AJ safe. Bring her back to me.*

Will came and sat beside Logan. "Will Stutely and Little John are not going to let the Sheriff of Nottingham keep Robin Hood prisoner."

Logan chuckled, a little bit of tension releasing from his muscles. "We have to find her."

Will nodded. Logan followed his friend's attention to Zara, who was struggling to keep her tough police exterior. She hugged herself. She and AJ had become such close friends over the last month or so.

Will said, "We'll find her if it's the last thing we do."

Zara joined them, and Will put his arm around his girlfriend.

The officers began dispersing, and Adam walked over to the three friends. "I got word that Miles's rental car has been spotted across town."

Logan jumped to his feet. "Let's go."

"I figured you'd say that." Adam motioned for him to follow.

Will said, "We're coming too."

Adam gave a thumbs up, and they all left.

Fifteen minutes later, they arrived at a rural park with a gravel lot between empty ball fields and a walking path. The officer on the scene nodded to them. "I looked around, but nothing stood out to me. This parking lot doesn't have any cameras."

Logan kicked at the gravel. "Miles wasn't the dumb kid in class. He thought this all through. It's possible he took her somewhere on foot from here."

Will pointed at the vehicle. "That car is backed in. I wonder if he had another car parked here and switched it up in case we figured out it was him and looked for his car."

Adam nodded. "Likely. The car being backward also helped delay identifying it since we couldn't see the license plate."

Logan agreed. "Now what?"

Adam said, "We search the area and the car. Logan, you and I are on the car. Everyone else spread out and look for any clues showing they walked rather than drove away from here."

Adam handed Logan a set of gloves, and they walked to the vehicle.

"Are you sure I'm not compromising evidence by being her husband? Conflict of interests?"

"Doesn't matter. You will know what is your wife's. If she left a clue, you're more likely to recognize it."

Logan studied the gravel as he approached the passenger side of the sedan.

"Adam, check out the gravel over here. Is it me or does that look more disturbed than it should?"

Adam joined him. "I'd say she did not transfer easy. And look, it stops abruptly here."

"Like she got into another vehicle?"

Adam nodded.

They searched the car but didn't find anything useful.

Logan walked away and yanked the gloves off. Despair loomed again. *Where is she? Please lead us to her.*

How many dead ends would they run into before they found her? Would it be too late? Was it already too late?

If AJ hadn't had her watch on, she would have been completely lost for time. But her watch said it was nine in the evening. Miles had been gone for hours. He'd told her he would sneak through the back door since a cop was sitting out front. He was pretty confident he wouldn't get caught. She wished he would but at the same time, if they did catch him and he didn't give up where she was, she could die in this place. The police had searched it, and she was there the whole time. Logan had been outside the wall and never knew she was behind it.

She distracted herself by quoting all the Scripture she had memorized, singing hymns and any other song she could think of, praying, and practicing what she would say to Logan if she got a chance. She wanted to tell him how much she loved him. But words weren't what they needed. They needed years, a future filled with opportunities to live out the love that overwhelmed her heart. They'd so easily taken each other for granted when they were younger. But if she got out of here, they'd live differently.

But how was she going to get out of this mess?

Logan had to be a wreck. He'd known pretty early she'd been taken and it was Miles. But how? She'd tried to figure it out, but she couldn't. There were pieces of the puzzle she had no way of knowing.

But what was Miles planning? What was he going to do with her? Did he really think he would win her over by keeping her hostage?

Stockholm syndrome was a real thing, but she couldn't imagine it working on her. She wasn't going to be stuck with Miles long enough for that. She'd find a way to escape or die trying.

The minutes seemed to inch by. She'd fallen asleep at some point and tried to do some exercise, but that was limited when chained up with hands still zip tied together. Despite her best effort to keep the zip tie from eating into her skin, it did anyway. Her wrists were raw, and one spot was at risk of bleeding if she didn't keep them still.

The door opened, and AJ sat up straighter. Miles came in.

"Hey, sweetie. It's about time to go to our next location. It's nice and hidden here, but a little cramped."

"Don't call me *sweetie*."

He raised an eyebrow at her. "Do you prefer pumpkin?"

"No." Was he really this delusional?

"We'll have to figure out what fits best then. A pet name will make changing our identities easier."

Yep, delusional. One hundred percent.

Would playing along give her a better chance of escape? Though completely revolting, it was tempting.

Miles walked over and knelt down in front of her, taking her hands.

It took everything not to pull away.

"I have wonderful plans for us. You'll appreciate it eventually. Now, let's get these cuffs off, so we can get moving." He inserted the key into the lock.

"Can't you take the zip tie off too? It's cutting into my wrists."

"Not yet, dear. We need to get you safely to dinner. Are you hungry?"

She was starving; the prepackaged snack food he'd provided earlier in the day was long digested. But if he made her food and it didn't come out of a wrapper opened by her, she wasn't going to eat it. She wouldn't risk him slipping some sort of drug into her system if she could help it.

"Not going to answer?"

Her stomach growled, giving her away.

"See, that wasn't so hard." He turned the key, freeing her from the cuffs, but he took her hands by the zip tie.

Her arms ached at being stuck in the same position for so long. She could use a chance to fully rotate her arms.

He jerked her to standing. "Now, we can't have you screaming or concerning any of the neighbors with something that is none of their business." He pushed her face first into the opposite wall and put a gag in her mouth, tying it behind her head. He then picked up a hoodie, wrapped it around her shoulders, tugged the hood onto her head, and zipped the front up over her bound arms.

So much for getting away.

He tucked the sleeves into the hoodie's pockets so it looked like she was strolling along. Getting really close to her ear, he said, "If you try anything, I won't just kill Logan, I will make you watch as I torture him before the final blow. Do you understand?"

She nodded, willing her nauseated stomach to keep its bile to itself. As much as she didn't want to go down without a fight, she didn't want Miles to lay a single finger on Logan. What should she do?

Logan would want her to fight. He wouldn't care about the risk to himself.

But when? Where? How?

With her mouth gagged and hands bound, she wasn't going to be able to get away easily. But she needed to think of something now before they left town. She had no idea where he was taking her.

He kept a tight grip on her arm as he led her through the dark house, out the back door, down the alley, and to a waiting car. A different one than he'd had her in earlier today.

He was entirely too thorough in covering his tracks. How was Logan ever going to find her?

She squirmed against Miles's grasp, but he held her tighter. Shoving her in the front seat, he reached in and buckled the seatbelt, locking it in place.

As he went around, she started working the zipper of the hoodie down. She had to get that free. She had to get loose. She had to get away.

Chapter Thirty-Nine

Logan poked at the Chinese takeout someone had shoved in front of him half an hour ago. Fifteen hours. It'd been nearly fifteen hours since Miles took AJ, and the police had nothing. No signs of where they could be, no clues as to what he was planning. Nothing.

Despite not eating most of the day, Logan couldn't stomach another bite of the fried rice, so he pushed it away and laid his head down on the conference room table.

They'd set up the command center in the conference room off of the detectives' squad room hours earlier. Logan had been there most of the day. The walls were closing in, and he was getting antsy.

Zara was curled up in a chair in the corner trying to get a little rest. Logan hoped she was actually succeeding. As soon as they had anything, they'd all jump back into gear.

The door opened, and Logan spun around. Maybe they had a clue.

Will came through the door and shook his head. "Wanna go for a walk?"

"What and risk missing something?"

"We won't miss anything. But I know you, and you need to burn off some steam."

Logan rolled the chair back and stood. "You aren't wrong."

The two friends went through the bullpen where Will told Adam they were going to wander around the parking lot.

Once outside, Will stayed quiet, but Logan's brain was spinning at a billion miles a second. His thoughts were running so fast, he couldn't grasp a single one. But they all revolved around what he'd done wrong.

"I really screwed this up, didn't I?"

Will shook his head. "No, Miles did."

"But I could have—"

"Stop. You can't do that."

"How can I not? I watched him take her."

"You didn't know."

"I assumed the worst. I should have intervened. I should have assumed the worst in the other direction and tried to save my wife's life. They could be in Arkansas or New York or who-knows-where by now. I may never see her again."

The thought hit Logan hard, and he stopped walking, unable to move or breathe.

Never seeing her again wasn't an option. It couldn't be. He had to find her. He had to save her from this supposed friend.

He had to hold onto the fact that Miles had made it clear he wanted AJ for himself. Surely that meant he wouldn't kill her ... at least not right away. But it did mean he would likely do other things to her.

Heat rushed through Logan, and he clenched his fists. He couldn't tolerate the thought.

Will's hand rested on Logan's shoulder. "Hey. We'll find her."

"How?"

"I don't know. We keep praying. Miles will mess up at some point. I know it."

Logan looked up into the clear night sky. "Lord, please. Help us find her. Bring her home safely. Make Miles slip up and do something to reveal himself."

After thirty minutes in the car, AJ had managed to work the zipper of the hoodie all the way down. Somehow Miles hadn't noticed. Or if he had, he didn't care.

But now they were miles out of town. She didn't even know where they were. She'd been so focused on the zipper she hadn't really paid attention. But if she could get away, find anyone who could help or even a place to hide, she'd be able to eventually get home. She needed to survive, and the best bet for that was getting away from Miles.

Miles turned the car down a long, tree-lined driveway.

Her window of opportunity was approaching.

Miles, who had been fairly quiet for the last ten minutes of the drive, said, "We can be grateful the owners of this house don't believe in home security and are out of the country right now. Not really sure why the doc told me all about their trip. Sure, I've been selling pharmaceuticals to him for years, but he had no idea what I was planning." He let out a sardonic laugh.

Was this man pure evil? The derision in his voice motivated her more to make a run for it as soon as he let her out.

He drove up in front of a large house. The owners were not going to be happy a sociopath had brought his kidnap victim to their pristine home.

But with any luck, she'd never go inside.

Miles parked and turned off the engine. "Sit tight, and I'll be right with you."

She was tempted to spit in his face but resisted the urge. She needed to act like she was submissive, so she could catch him off-guard.

He opened the car door and reached in to unbuckle her. "All right, let's go have a nice dinner." He stepped back to give her enough room to climb out.

She had to time this right or he'd grab her, and she wouldn't get anywhere.

She walked toward the house without waiting for him to take her arm. He pushed the door shut, then put his hand loosely on her back.

Wait for it. He'd have to open the door ... maybe he'd step ahead.

He did just that. As soon as he moved slightly past her, gaze fixed on the front door, AJ spun and ran. She let the hoodie fall from her shoulders.

Miles swore and came after her.

As she ran, she lifted her arms into the air and slammed them down against her abdomen. The plastic gouged into her wrist before it finally snapped. She reached up and ripped the gag out of her mouth and tossed it to the ground.

With her arms free, she increased her speed and ran down the driveway.

She didn't know where she was going, but she didn't care. She had to get away from Miles.

Lights from a neighbor's house flashed as she ran past the trees. She dared to dart that direction. She couldn't see, but neither could Miles. If she could get to someone, she could call 911. She could call Logan.

Miles gained on her.

Her toe caught on a root. She flailed but managed to keep her feet underneath her and not fall. But it slowed her down.

She needed to get out of the woods. Once on the neighbor's lawn, she'd be able to pick up her speed again.

But was it worth running to the front door? What if they weren't home?

As soon as she broke through the trees she yelled, "Help! Someone please help me."

Miles caught up, and he tackled her.

She flew forward and slammed into the grass. Her head narrowly missed an edging stone around a flower garden.

Her breath was gone. She couldn't scream. The seizing of her lungs finally eased, but with Miles's weight on her, she still couldn't catch her breath. Not enough to scream anyway.

No lights flicked on inside the house. No curtains shifted to indicate someone was checking on the noise. No one was home.

And she was back in Miles's grasp.

God, no, don't let him—

Miles cut off her prayer by flipping her over and slamming her onto her back. Nasty words flew from his mouth. He slammed his fist into the side of her face.

She swung her arms at him and hit him as best she could. It wasn't much, but it blocked his attempts to punch her again.

He caught her wrist. "Stop it. All I wanted was a nice dinner with you. Why would you run from me?" He called her a derogatory name.

He jumped to his feet and yanked her up too.

She jerked her arm and twisted it trying to break free from his grasp. But his hand was too large, and he had a tight grip on her.

He hauled her back through the woods and to the house. He didn't let go, and she couldn't get free.

He took her into the kitchen and to a dining-room table set with candles and beautiful china.

If this man wasn't a deranged stalker, it might have been a beautiful dinner.

He shoved her into the chair. With his free hand, he grabbed a roll of duct tape. He pressed his knee into her lap and wrapped the duct tape around her body and the chair. Then he taped each of her legs to the chair.

She wasn't going anywhere until he decided to cut her free. The adrenaline from running faded, and exhaustion hit her. What was she going to do?

Miles snatched the plates off the table. He was fuming.

His behavior confirmed he was indeed a sociopath and not a psychopath. That anger was indicative of someone who still had emotions, unlike a psychopath. Why did she know so much about this? Probably the podcasts her co-worker Emily liked to listen to at the station.

Miles came back with plates filled with pot roast, potatoes, and carrots. It smelled amazing.

Against AJ's will, her stomach grumbled.

"See what wonderful food I've prepared for you? Now because you've been so naughty, I'm going to have to feed you, aren't I?"

"You could always free one of my arms." *Then maybe I could stab you in the eyeball with a fork.*

"Not hardly. It'll be more romantic this way anyway." He put a small piece of potato on the end of the fork and lifted it to her mouth.

She refused to open it. She wouldn't eat anything he made for her. Her conviction about that had not changed.

"You will eat the food I made you."

She shook her head.

Miles leaned closer and took her jaw in his other hand, working his fingers into her cheeks and between her teeth until he was able to slip the potato in her mouth.

The savory flavor touched her tongue. It tasted incredible, but she wouldn't eat it.

He leaned back. "It's good, isn't it?"

She spit it in his face. It landed square between his eyes. She'd have to thank Logan for teaching this homeschooled kid how to shoot spitballs.

Miles set down the fork and slapped her, hitting the same place he'd punched her not ten minutes ago.

Her cheek stung. The metallic taste of blood filled her mouth. Her lip was split.

Yet she didn't regret her actions.

"You going to eat now?"

"No." She hoped her defiance came through her eyes as much as her word.

"I will—"

"Do your worst, I don't care. I will not do anything willingly."

"You better think again."

She glared at him.

"Fine. I'm going to eat, but by morning you will pay."

A shudder rocked her body, but she tried to contain it. She didn't know what he planned to do to her, and if it would be before or after he tried to kill Logan again. As much as it all horrified her, she wouldn't take back or regret her actions. She'd best him ... somehow.

Chapter Forty

God hadn't answered Logan's prayer. It was nearly two in the morning, and they still had nothing to go on. It was as if Miles and AJ had disappeared off the planet. They had no idea what he was driving or which direction he would have taken her.

Logan sat on the couch in Captain Baker's office. He'd been trying to sleep, and probably had dozed off at some point, but he couldn't sleep any longer. He needed AJ in his arms. How had he slept for five years without her? Why had he let that separation linger?

If he lost her for real, if she didn't come home, he'd never recover. All that wasted time.

He dropped his head into his hands. All of the emotions swelled in him. He wasn't sure if he wanted to sob uncontrollably or punch a hole in a brick wall.

His phone rang, and he jumped. Who was calling him? Everyone who would call him was still there. Could it be AJ?

He snatched his phone from the table. It was an unknown number.

He answered it and walked out to the bullpen.

"Hello?"

"Hey, Logan."

Miles. Logan tapped, more like smacked, Adam on the shoulder and pointed at the phone.

Adam started the search.

"Where is she, Miles?"

"She's still alive, if that's what you want to know. But I'm not telling you where she is. Not yet. If you want her back, you're going to have to play my game. You, by yourself, on your motorcycle—that way I can tell you're by yourself—are to come to the address I send you. No cops. No backup. Just you and your bike. Otherwise, AJ will pay the price."

Click. The line went dead.

"Tell me you were able to triangulate that."

Adam shook his head. "Wasn't long enough. I was getting close. He's in the general area at least."

Relief washed over Logan at the thought that Miles hadn't taken her off to another state. She was still nearby.

"I have to go." Logan took his keys from his pocket.

Adam grabbed the keys from Logan's hand. "No. It's a trap."

"Of course it is, but I have to go. I can't sit here and let her be hurt even worse than what he might have already done to her."

"But you need a plan."

"He said no backup. I have to go by myself."

"Doesn't mean we can't be two minutes out instead of twenty. I can't in good conscience let you face this alone."

Logan nodded. He understood, but he had to save his wife if at all possible, even if it meant giving his own life. He was prepared for that.

A text came through on his phone. A clue from Miles. But it made no sense.

> *Frost. Elliot. Swift. Whithers.*
> *38 14 57*
> *2:58*

"What on earth is that supposed to mean?" Logan turned his phone to Adam as well as Amelia, who had wandered in with fresh cups of coffee for them.

She said, "A riddle maybe?"

Logan groaned. He hated riddles.

Amelia pressed the cup of coffee into his hand. "You're gonna need this. The last line looks like a time. Guessing you have until then to solve the riddle."

"I guess that makes sense." Logan stared at the other words. But he tried so hard to make sense of it that it seemed to make less sense.

Will and Zara came in the room. Will asked, "What's going on? News?"

Logan nodded and told them about the call and the text.

Zara gripped his arm while reading at the riddle. She squeezed his arm. "The numbers. It's like a lock combination. The one on my locker is really close."

"Why a combination?" Logan ran his hand into his hair, willing his brain to unravel the mystery.

"Frost, Elliot, and Swift are all authors. But Whithers?"

Adam raised his finger in the air. "Mr. Whithers is the principle at Lincoln Elementary."

Logan snapped his hand. "And was our English teacher in high school."

Will said, "The bell rang at 2:58. I bet the next clue is at the high school."

Logan glanced at his watch. It was 2:10. "I don't have much time if it's supposed to be a.m." He moved to leave.

251

Adam glared at him. "You aren't going without a wire. We need to know what's going on, even if we do stay back. Which we will only do because we don't want AJ hurt either."

Logan agreed and didn't leave until he had a mic and an earpiece along with Adam's extra gun and ankle holster hidden under his pant leg. When all was set, he left on his bike and headed to their old high school.

AJ's entire body ached. She was still taped to the dining room chair. Besides being hungry and needing to use the bathroom, she had a crick in her neck. She'd fallen asleep for a little while but woke to the sound of Miles talking on the phone. He had it on speaker, and it had only taken a second for her to realize he was talking to Logan. Hope stirred in her until she realized Miles was trying to lure Logan to his death. Then dread overwhelmed her heart.

Surely Logan knew it was a trap, but he wouldn't let Miles's challenge go unanswered, not when AJ's well-being was on the line.

But what was Miles planning? Was there anything she could do or say to help? She couldn't think of anything.

Her head pounded, and her cheek throbbed.

Miles walked into the room. "Everything is set in motion. It's almost time for you to leave, my dear."

"Me? Just me?"

"Yes. I have to meet Logan and dispose of him, and then I will come get you, and we will run away together for good."

"But where am I going to be?"

"Somewhere that if things go poorly, no one will ever find you—alive anyway. But don't worry. I'll rescue you before it's too late."

His words were unnerving at best. He looked around as if he was making sure everything was still set.

"But before we leave, let's watch and see if Logan figures out the first clue. The second will take a while, so we'll have time to get you situated."

He set his computer—which she hadn't realized he'd been holding—down on the table and opened it.

She shouldn't be surprised he would have set up cameras to watch whatever he had planned.

He opened several camera views. All in the same program as before, except one. The different one took him a few minutes of what she guessed was hacking before he pulled up the feed.

"Is that our old high school?"

"Yep, that's were your *husband* will find his next clue. If he's smart enough."

Disdain filled Miles's voice when he said the word "husband."

Logan was plenty smart. AJ had heard Miles tell him he was to come alone, but that didn't mean a team wasn't close by or even in his ear helping him. She prayed Logan would be clever enough to not let Miles onto that fact. She wasn't ready for another beating or anything else Miles might do.

He reached over and ran his hand down her arm. "Soon, my dear. Once he's out of the picture, I'll be at peace, and we can be together." He kissed her cheek, brushing the swollen area.

She winced and tried to contain a painful moan, but it slipped out.

"Just a reminder I love you. And you shouldn't cross me." His voice had changed from sweet to creepy.

Every hair on her neck stood up. *Lord, please help Logan. Protect us both.*

Chapter Forty-One

Logan rode his motorcycle up to the front door of the school. He and Adam had talked about this part. He'd have to break in. Adam was dealing with security and heading off any potential problems. But for Logan to look like he was being unaided, he would need to pick the lock on the front door and find whatever locker that combination opened. He'd tossed around a few ideas with the others, and they decided it had to be one of three lockers: Logan's, AJ's, or Miles's. AJ had only gone to public school for her last three years before graduating. So since this all revolved around her, that narrowed it down to probably nine lockers to check.

But that required him to remember which lockers they all had more than fifteen years ago. He was pretty sure he remembered his and AJ's lockers, but Miles ... he had no idea. AJ's seemed like the most obvious choice, so he'd start with those three.

He knelt in front of the door and inserted the lock picks. This was not something he ever thought he'd do. As kids, Will, AJ, and he had done plenty of goofy stuff but breaking and entering was not on their lists. Logan and Will had both wanted to be cops, so they had been intentional not to do things that would tarnish their records ... well, other than trespassing at the old asylum.

The adrenaline and exhaustion made his hands unsteady, but eventually he was able to get the bolt to slide into the unlocked position.

One hurdle down.

After glancing over his shoulder, he slipped inside the building. It looked almost exactly the same as he remembered it.

An alarm sounded. He jumped. At least he knew Adam was taking care of it.

Now think. Where were AJ's lockers? He went to the first one he remembered, which wasn't too far from the front door.

It was a bust. The combination didn't work.

He checked the time. Two forty-eight ... he had ten minutes.

Her locker from sophomore year was on the other end of the building, but that was the one she'd had when she went to homecoming with Miles. That was probably it.

He sprinted through the halls, illuminated by very few lights. This locker had seemed so much farther away when he'd had to walk to it through a sea of other students.

Grabbing the lock, he spun the dial to the first number, but he passed the second number and had to start over. He grunted.

A voice softly said in his ear, "Slow down."

Amelia was right. He took a deep breath and focused on getting the combination correct.

The lock popped open.

His heart thudded harder against his chest, nervous about what he might find inside.

He opened the locker and clicked on his flashlight. The walls inside were covered with photographs of AJ, a bunch from high school—including a larger one of AJ and Miles from homecoming—and many from the last month or so.

Taped to the locker shelf was a note written in bold ink:

The game is on. Madness it is.
Capture the clue hidden with the dead,
but don't tarry long or too deep she will be.

Logan smacked his palm against the neighboring locker. Another riddle. He hated riddles.

He wanted to talk to the team about it, but the camera in the top of the locker told him Miles was watching.

He glared straight into the camera but opted not to say anything. If only he knew whether AJ was right there too.

Logan jerked the clue off the shelf and slammed the locker shut. He needed to get out of this building before the cops showed up, even if they knew he was there. Logan had no clue where else Miles might have hidden cameras. If he was watching, it was best for Logan to be gone and the police to actually show up in a reasonable amount of time.

He ran out of the building and hopped on his bike. He sped away just as the sirens approached.

Pulling into a parking lot, Logan stopped and removed his helmet. He needed to breathe. What did this riddle mean?

God, give me wisdom and direction.

Out loud he said, "You guys have any idea what this could mean?" He read the riddle.

Amelia asked him to read it again a little slower. She was probably writing it down on their end, which was in a car only a mile away.

Zara spoke up, "'With the dead.' Could that mean the cemetery?"

"Maybe. I have no idea if he knows about Bree. I've never talked to him about her."

Adam said, "Most people in Hazel Hill know what happened."

"But he had no clue AJ and I were even married." He put on his helmet again. "I can go and look. It's not that far away."

Will said, "Go. We'll keep working on the riddle."

"Thanks, guys." Logan drove off toward the cemetery where his daughter was buried.

AJ's jaw quivered. Seeing Logan look so intense as he stared at whatever clue Miles had left in that locker had broken her heart. She wanted to hold Logan so bad and be held by him. But Miles was set on killing Logan and stealing her away forever.

There had to be some way out of this. Miles was strong; it didn't matter that AJ could carry a hundred pounds of gear and a full-grown man on her shoulders. She hadn't been able to get out of Miles's grip. He was taller, bigger, stronger. He seemed to be able to counter every defense she tried. She didn't want to give up hope, but at this moment in time, it seemed impossible to get away. She needed an act of God or at least for Miles to slip up.

Miles had closed his laptop and exited the room after Logan had left the school. Miles seemed quite satisfied by Logan's reaction. If only she could tell Logan she was fine and she'd find a way out. But she didn't know if she'd be able to get away.

Miles came back into the room and opened his knife in front of her.

Her chest tightened. "What are you going to do with that?"

"Cut you free, pumpkin." He paused and glanced to the side. "No, I don't like that one. I'll stick with dear. It's better." He looked at her again. "Time for us to leave. If Logan is smarter than he looks, the fastest he could get here is about forty-five minutes.

But I need to be ready for him. Although I do doubt he'll get here *that* fast."

"He's coming here?"

"Eventually. But you won't be here."

"You're going to kill him at some stranger's house?"

"And dump his body in the river where no one will find it. It's perfect. I'll clean up, don't worry. They won't even know we were here."

She grimaced at the thought. *Lord, please protect Logan. Don't let this vile man hurt him.*

Miles cut the tape around her body and freed her from the chair. It pulled at her skin, but she couldn't rip her arms away from the tape still attached to her.

He pushed her body forward and yanked her arms back behind her, releasing them from the tape.

She yelped at the pain as her skin and arm hair went with the adhesive.

"Sorry, dear, but you are proving to be too combatant. When you learn to behave, I won't have to be so rough." He leaned near her ear. "Or do you like it rough?"

She flung her head into his. Pain radiated through her skull, but she'd do it again, even if his noggin was harder than a soccer ball.

"You little ..." He slapped the back of her sore head.

If she made it through tonight, she was going to have a doozy of a headache tomorrow. Nope, she had a doozy of one now. Pain surged and ebbed. She squeezed her eyes shut for a moment. She needed to stay alert and actively fighting against Miles.

He let her sit back and then cut her legs free. When they were, she tried to kick Miles, but he stepped too close for her to be able to hit him with any power.

"Would you stop already? Have you not figured out you can't beat me?" He gripped her arm and yanked her to her feet.

Her legs didn't want to work, and she stumbled.

"Pull yourself together. I will throw you over my shoulder if I have to." He turned to her stopping only inches from her nose. "And who knows where I might have to touch you."

She spit in his face.

With his free hand he punched her in the gut.

She doubled over. She'd been ready for another slap, but the punch sent her stomach into a tizzy.

Before she could recover, he dragged her forward and out the back door onto a large deck. He pulled her down the steps and across a stone patio. She was barely able to keep her feet beneath her.

Where was he taking her now?

He continued to tug her through the back yard, down a tall set of stairs that led to the river, and into a motorboat docked at a small pier.

The river. The same river in which Bree had drowned.

Chapter Forty-Two

Logan rode slowly along the paths in the cemetery. He didn't see anything. He parked his bike as close to Bree's grave as he could and jogged toward the tombstone with his daughter's name.

The light of his flashlight caught the wilting flowers AJ had left there only a little more than a week ago. Emotions washed over him, but he wouldn't let them take control. Holding them in check, he looked around. Nothing.

"Guys, there's nothing here."

Will's voice came across Logan's earpiece. "I'm not surprised. The more I think about it, the more I think he's indicating something else. Capture. Madness. Do you think he's referring to the asylum and Capture the Flag?"

"Oh, duh. Why didn't I think of that first?" A memory rushed into Logan's mind. "One time when we were playing, Miles was looking for AJ, hoping to get a kiss out of her. It was right after homecoming."

"Didn't you kiss her that night instead?"

"Yep. Do you think he knew?"

"I remember that night; you two were awfully cozy after the game. So there's a good chance. That's got to be it. It's not like you didn't associate it earlier today too."

"Indeed. That place is huge. It's going to take forever to find the clue unless it's on the front steps."

"Maybe *dead* is the clue. Try the asylum's morgue."

"Will do."

Logan stared at Bree's tombstone, kissed his fingertips, and laid them on top of the marker. "I'll find your momma and save her. I promise."

He ran to his motorcycle. Time was ticking.

AJ shivered as the cool September night air rushed across her body. Miles had plopped her inside the bottom of the small boat and tied her legs together. She was half tempted to fling herself over the side of the boat and take the risk with the water, but with her hands and feet bound, she'd never make it to shore.

He drove the boat upstream from the house for about a mile but slowed as they approached a bridge that took a road across the river. He stopped beneath the center of the bridge and went to the side of the boat and clipped the boat to a rope wrapped around the concrete column that came out of the dark water.

Whatever he was planning, he had already prepared for it.

Grabbing a second rope hanging from the bridge towering so high above them, he tugged on it. "Perfect. Come here, dear."

She didn't budge. Not that she could. She glared at his shadowy figure, unable to process what his plan was.

"Oh right. You can't." Miles crossed the boat to her and lifted her to her feet. "Now it's not too cold, so that won't kill you. As long as you stay above water, you'll live. It's that simple."

Was he going to put her in the water somehow? Her insides quaked at the idea. Ever since Bree had drowned in this very river, she had vowed to avoid it at all costs. She loved swimming, but she hated this body of water.

He tugged her to the front of the boat and wove the rope under one arm, around her front and under the other arm. "I'm very skilled at tying knots, so this will hold just fine." He tied what seemed like an intricate knot behind her back.

"What are you doing?" She couldn't keep her voice from cracking.

"You'll figure it out." He turned her around to face him and gripped her arms. "I'll be back for you in about an hour." He looked up. "Unless of course that stupid husband of yours takes too long to figure out these simple clues. But either way, as long as nothing happens to me, you'll be safe."

With one hand still tightly gripping her arm, he cupped the side of her head with the other. She tried to squirm away, but his hold was too strong.

He leaned his face in toward hers. His hand on the side of her face prevented her from headbutting him again. "Stop looking so scared. You'll be fine. You just have to hang in there. Now for something I've waited for since I was fifteen years old."

He closed the distance and planted his lips on hers.

She scrunched hers up and tried to pull away.

He backed off and once more she spit in his face. He swore and shoved her off the side of the boat.

AJ splashed into the water. The inky darkness swallowed her whole. Her lungs screamed for air, but she couldn't do much of anything to get to the surface. She wriggled her body like a mermaid as best she could.

But the rope under her arms became taut and raised her out of the water. She spit the river water out of her mouth and gasped for air.

Miles stood in the boat with his phone glowing in his hand. "Now you understand. You'll slowly sink into the water, but every ten minutes I will press this button"—he pressed a button, and she rose another foot, putting the water line at her waist—"and you'll come up, but if I don't push the button, you'll sink farther. Better hope Logan doesn't distract me too long."

He unhooked the boat and drove away.

The current of the river pulled on her legs. Her shoes were already waterlogged, weighing her feet down.

The Catawba River was big and broad. It looked quiet here; however, it was anything but. The current was strong and the water cool.

Thankfully, it was probably in the upper seventies as far as temperature, although the air was only in the sixties. Cool enough in her short-sleeve polo to make her uncomfortable when dry, yet now that she was wet, she began to shiver.

She tried to push away the thoughts about how little Bree had breathed her last in this very water. She couldn't think about it. Yet thoughts that she was going to meet the same fate as her daughter bombarded her mind, attempting to squash her hope completely.

God, help.

Chapter Forty-Three

Logan sped down the driveway to the asylum and skidded to a stop in front of the large building. He'd passed the unmarked car where Will, Zara, Adam, and Amelia were keeping their distance but ready to come in as soon as needed. They'd followed him to the entrance to the dilapidated institution and drove past. Although they wouldn't be far away.

He hated having to do this on his own, however, playing by Miles's rules was the best for keeping AJ safe.

Maybe it was the adrenaline or the immense quantities of caffeine pulsing through his veins, but his sense of urgency was mounting.

He ran up the front steps and shined his flashlight across the front of the building. One of Miles's stupid little cameras stared back at him. He was in the right place.

Logan yanked open the ancient doors that hadn't been locked in twenty years. He dashed down the stairs. As teens, they'd mostly avoided the morgue because it freaked him out. Except that one time he'd let AJ convince him it would make a good make-out spot. She hadn't been wrong until a rat scurried across the room, sending them both into a screaming fit. He chuckled at the memory, despite the current situation.

Down the hallway, he slowed in front of a pair of swinging doors, one of which was only half on its hinges. He hesitated for half a second before pushing through the intact door.

He swept the flashlight beam across the room in slow incremental passes. It had to be here somewhere.

Logan spotted a couple of Miles's cameras. He hadn't tried to hide them here.

But where was the next clue? And how many of these would he have to go through before he found Miles and AJ?

"Where is it?" he voiced out loud. He needed ideas of where to look but knew better than to ask his friends directly.

Zara's voice came into his ear. "Did you look in the pull-out thingies?"

He grunted. He had hoped to avoid that. When they were in high school, the kids had joked about bodies having been left in the coolers.

He shook the thought away. He'd risk random skulls staring back at him for AJ.

He gripped the handle of the first one. For AJ. And he hauled it open. Nothing. He tried another. Finally, in the sixth one, a little camera stared back at him along with two sheets of paper.

Logan pointed his flashlight at them.

One had a riddle, the second had a bunch of seemingly random numbers. They meant something, but what?

He read the riddle:

A beautiful view but not for you
Watery grave is your fate but hopefully not hers
Don't be late.

Logan picked up the little camera and chucked it at the ground, then stomped on it for good measure. He was tired of this ridiculous game. He wanted his wife home and safe. If it took killing Miles, he would. He hoped he wouldn't have to, but if it came down to it ...

Logan swiped the papers from the tray and bolted back out of the building.

Same drill as before. He left the site of the clues and drove down the road, but this time he pulled into the same parking lot where Adam had parked in front of an old gas station.

As he got off his bike, the four others exited the car.

Logan slapped the papers down on the trunk of the car. "What does it mean? My brain is done. I can't figure out what he's talking about. I need to get AJ. But I don't know where she is. How can I save her if I can't find her? I can't do this."

Amelia came to him and rubbed his arm. "First, you have to calm down. I get how you're feeling, but you have to breathe. We're all here to help you figure this out. You are not alone. You will find her."

He nodded at her motherly reprimand, rubbed his eyes, and looked back at the numbers.

35
41 14.6
80
58 55.2

He laid a hand on the bottom of the page. "What on earth does this jumble of numbers mean?"

Everyone stood around the trunk staring at the pages. Silence reigned for at least two minutes; to Logan it felt like two hours.

"I don't know. I don't get it." A sob shook Zara's voice.

Will pulled her against his chest.

Logan watched the two of them. Zara had lost too many people. She needed her friend back. Determination swelled within him. This wasn't just about getting his wife home.

He read the riddle again. "Watery grave. There are plenty of bodies of water around here. View ... the river has beautiful views."

Adam said, "Both previous clues pointed to a specific location. This has to be doing that too."

"That's it." Amelia tapped the numbers on the page. "Yep. I bet it is." She looked at Logan. "I think they are coordinates."

"Really?" He didn't know enough about navigating to see it.

She took out a pen and wrote it out with degrees, feet, and directions. "Makes sense to me. Where is it?"

Adam grabbed his phone and entered the coordinates into a map app. "It's right in the middle of the Catawba River."

Dread filled Logan. "It fits. How far from here?" The Catawba River stretched from the mountains all the way into South Carolina.

"Only about twenty minutes away."

Logan entered the coordinates into his phone. "But where does he want me to go? Other than the middle of the river—no doubt that's where he wants me to end up."

"Maybe try the house closest to the coordinates?" Zara suggested. She looked at his phone with him. "This one." She tapped his screen.

He nodded. "It's worth a shot." He turned toward his bike.

"Wait," Amelia said. "Let's pray together first."

"Please." He put his arm across Zara's shoulders.

Amelia, Adam, and Will all placed their hands on Logan, and Amelia led. "Heavenly Father, we implore you for help saving our sister, friend, loved one from the grips of a madman. Strengthen her and keep her hoping in You. Go with Logan now as he faces the unknown. Give him peace and wisdom and strength to face and defeat the evil in front of him. Guard both Logan and AJ with

Your supernatural protection. And please bring Miles to justice. We pray this in Jesus's holy and powerful name. Amen."

Peace and fresh energy surged through Logan, no doubt courtesy of the Holy Spirit. *Thank You, Lord.*

To Amelia he said, "Thank you. I have to go now."

They all nodded, and he started to walk away.

"Logan." Zara's voice held heavy emotion.

He spun back to her. She embraced him. He held her, and Will came over and wrapped his arms around both of them.

They stood there for a moment before Zara let go and said, "Bring her home. And bring yourself home too."

"Yes, ma'am." Without looking back at any of them for fear the emotions would become too heavy, he slid his helmet on and straddled his bike.

"We'll be right behind you," Adam said before Logan started the engine.

Logan gave them a salute and drove off, following the directions on his phone. He had to get there as soon as possible, especially if he had to search more than one location to find Miles and whatever trap he had set.

The riddle had said not to be late, but what did that even mean? With no time set, he was working against a clock with an unknown amount of time.

Chapter Forty-Four

AJ's fingers were growing numb as she slipped lower and lower into the river. The water lapped her ears. She was almost as low as she had been the last time Miles had raised her up, so she'd been in the water for about twenty minutes already.

She hoped Miles didn't forget to hit the button.

The rope let out a little farther, and AJ had to crane her neck to keep her chin out of the water.

With a jerk the pulley began to raise her out of the water again until she was hanging with only her hips and legs in the water.

The gentle night breeze felt like tentacles of ice wrapping around her wet body. How long could she endure this?

Her already-sore body screamed as she shivered. She should probably be grateful she wouldn't get hypothermia. The water wasn't cold enough to do anything but make her uncomfortable.

She was so tired. She'd rather be locked up in Miles's panic room. At least there she wouldn't drown if she fell asleep.

In her exhaustion, her mind wandered back six years. Her daughter's lifeless face stared back at her, Logan's anguish matched only by her own.

What if she drowned tonight? What if Logan found her too late? It would wreck him beyond repair. She'd seen what losing Bree had done to him, and she wasn't sure he could handle another blow.

He'd made such growth in the last week. Would this undo it all? Would he lean into Jesus this time? Or would he turn to a bottle of whiskey?

Lord, help Logan. Draw him to Your heart.

But what if Logan didn't survive whatever Miles had planned?

Her breath caught in her throat. She wasn't sure *she* could handle that loss.

Logan turned into the long driveway in a nice neighborhood near the river and stopped. This was the address nearest the coordinates, but was it the right place? Was AJ here somewhere? Was Miles?

He didn't know what kind of trap he was walking into. Was he even going to see it coming or would he be dead before he made it down the driveway?

How he wished he had a clue what he was headed into. He was tempted to draw his concealed pistol before he rode closer to the house, but at the same time keeping it hidden longer might be the better bet. He didn't know if AJ was here or somewhere else. He might need to let Miles talk before he shot him.

Adam's voice came across his earpiece. "We're down the street and will come in at the first sign of trouble. We'll keep listening."

Logan wanted to say thank you, to say anything. But he was sure Miles already had eyes on him, so he didn't dare.

With a hefty breath, he drove down the driveway. A strip of fabric caught his eye. What was that?

As the house came into sight, his ear filled with static and a high-pitched buzz. He had to remove the piece. Coasting down the driveway he yanked off his helmet and popped out the screaming earpiece.

His phone vibrated that it had lost signal. No surprise, Miles was jamming communications. Logan should have seen that coming.

He slowed. The house came into view completely. A sweatshirt lay discarded on the driveway.

Miles sat on the front steps, computer on his lap. He looked up as Logan parked his bike and got off, keeping the bike between him and Miles.

"Well, it's about time. I was beginning to wonder if we were going to have to contend with daylight." Miles stood. He pressed a button on his phone before sliding it into his pocket. The laptop stayed in his other hand.

"What did you just do?"

"Oh, nothing you need to worry about. What you should worry about is that red dot on your chest."

Logan looked down at his chest, then up to a drone flying above him. He drew his gun and pointed at the drone.

"I wouldn't do that. I hold AJ's life in my hand."

Logan lowered his gun.

"And while you're at it, put that thing down."

Logan set his pistol on the ground at his feet.

"Nice try. Kick it away."

Logan kicked it behind him. "You didn't say where." At least he still had Adam's extra pistol strapped to his ankle.

Miles's eyes narrowed. "It doesn't matter. Come over here."

"Why should I listen to what you say?"

"Because I'm the one who knows where your wife is. I'm the one who has control over her life."

Miles had him beat there. Logan walked toward Miles, the drone hovering not too far away.

With a few clicks on his computer, Miles flew the drone down and landed on top of a car parked nearby.

Miles closed the computer and set it on the stoop.

Logan seized the opportunity and rushed toward Miles, but the madman spun around, pointing a knife at Logan.

He raised his hands and took a step back.

"Do you forget so quickly that I hold her life in my hands? With the push of a button, I can decide if she lives or dies."

"Where is she?"

"It's irrelevant to you. I'm truly sorry I can't give you the opportunity to say goodbye, but it's not possible." Miles pointed the knife toward the side of the house. "March."

Logan needed a plan. What little plan he did have had faded when the coms went down ... and why did he draw his gun on that stupid drone? It probably only had a laser light on it and nothing else. Drawing a gun from an ankle holster was a lot more difficult than from a waistband.

He followed a path lit with sunken lights around the side of the house. The ground sloped so much that by the time they were at the back, they were level with the basement. A large stone patio spread out behind the house. Beyond that, a set of stairs led down to the river. No doubt this house had a beautiful view during the day. The full moon reflecting off the surface of the river was amazing at the moment. Too bad Logan couldn't linger to take it in. He needed to figure out how to get control of the situation.

"Walk toward those stairs."

To the river it would be. But Logan couldn't let them get there. He could sense where Miles was behind him, but without line of sight, he was hesitant to turn.

Miles was decently built and easily matched Logan in height and weight. He hoped they were evenly matched enough that Logan could get the upper hand.

They walked past a built-in grill with a chrome lid. The bright moon filled the area with light, and the surface of the grill lid reflected Logan's image back to him. He slowed.

Miles came closer and into the reflection. Logan now knew exactly where the knife was.

He spun around and caught Miles's wrist, seizing at least some degree of control.

Chapter Forty-Five

AJ kicked her legs in the water, trying to free them from the rope that bound her feet. She'd worked at trying to get the duct tape free from her wrists, but it had simply rolled up and become impossible to dislodge. Miles had used entirely too much tape for her to get it off.

The rope wouldn't budge either. Part of her was grateful Miles could tie a good knot. At least she could trust the rope under her arms was tied well too.

The pulley continued to lower her into the water. It was about time for Miles to hit the button again.

She leaned her head back against the rope right behind her head as she had for what seemed like forever. She'd lost count of how many times she'd been raised from the water.

Not wanting to fall into the despair that lapped at her like the river's current, she prayed. The words were the same. Pleas for rescue. Petitions for Logan's safety. Cries for help.

The pulley lowered her farther into the water. Farther than she'd been yet. Why hadn't Miles pushed the button?

"Come on, Miles. Hit the button already."

Logan held Miles's wrist tightly and thrust it upward, bringing Miles's body closer to his. Break the knife free, and let it be a fair hand-to-hand fight. Logan needed to get him to the ground and restrain him.

But Miles countered and swung his leg behind Logan's in an attempt to push him over.

Logan kept his footing and twisted Miles's arm down and around, jerking it back and forth. Using his other hand, he pressed his thumb into Miles's wrist until he dropped the knife.

It clattered on the stonework.

Miles other fist collided with Logan's side. He let go of Miles's wrist and shoved him. Logan kicked the knife farther away.

Miles charged at Logan. He waited for Miles to get closer, then swung up and punched him in the cheek.

Miles's head flew to the side, but he rebounded quickly and seized Logan's shirt. He fought to stay on his feet. Miles wanted to take this to the ground, but Logan would only go down on his own terms. He was a better boxer than wrestler.

He dodged a punch from Miles and sent one of his own into Miles's other cheek.

He stumbled but sent an uppercut into Logan's ribs, then grabbed him.

Logan repeatedly jabbed Miles in the back. They twisted and turned, trying to get the other one to lose control and footing. But it wasn't accomplishing much.

They truly were equal in build and strength.

Miles pushed off of him and scurried backward toward the knife. He took his phone from his pocket and clutched the knife.

Logan drew the pistol from his ankle holster and aimed it at Miles. "Drop both the phone and knife."

"No. You drop the gun. I told you I have AJ's fate in my hands. The app on my phone controls if she goes under or not." He walked toward Logan.

"Don't push it."

"I'll do what I want." He raised the knife toward Logan and swiped open his phone, then positioned his thumb over the red button on the screen.

"Drop them."

Miles moved his thumb to the button.

Logan couldn't let him push a button that would hurt AJ. Logan fired a shot. The bullet went through Miles's hand. The phone flung to the ground.

Miles screamed in agony. "You fool. Are you trying to kill her?"

Logan didn't understand, but he didn't have time to consider. Miles ran at him with the knife.

Logan fired again. Three more bullets, each one hit Miles center mass. He dropped at Logan's feet.

Logan leaned over and breathed.

He hadn't wanted to kill Miles, especially not before learning where AJ was. And what did Miles mean about Logan trying to kill her? Miles was the one wanting to push the button.

Adam and Will ran out from the woods nearby. Amelia and Zara came around the side of the house.

Zara holstered her gun and ran to hug him. He returned his firearm to its holster before embracing her for a brief moment.

Will came up. "Sorry, man. When we lost coms we decided it would be better to walk in. That driveway is long."

Logan nodded. "I don't know where she is. He had a button. I don't know what he was doing to her."

Adam picked up Miles's phone. "Plus or minus. Those are the only buttons."

"Plus or minus what? Was he shocking her?" The horror in Zara's voice matched how he felt.

Logan tried to rack his brain for anything Miles might have said. "Goes under ... he accused me of killing her by not letting him push the button. Did I?"

Will put his hand on Logan's shoulder. "Don't think like that right now. Let's find her first."

Adam's phone vibrated, and he answered it. Whatever blocker Miles had either stopped working or didn't cover the backyard. "Megan and Wesson are here."

Logan ran to the front of the house. Megan's German shepherd had a sharp nose. If AJ was here, he'd help them find her.

"Logan." Megan held out her arms, and they embraced.

Wesson nosed Logan's hand.

He squatted down and petted the dog. "Can you find AJ for me? Where has she been? Where is she now?"

Megan opened a large Ziplock bag with a t-shirt in it. "Zara gave me this this afternoon, just in case." She gave Wesson a command and unhooked his leash. Searching for people wasn't his normal job, but he was still good at it. Megan continually worked on developing new skills with Wesson, while maintaining the dog's other abilities.

Wesson sniffed the bag then started smelling the ground. He bolted away from the house, back down the driveway.

Logan grabbed his powerful flashlight from his bike bag and joined Megan in following Wesson. He stopped and sniffed the sweatshirt that had been discarded before leading them farther down the driveway, into the woods, and onto a neighbor's lawn.

Logan shined his flashlight around. The ground looked smashed in one area as if a large person or two people had hit the ground. Had AJ tried to get away but Miles caught her here?

Wesson didn't linger long before dashing back through the woods, retracing his path down the driveway, and running to the front door of the house. He darted past Amelia who sat on the front step with Miles's computer.

She said, "With all those cameras I bet he was watching her wherever he had her. I'll see what I can find."

Logan nodded. "Thank you."

Wesson scratched at the door.

AJ had gone inside the house.

Megan opened the door, and she and Logan went with Wesson through the house. In the kitchen, a chair was covered in duct tape where someone had clearly been bound.

Logan's stomach churned at the sight. AJ. She'd been in the house, taped up. But she wasn't here now.

"Where is she, Wesson? Where'd he take her?"

Wesson barked at Logan as if he understood what he was asking. The dog went to the back door and pawed at it.

Megan again opened the door, and they let Wesson lead the way down the steps to the patio. He barked at Miles's dead body but ran around it and down the steep stairs that led to the river.

The river.

Miles had said he planned for Logan to go in the river ... the riddle. *Hopefully not hers.* Was she in the water somewhere?

She hated the river. As a kid she'd loved going, but after Bree died she swore she'd never go again. *Oh, AJ!*

Wesson bounded down the steps and ran to the end of the dock where a small motorboat was moored. The dog jumped in the boat, sniffed around, then barked.

"Logan!" Amelia called from the top of the stairs. "There's a camera focused on the water beneath a road bridge over what looks like the river. It also looks like there's a rope coming off the bridge."

Logan turned to Megan. "Is there a key in that boat?"

She got in. "Yep. In the ignition. Lucky for you, I know how to drive one of these things. Get in."

Logan hopped over the side. They didn't wait for anyone else and set out on the river. They had to find AJ.

Chapter Forty-Six

AJ wriggled her body up, and as soon as her face broke the surface, she sucked in a giant breath before the current dragged her under again. She couldn't keep this up much longer.

She hoped and prayed the fact Miles hadn't pushed the button again meant Logan had bested him, but that also meant she was probably going to drown.

Just like Bree.

At least she'd get to be with Bree at last. The two of them could curl up with Jesus and talk for hours.

But Logan.

She was sure she added to the river, probably enough to make the water brackish. But she couldn't sob, or she'd drown that much faster.

Keep it together, AJ. God, help me.

The rope let out more.

She tried to float. But without her arms and legs free, she couldn't get her body at the right angle to lay near the surface. Plus her work boots were too heavy. Again she tried to kick them off, but they were laced too well, and the rope around her ankles was too tight.

Propelling herself upward, she took a breath.

A dog barked in the distance.

But she sank back into the water before she could yell for help.

God, am I going to die now? I'm Yours. If this is my time, so be it. Help Logan. Tell Bree I can't wait to see her.

Logan sat at the front of the boat with Wesson, who continually sniffed the air and barked upstream. A bridge came into view. Was that the bridge Amelia had seen? He probably should have taken a minute to look at it.

But his sense of urgency was growing exponentially by the moment.

"God, help us find her!"

The wind blew through his hair as Megan sped the boat forward. She slowed as they approached the bridge spanning the river, which was nearly a quarter of a mile wide. Where was she?

What if this wasn't the right bridge? There weren't too many that crossed this river, so there weren't many to choose from, but it made logical sense that Miles would use the closest one.

Did Miles know they'd lost their daughter in this river? Is that why he chose it? To be as cruel as possible?

What if they didn't make it in time? What if she was already gone?

He braced against the boat, willing himself to stay positive. Silently he begged God to keep her alive.

Sweeping the flashlight beam under the bridge, he looked for any clue.

A line coming down from the bridge caught his eye. A black rope.

"There!"

"I see it." Megan directed the boat that way.

The rope was attached to an elaborate pulley system.

"Logan!" Megan yelled.

He followed the rope down. "I don't see anything."

"She's under the water. I saw her bob up for a second."

He tossed the flashlight to Megan then whipped off his shoes. It was all he could do to wait until Megan had gotten the boat closer, but as soon as it was, she cut the engine, and he dove in.

The cool water shocked his body, but he ignored it.

Megan shined the flashlight into the water. Thankfully, there hadn't been a huge rain recently to churn up a bunch of mud, so the water was fairly clear. The coolness stung Logan's eyes.

AJ.

He spotted her. She was struggling, hands and feet both bound, but her movements were slowing. He needed to get to her quickly.

After surfacing for air, he dove again, straight to her.

He wrapped his arms around her and propelled them both upward. They surfaced.

Splash.

Wesson swam to them. He clasped the rope that came from AJ's back in his teeth.

"Good boy," Megan called. "Bring 'em here."

Wesson swam toward the boat. Logan helped.

AJ was limp in his arms.

Oh Jesus, please! Help her!

He reached the boat, and Megan leaned over the side and hauled AJ up.

Logan got in the boat as fast as he could, and Wesson jumped in the back.

Megan was working to untie the rope. She tossed Logan a knife.

He cut the duct tape, and they laid AJ on her back. She wasn't breathing.

"AJ!" Logan threw himself down to her and patted her cheek. "Come back to me."

"Rescue breaths." Megan's voice was strong and demanding.

Logan repositioned himself, pinched AJ's nose, and covered her mouth with his own. He gave her two forceful breaths. He sat back.

Megan did thirty compressions. "Come on, AJ."

Logan breathed into his wife's lungs two more breaths.

Megan started compressions again, but AJ sputtered.

Relief filled Logan. They turned AJ on her side, and she coughed up water.

She moved her arms and pushed herself up some, and she continued to expel water from her airway.

He'd almost lost her ... and in the same way he'd lost Bree. But AJ was okay. She was breathing. *Thank you, Jesus.*

AJ looked up at him. So much love and joy filled her eyes.

He scooped her up and held her against his chest. She wove her arms around him.

Megan untied the rope around her legs. "Let's get you two back, then warm and dry." She squeezed AJ's knee. "I'm glad you're okay, friend."

AJ let go of Logan for a moment and gave Megan a hug.

While Megan started the boat and turned them back toward where they had come from, Logan took AJ's face in his hands. "I'm so sorry."

"Stop. You don't have—"

"But I do. I could have prevented this whole day. I saw you get in his car. I made wrong assumptions."

"What do you mean you saw?"

"I wanted to take you to work, because I had a bad feeling. But you were gone, had just left, so I jumped on my bike and tried to catch up."

"We never suspected Miles. He was supposed to be our friend. And it's not like I didn't give you reason in the past to suspect me of such ..." She looked down.

He lifted her face until her eyes met his. "You have changed. I know you wouldn't ..."

"But past hurts reared their ugly cheating heads."

He nodded. "So I'm sorry. Forgive me?"

"Of course. I love you. Forever and always."

He met her lips with his and kissed her with all the joy, relief, and hope he had.

Breathlessly he came out of the kiss. "I love you."

Chapter Forty-Seven

AJ held tight to Logan as Megan drove the boat back. She was alive and safe. Her brain couldn't quite process that. She had almost died. She'd fought so hard, but it had gotten too difficult to get to the surface again, and she'd run out of air.

Thank You, Lord, for getting Logan there in time. Any later and ...

The thought of seeing Jesus face-to-face and holding Bree again had made the idea of death not so bad. She wasn't scared of dying. But she was a little scared of what losing her would do to Logan.

She squeezed him a little harder. God was good and knew what Logan needed. And if it had been her time, she trusted Jesus would have taken care of her husband.

Megan pulled up to the dock where the moon illuminated Will and Zara standing there, holding one another.

AJ lifted a hand and waved.

Zara's face lit up.

Once the boat was moored, Logan stood and offered his hands to AJ. She was too weak to stand on her own, so she let him lift her to her feet. He helped her out of the boat and onto the pier.

She fell into Zara's arms. Her friend held her tight. "I was so scared."

"You're telling me. I was tied up under a bridge in the water."

Zara held her back and looked in her face. "For real then, huh?"

AJ nodded. "What happened here?"

Zara said, "Your husband outsmarted the bad guy."

AJ turned to Logan, who half shrugged.

She shivered.

Logan took her hand. "Let's get you warm."

They took the hike up the 150 billion stairs. Her body did not like it, but she pushed and tried not to let Logan see that she was struggling. But the exhaustion was too much.

She wasn't able to lift her foot high enough and tripped on a step. She landed on the stairs.

Logan stooped down beside her. "Are you okay?"

"I'm so tired. I'll be fine. Just need a moment."

They sat there for a minute until she regained a tiny bit of energy, then finished the trek up. The patio was filled with police officers. Adam and Amelia were in full-detective mode until they saw AJ.

Both of them ran to her and gave her hugs and expressed their relief that she was safe.

Amelia rubbed AJ's arms. "Go get dry and warm. You let us know when you're ready to give us your statement."

The detectives stepped away, and that's when AJ spotted Miles lying on the ground in a pool of blood.

She gasped. Emotions hit like a freight train, one car after another. Horror. Relief. Guilt for feeling relief. Grief—he had been their friend.

She couldn't breathe.

Logan wrapped his arm around her shoulders. She turned into him and sobbed. The pent-up tears from the last twenty hours released in a storm.

But they were safe. Both her and Logan. Miles was gone and would never torment her again.

When her sobs let up, Logan led her away and around to the front of the house where an ambulance waited. They climbed in the back and accepted space blankets from the EMTs. Logan rested his hand on her back, while the medic listened to her lungs and examined the wounds on her wrists.

She leaned her head on Logan's shoulder. As ready as she was to go somewhere warm and cozy, she was already home.

Logan opened the door of AJ's apartment for her. It was the first time they'd been there since Miles had violated it. But it was all clean and didn't look like he'd ever been there. And for that, Logan was grateful.

They hadn't left the crime scene until after they'd both given their statements. And despite being fairly dry, riding his motorcycle back left them both cold.

AJ wandered toward her bedroom but stopped and turned before she'd even made it halfway.

"You okay?" he asked.

The weariness on her face morphed into a mischievous grin. "I know how we can get warm."

He laughed. "Will and Zara will be here in like ten minutes."

Her eyebrow quirked up.

He shook his head and chuckled. "Tempting, but maybe now's not the moment."

She giggled. "I know." She came back over to him and threw her arms around his neck.

Maybe he should call Will and tell him to take his time.

He kissed his wife. "Go take a shower and get changed."

"I'm too weary to stand up in the shower. I'll stick to clean clothes and shower later." She gave his lips another quick peck and disappeared, leaving him reeling. How had he ever sent her away? It seemed so ridiculous now. Yes, she had betrayed their wedding vows, but she had repented. Why had he had such a hard heart?

He dropped to his knees in the middle of the apartment. *God, I'm so sorry. I never want to walk away from You or her ever again. I'm done keeping You at arm's length. I'm done living for myself and wallowing in self-pity. You gave me a woman who knows me better than I know myself, who loves me in spite of it. Heal us both. Thank You for the work You are already doing in us. Forgive me for failing to protect her. And thank You for Your safety and provision.*

He leaned his hands on the floor as sobs shook his body. He had only spent half of his bottled-up grief at the cemetery last week, and now the rest of the suppressed emotions made their way to the surface. Why had he ever held it back?

"Logan?" Panic filled AJ's voice.

He sat up. "I'm fine."

She dropped to the floor in front of him. "You don't look okay."

He opened his arms to her.

She closed the space and took his face in her hands. She searched his eyes and smiled. "We're gonna make it."

"I regret so much wasted time."

"I know. But God is one to make up for that time. He's good at that kind of thing. And we'll just have to make up for it too. And we can. We will." She winked at him.

"You are so good to me."

She shrugged. "I haven't always been. But I promise to be from now on. As best I can anyway."

He chuckled. "I know." He leaned forward and seized her lips with his own.

The rumble of a pickup engine sounded in the driveway, so Logan drew out of the kiss and tugged AJ to her feet.

He wiped his face, hoping he didn't look like a weepy mess. "You're fine. Plus, I think they'll understand."

AJ went to the door and opened it for Will and Zara. They came in, and Will passed off a bag to Logan, who went and changed.

While Logan changed, AJ rummaged through the kitchen for something to eat.

Zara joined her. "You need to get some sleep."

"I will. But I'm starving."

"Fine. Food first. I wanted to talk to you about something. This isn't a great time, I know ..."

"No time like the present. If life has taught me anything, it's to embrace what's in front of you." AJ grabbed a Greek yogurt and a spoon.

Zara nodded. "I was talking to Granny the other day."

"I love that you call her Granny now too." AJ dug into her snack.

"It's such an honor really. I love that woman. But she offered me a room in her house until Will and I get married."

"Really?" The spoon stopped halfway to AJ's mouth.

"Yeah, so you and Logan can have this place to yourselves."

What Zara was saying fell into place in AJ's sleepy brain. "Oh. Really?"

Zara chuckled. "Really. You two shouldn't have to wait any longer to get back to being married."

AJ ate a giant spoonful of yogurt. She wasn't about to tell Zara they were already working on it. "Are you okay with that?"

"Of course. I'll be across the driveway and, maybe sooner rather than later, across town with *my* husband."

"I like the sound of that." AJ set down the now empty yogurt and gripped Zara's arm. "Thanks for helping look for me."

"That's what friends are for. They don't let them be murdered by crazy lunatics. It's part of the code."

"Indeed."

The women chuckled and went back to the living room where the guys were sitting. Zara sat with Will on the couch, but AJ couldn't quite bear to sit in the chair opposite Logan. So she wandered toward him, aiming for the floor in front of him. He lifted his arm, inviting her to join him. She sat on his leg and wrapped her arms around his neck. His hand tugged her close.

The friends decompressed by talking about what happened and then about nothing, until everyone started falling asleep.

Zara stood. "I don't know about the rest of you, but I'm going to sleep in my bed."

Will and Logan exchanged a look, and Logan nodded slightly.

Will said, "If it's okay with you, ladies, we'll both crash here. I'll be on the couch, of course."

Zara smiled. "Fine by me." She kissed Will then left the room. A brief moment later, she came out with pillows and blankets for him. "Good night, y'all."

They told her good night despite the sun starting to make its appearance.

Will looked at Logan and AJ. "Don't keep me company. Please, go get some rest."

AJ stood. "You too." She took Logan's hand, and they went to her—their bedroom.

She curled up next to her husband, and in minutes they both fell asleep. The horrors of the day faded away like a foggy mist. They were as they should be. Together.

Three and a Half Weeks Later

The sun peeked through the blinds, and AJ rolled over in bed and found her husband snoring beside her. She still couldn't believe they'd reconciled. After so many years of being estranged, hoping that reconnecting would be possible, it seemed like a dream. She was afraid she'd wake up one day to find it was, in fact, a dream, but the scars on her wrists from the zip ties told her it had all been too real.

But so good now.

Was this a reflection of how God works all things together for the good of His people? So many bad things, hard things, horrible things ... but here they were—childhood friends turned lovers. A marriage reunited. A family reconnected despite tragedy and betrayal. God was so good.

They both had today completely off, so it was a good opportunity to go through the boxes that had arrived yesterday from the restoration company. Part of her dreaded it. Ninety-five percent of what was in those boxes had come from Bree's room. The day would be full of memories and tears. But hopefully it would be cathartic. AJ prayed it would be healing for both her and Logan.

She traced his face, running her finger along the stubble on his jaw.

He stirred. His eyes didn't open, but a smile nudged his lips up.

He reached for her and tugged her closer.

She scooted into his arms. "Good morning."

He grunted.

"Oh come on, get up sleepyhead. The sun is awake."

"Why does that mean I have to be? Let me sleep in for once." He still didn't open his eyes.

"You can sleep in when I go to work tomorrow. But today it's you and me, no outside commitments." She rolled onto her stomach and propped herself up on her elbows.

His eyes cracked open. "You're gonna make us go through those boxes, aren't you?"

"Isn't it time? I'm afraid if we put it off, we won't do it."

"That's probably true." He ran his hand up and down her back. "Big breakfast and then dive in? Or quick, easy breakfast?"

"I'm not super hungry, but I can help you make something if you want bigger."

"Cereal is okay with me. I'd be fine waiting another two hours before I got up and ate."

She chuckled.

He closed his eyes and shook his head. "Morning people."

She swatted his chest.

He flipped her onto her back and leaned over her.

"A sudden spurt of energy? I thought you wanted to go back to sleep." She could barely get the words out around her giggles.

He shook his head again but didn't say anything. Instead, he lowered himself to her and kissed her.

She reveled in the passion of his affection and melted into his kiss.

With a contented sigh, he lay down next to her, holding her close. "Nah, I could still go back to sleep."

She pushed herself to a sitting position. "Get up, mister. I want coffee. And you need to brush your teeth."

They crawled out of bed and brushed their teeth before finding some cereal to start their day. They moved around one another in a beautiful dance of ordinary life as husband and wife.

Still in their pajamas, they settled on the couch with the first of the boxes in front of them.

AJ's hands shook as she removed the tape off the top of the box. Logan gripped her hand. "Are you okay?"

"Nervous about all the emotions that are going to come out of these boxes."

"Let's pray."

"Please."

Logan opened his hands to her, so she slid hers into his. "Lord, help us as we face a new layer of grief. We know that grief is a road we will have to walk for the rest of our lives, but with Your hope and comfort, we can face this together. Give us what we need right now as we go through these things that belonged to our little girl. Hold her for us today. Thank You for Your assurance that she is safe with You right now."

AJ opened her eyes when Logan didn't continue. Tears already streamed down his cheeks. She let go of his hands and wrapped her arms around his neck.

He held her, and they cried for a moment together, but then AJ turned to the box and ripped the tape the rest of the way off. They pulled out one item after another. Mostly little girl clothes. The outfits Bree had worn to church the summer before she died.

AJ could picture each article on Bree. It was good to go through them and remember, but also to admit they could pass the clothes on to someone else.

Logan opened another box. He removed the first item and unwrapped it.

AJ gasped. Bree's purple hippo. She took it from Logan and held it close. "I'm keeping this."

"I was going to say that if you didn't."

For the rest of the day, they slowly went through each item. Most things would go to others, but the favorite—clothes and toys alike—would be kept. More children would come, Lord willing.

Plus they decided they would put together a shelf of special items as a little memorial to Bree, wherever they ended up living.

Together they decided they would talk about her, unlike that first year and the years since. They would talk about her to one another and to anyone who entered their lives and home. They would tell the world how God had blessed them with the most darling little girl for a short while and how God had worked in their lives despite the tragedy of her loss. Because God was good no matter how difficult life was, and more than ever AJ was convinced of that. Bree would want them to tell the world about Jesus and His love, and that's exactly what they would do.

Two Months Later

The cold December wind whipped around the car, so Logan jogged around to open the door for his wife. They had just come from the title company's office, where they'd signed the papers to become homeowners once again. The insurance was going to take a while to come through, but God had blessed their socks off, and they'd been able to get a mortgage to buy a new-to-them home.

He opened the car door, and AJ bounded out. She'd had entirely too much caffeine already.

"Logan, it's really ours!"

"Yep." Logan offered his elbow.

She wound her hand around it and tugged him to the front door of the two-story, four-bedroom house on two acres. Their favorite part was it was only two blocks away from Will's house. There were old-growth trees too. It was everything they could have hoped for.

Logan removed the key out of his pocket and unlocked the front door.

AJ nearly shoved him out of the way in her effort to dart inside, but he gripped her arm.

"Wait up there, babe. Tradition."

She dropped her head to the side. "You aren't serious."

"I am."

"Maybe I should carry *you* across the threshold." The teasing glint in her eyes made him laugh.

"You may be a firefighter, but I'm the husband."

"Just don't hit my head on the door frame this time."

"I'll try not to." He slid his arm under hers and around her back before leaning over and placing his other arm beneath her knees.

He lifted her and stepped over the threshold into the next chapter of their lives.

"Now put me down." She tapped his chest.

He lowered her to the ground and watched her spin around.

"I love this house." She stopped and grinned at him. "I can't wait to see ... to see all the things. Hopefully, we can afford some furniture for this place. It's so empty right now."

"We'll be fine."

She clasped his hand and dragged him into the living room at the front of the house. "The Christmas tree can go right here." She stood by the front window.

He nodded.

They walked through the rest of the lower level with a dining room and kitchen and the family room. Then they wandered upstairs to the bedrooms and loft.

"Logan? How many kids?"

"Pregnancy and childbirth went all right for you so ... as many as God gives us?"

Her eyes nearly bulged out of her face. "You want to go that route?"

He shrugged. Despite years of not being careful to avoid pregnancy, they'd only ever conceived the one time.

"I think we should wait a little while to try, but do you think we can handle four kids?"

"Of course. Isn't that what we talked about way back in the day?"

"When we were seventeen?"

He nodded. "So five total."

She deflated slightly. "Five. Maybe six total."

It was his turn to raise his eyebrows. "How about we get our feet under us, get used to this whole healthy marriage thing again, and then let God guide how many."

"I love that idea." She tucked herself up against him. "What if we had twins?"

He closed his eyes. Twins would be a lot. "A double blessing, I suppose."

She laid her head on his chest. "What if we can't get pregnant again?"

He ran his hand up and down her back and cupped her face with the other. "We'll take on those challenges as they come. But maybe we can adopt or open our home to families that need help. God will use us and this home however He chooses. We're His, and I pray we'll be a part of furthering His kingdom."

"It is so good to hear you talk like that."

God had done a major work in Logan's life. He had a long way to go, but he prayed he'd be the husband AJ needed him to be. He prayed he'd love her the way Christ loved the church.

"Whatever comes, I love you." Logan kissed her forehead.

"I love you too."

He held AJ close. And he would continue to do so. Forever and always.

Author's Note

Phew! What a ride! Logan and AJ have been kicking around in my head for a long time, but while I was so excited to write their story, I was terrified once I discovered the piece of their past that had caused the rift between them. I never wanted to tackle the loss of a child in a story, but no matter how much I tried to talk myself (and God) out of making that a piece of it, I knew this was what God had for this story (FYI you can't talk God out of his plans). By His grace the story flowed as I wrote it (along with tears -yes, I make myself cry while I'm writing even though I'm not typically a crier).

God is so good.

And that's what I hope you saw in this story. That even when terrible things happen in our lives, He works it all together for His glory and our good, even when what happened is the farthest thing from good. We can trust that He is good. He loves us and holds us when tragedy hits. But we have to turn to Him. Unlike Logan.

Like Logan eventually did in this story, we have to learn to surrender to Jesus and to forgive others. Bitterness will fester in our hearts if we let it, but something sweet can grow when we surrender to Christ. Whether it's hurts, disappointments, tragedy, or our own sin, we have to surrender it completely at the cross. I pray that you find solace and healing in Jesus's arms.

I'm glad Logan and AJ's story is the second in this series so we can see how God works in their lives while their friends and co-workers have their own adventures. Hang on tight for Brennan and Megan's story. Will Megan's ex restrain her to the point that she never gives Brennan the chance to win her heart?

Keep in Touch

Be sure to sign up for Liz's newsletter. By signing up you will have a short story delivered to your inbox. You'll also be able to stay up to date on release dates and sales!

Sign Up for Liz's mailing list by going to:
https://bit.ly/lizbradfordwritesnewsletter

You can also find Liz at:
www.facebook.com/lizbradfordwrites
www.instagram.com/lizbradfordwrites
www.pinterest.com/lizbradfordwrites
www.goodreads.com/author/show/18532678.Liz_Bradford

Also By Liz Bradford

The Detectives of Hazel Hill

A FRIGHTFUL NOEL - Prequel - Christmas Novella
NOT ALONE - Book One
PURSUED - Book Two
ON YOUR KNEES- Book Three
A SHOT AT REDEMPTION - Book Four
GIANTS FALL - Book Five
Book Six is in the works

Knoxville FBI

REVENGE IGNITED - Prequel - Christmas Novella
INTO THE FLAMES - Book One
UNDER FIRE - Book Two
SMOKY ESCAPE - Book Three
OUT OF THE ASHES - Book Four

Tracking Danger – A K9 Search and Rescue Series

TOO LATE - A Novella - Book One (previously in the Winter Deceptions Collection)
SWEPT AWAY - Book Two (previously in the Small Town Danger Collection)
More books to come with Josh, Chloe, and Poirot

Stand Alone

STONE COLD CHRISTMAS (previously published in the Silent Night collection from Two Dogs Publishing)

Hazel Hill Police & Fire

ABANDONED – Book One
BETRAYED – Book Two
Book Three (Coming 2026)

Acknowledgements

First and foremost, I must thank my Lord and Savior, Jesus! Thank You for the gift of story and allowing me to pen words. I hope and pray that You will use them to touch hearts and draw readers closer to You!

Thank you, Ken for being so supportive as I pursue my dreams and make the voices in my head earn their keep.

Thank you to my daughters for doing your school work without complaint eventually and helping me by not fighting not killing each other while I'm working.

Thank you, Mom for always being just a text or phone call away when I get stuck on a medical issue, a word, or whatnot.

Thank you to my partners in crime and dearest friends, Crystal Caudill, Angela Carlisle, and Voni Harris for your accountability, wording advice, and general mayhem fun. This book definitely wouldn't have happened without all y'all support, advice, and prayers! Love you, girls!

Thank you to my friends on Discord! May your sprints always be productive and GIF filled.

Thank you, Teresa for helping me make my story all that it could be!

Thank you, Sharyn for your ruthless cutting of the word *that* and for making me use my thesaurus!

Thank you, Emilie Haney for an incredibly beautiful cover!

About the Author

Liz didn't always know she a writer, but she was. Before she even knew it, God was plotting out this path for her. From her earliest days, stories were a natural part of her imagination. In high school, she toyed around with writing, but it was nothing more than a secret hobby. But one day, when her middle daughter was a little over a year old, a story idea crept in her mind and wouldn't leave her alone. So, she started writing. She would stay up late after everyone else was in bed and frantically write the words that brought her characters to life.

That first novel lives buried deep in her hard drive, and maybe one day it will see the light of day, but that would take a LOT of editing. About the time she couldn't figure out where that first book would end, another idea persisted in her mind. That was Becca and Jared's story, book one in *The Detectives of Hazel Hill* series. Before she knew it, what started as a single novel turned into a trilogy... but wait, there's more. In that series, she now has six stories published (including the prequel novella) and many more percolating. She also has several more ideas for the characters of Hazel Hill, North Carolina. The *Knoxville FBI* series is now complete. Her *Tracking Danger* series currently has two books out with more coming. Liz also has numerous other series forming in her mind!

Liz is a member of Faith, Hope, & Love Christian Writers, American Christian Fiction Writers, and ACFW Louisville Chapter. Her heart longs to live in the mountains of North Carolina (where she was born) or Tennessee and that is why she sets most her stories there. But, for now, she and her husband live in Southern Indiana where she homeschools their three daughters.

Made in the USA
Middletown, DE
21 June 2025

77324256R00172